Claire Gillies

X

Girl of the red-gold hair,
    far from you, o love, my aim;
    girl of the red-gold hair,
    far from you my sorrow.

— SORLEY MACLEAN

1

Catherine brushed her hair out of her eyes and sighed. Another day stuck in a grey office, looking out at the interminable rain falling from dark Glasgow clouds.

"Come on guys, I want to see another sale up on the board!" Adam, her supervisor, looked high-flying and important with his pristine white shirt and colourful tie, as he tried to infuse the room yet again with his own brand of corporate enthusiasm. Yet all the while never really doing anything, thought Cat. She cringed; he would surely give his time-honoured motivation speech in an hour, taking everyone into one of the small cupboard-like office rooms next to their groups Pod. There he would share his sales expertise for the hundredth time, ending by getting everyone to shout: "Yes we can!".

She looked around her and saw her colleagues all chatting on the phone, looking brilliantly professional, and always getting more than the three stars on the board for each sale made. If three sales were not achieved within a three day period, then the employee would be asked to leave the company. As bad as her job was, Cat did not want to leave - not just now, anyway. She was the only one making money to pay rent, bills, and put food on the table while Dave was out of work. Thinking of their finances again, she bit her lip as her stomach tightened; she barely had enough to cover their outgoings, and needed this job, even if she hated it. Cat wondered how she could be more like everyone else and get more sales, to win herself enough stars on the board to keep her job for another week. Cat fidgeted with her nail-bitten fingers, reflecting, as she waited for her next call that she must try to be happy in this job - everyone else seemed to be, and a part of her, she admitted, wanted to be like everyone else, and enjoy the nine to five. She sighed, and tried to drum her fingers on the desk, but without nails she had little effect, and the dull ache made her stop. She looked across to Shelley who sat legs-crossed filing her nails and talking merrily to the person she would make money from at the end of the call. Her bleached blonde hair was scraped into a ponytail, showing off her new gold earrings. Shelley giggled at something her customer was saying, glanced over to Cat and gave her a wink. Cat smiled back, not wanting to appear rude or unoccupied, and pretended to write down some notes, which really turned into doodling.

"Cat...you have only one star beside your name! I want to see at least two more by lunchtime." Adam said in his softest and most patronizing tone, standing and pointing his marker pen at her with his hand resting elegantly on his hip. Noticing her smiling affectionately at his posture, he sat down immediately. Cat knew Adam was gay, but for some reason he tried to hide it. It was useless though, no matter how straight he tried to act, everyone in the office knew his real preferences.

She cringed and took another sip of her instant coffee. It was already her third cup and it wasn't even 10.am.

The automatic dialler rang to her next cold call.

"Hello?"

Cat cleared her throat quickly. "Good Morning, am I speaking with the house-owner?"

"Yes dear, it's Mrs MacIntrye," an old woman said in a shaky but friendly voice.

"Hello Mrs MacIntyre, my name is Catherine and I'm calling from SunnySkies UK. Have you ever thought about Life Insurance?"

The women paused. "No dear..."

"Well Mrs MacIntyre, you could be leaving your family more to deal with than you anticipate when you die. We could have the right policy for you, to ensure you have peace of mind and protection for your family financially". Cat continued her sales pitch and doodled in her notebook once again.

"Three stars Cat!" Adam said fifteen minutes later, with such excitement that she almost felt he was going to hug her. "Great job - amazing! And here was me thinking you wouldn't last too long here - you've managed to prove me wrong!"

Cat smiled thinly, gritted her teeth, and went slowly back to her desk. Oh, how she hated this job and how she hated what she had become!

~

When she was safely on the bus, Cat put her headphones on and began listening to Boccherini, sighing as she debated what to make for dinner, while the enchanting strings comforted her tired brain. This was her favourite part of the day; just her and her own thoughts. The bright traffic lights danced on the wet streets as the bus lurched and skidded through the rain. She couldn't remember the last time she saw sun, surely it wasn't that long ago? She felt she was slowly going mad as winter clung onto the heavy Glasgow skyline, not wanting to relinquish the city to spring. Squeezing past all the wet and grumpy faces who tried to steady themselves as the bus stopped, she stepped off the bus and emerged back into the rain. She tried dodging giant puddles and the splashes from cars driving past, but to no avail, the road was becoming a river and her feet were completely sodden. *This is ridiculous!* Cat thought to herself as she finally reached her street. Home was her flat, which she rented with Dave, a nice little one bedroom on the top floor of a tenement building. Tonight, the many windows were all lit up, casting a warm glow onto the road, their deep red walls standing strong after many years. Cat thought of the families and couples who lived there too, neighbours she didn't know, whose everyday lives she liked to imagine. They'd eat good wholesome food from the organic markets, say "grace" at dinner, and read to their children every night. Cat ran up the stone flagged steps to the large front door, then up a further four flights of stairs until the end was in sight. Gasping on the final step, she had thought at one time that after a few years of living here she'd be fit enough to just glide breezily up; oh how wrong she had been! The key turned and opened to their small hall, which led to all the tightly packed rooms, but the ceilings were high, giving the illusion it was bigger. Cat allowed herself the romantic notion that perhaps their tiny flat was where the servants had lived; maybe this big tenement had once housed a rich family and they of course would have needed servants. Images of housemaids dusting mantelpieces popped into her head like an episode of Downton Abbey as she popped her keys on a small array of hooks next to the door labelled "Home Sweet Home" that Dave's mum had bought them. Janet had bought them so many tacky home decorations that Cat had stopped putting them up, and was now keeping them in a box for the times Janet would visit. On those occasions she would re-adorn her flat with all the many homely items; pink china sets, vulgar doll-like ornaments or small wooden signs saying things like "Because someone we love is in heaven, there's a little bit of heaven in our home," or "The opinions expressed by the husband in this house are not necessarily those of the management," the latter of which Cat actually liked, but Dave hated; probably because they weren't married, much to Janet's disappointment.

"Hello sweetheart." Dave shouted from the couch as Cat's head appeared round the door.

Dave and Cat had been together for years. He was a friendly soul, a 'man's man', funny, chatty, and occasionally capable of the odd spark of old-fashioned charm. He was also prone to mood swings, laziness, and was now living off Cat's current wage after leaving his job three months ago. She tried to not let this bother her; it wasn't his fault he had been made redundant. She knew however that today he had probably spent the day playing computer games, and would have left the cleaning and cooking for Cat to do. A familiar feeling of irritation crept up on her, this time however, she managed to shrug it off.

"Hiya!" she called back, and seeing that he was too enthralled in his task of shooting zombies, she went straight to the kitchen to make dinner. The pokey room could only really fit one person anyway, so she got to work and made them a quick bolognese, and cut the last of the cake she had made the day before, with a dollop of cream on top.

They both ate at their small dining room table beside the couch, watching the TV. This had become their routine now and though Cat remembered all the talking they used to do at the dinner table, catching up on what they had done each day, now, every evening seemed the same, sitting distracted by the box in the corner until she broke the silence between them.

"Did you go to the Job Centre today?" she asked him while watching the screen.

"No, not today," he said with a sigh.

"Don't you think you should go at some point this week?" Cat tried not to sound like a nag.

"Yeah, yeah I will, definitely."

"Well it's Friday tomorrow and they will be closed on Saturday so what if you went and spoke to someone about work before the weekend?" She offered in a calm breezy voice.

"Yes." He paused for a few moments. His crew cut of brown hair was starting to get long, and Cat realised in surprise that this was the longest she had ever seen his hair. Dave was always fairly smart-looking, quite athletic in build, and usually to be found in a suit. Looking at his stubble and messy sports clothes, Cat knew he couldn't possibly be happy like this. He continued eating his dessert, looking down. "You're right, I'll do my resume in the morning, and go down to the Job Centre in the afternoon," he said through mouthfuls of cake. Cat was not convinced by this statement but decided not to press him; it was late and she couldn't face an argument. She collected the dishes and went to do the washing up. The lack of space meant that every kitchen utensil had to be put back in the cupboards after use, and everything had its own place, but Cat didn't mind. She enjoyed keeping a tidy house, and sometimes wondered if this made her a little pathetic. She even found herself more often than not preferring to clean the apartment rather than going out on the town for a weekend, although she wouldn't admit it to anyone. As she wiped down the worktop, she opened a bottle of red wine and poured two glasses. She had heard from the girls at work that a new costume drama was scheduled for 8pm tonight, so she carried the glasses through to the living room and snuggled up to Dave on the couch. TV on, costume drama credits starting and glass of wine in hand, Cat was content. But just as a woman in an empire dress walked into view with a manor house in the distance, Dave's phone buzzed loudly beside them making her jump.

"Hello? Barry! How's it going my son?" Dave spoke in the typical laddish tone he adopted whenever he spoke to his friends, at which Cat cringed and pushed him off the couch, so he would talk to his mate outside. Cat sprawled out on the couch, trying to not feel irritated again, and focused her attention back to the drama. The heroine marched off down to beautiful gardens where she seemed to be passionately angry at something. Just then an aesthetically pleasing man in a tailcoat came after her.

"Leave me, sir, I beg of you!" she said with utmost authority, but he walked up to her, about to take her arm, stopping himself at the very last moment. Cat was instantly hooked, and imagined herself being chased in a similar fashion, how fun it would be! Moments later Dave came back into the room with a grin on his face, tucking his phone into his back pocket.

"Let's go out. Barry and some of the guys are going out.

What d'you say, you could call up some of your old mates from college, it's been ages!", exclaimed Dave, bright-eyed.

"I've just sat down to watch my show," Cat protested with a sigh, her eyes glued to the screen, trying not to miss a moment.

"Oh come on you old bore! We never go out, I feel sometimes as though you just want me to behave like a fifty year old!", snapped Dave suddenly. Cat knew she would not get any peace tonight unless she gave in. She got up, went over to her handbag, which drooped on one of the hooks by the door. She opened her purse, and gathered up the few notes of money remaining there. It wasn't much, but it would do.

"Take it," she said, in a fed-up tone, stuffing the notes into his outstretched hand. Every week they argued, and every week it generally concluded with Dave wanting to go out and do things, and using her money to do it.

After ten tense minutes she heard the door slam. A part of her was relieved to be on her own tonight, with space to breathe. He never would thank her for giving him the money. She paid for food, rent and even gave him spending money like his mother... The never-ending cycle was already beginning to grate on her, leaving her unsure how things had become so bad between them. But tonight she let go of that tight, uneasy feeling, and allowed herself to escape into her costume drama; surely it would have a happy ending?

2

———————

A week later, back in the office, Cat looked at the calendar on her desk. It was only Wednesday. *How has the week taken this long?* She mentally counted through the days in her head, hoping her calendar was wrong and it was really Friday. Lost in her thoughts, she didn't notice that Shelley had been trying to get her attention.

"Psst!" came the sharp noise for a third time from across the desk.

"Oh Shelley, I'm sorry I was far away there!"

"You normally are darling," Shelley responded, in a short manner. Her lipstick was a pink shade that Cat would never dream of wearing, and her cream blouse clung to her torso, showing all manner of curves, with her large cleavage spilling out from its ruffled collar. Shelley looked around quickly, and then said mysteriously: "Meet me in the ladies, in ten minutes". Cat, feeling confused but intrigued at the same time, nodded promptly, and Shelley went back to her phone call.

Cat waited in the girl's loo for some time. After playing

with the hand dryer and looking at her pores in the mirror, she decided the star tele-seller had forgotten all about their meeting. Just as she was about to leave, Shelley flung the door open dramatically, then closed it gently just as suddenly, all the while suspiciously looking around the door for passersby. She peered into each toilet cubicle ensuring they were the only occupants. Cat couldn't help but feel that she was a spy, and a top-secret unmarked envelope was about to switch hands.

"We are alone, Miss Money-Penny!" Cat joked, but judging by Shelley's blank face she wasn't quite on the same page.

"Cat darling, you're doing it again"

"What?"

"That look! What goes on in that head of yours?" Shelley put her hands on her hips, waiting for an explanation.

Cat reddened. "Oh I don't know... I just daydream a little."

"Where do you go?" Shelley raised one eyebrow, but her expression had changed to one of mild concern.

"Anywhere but here," Cat sighed. "So - what have you brought me in here for?"

"Oh - just that I heard a bit of gossip, and I'm only telling you as I couldn't actually believe it." She paused a little, with a pregnant suspense. "Well, Tim, Jane, Francis and Joan know, but I told them not to tell anyone else, so you can't either, swear it!" She pointed at Cat, waiting for her agreement. Once she had received sufficient proof of Cat's intent at silence, she continued. "My friend Lucy is going out with the guy in HR, you know, the one with the goatee and the glasses? Well, apparently he's told her that the company will be letting a lot of people go. They're giving the business a restructure, it seems they have too many people employed in the life insurance department, or something, I don't know." Shelley rattled on while Cat listened numbly. "It ties in with what Adam said the other week, he emphasized to our team that we need to work really hard to get even more sales... I think he knows what's going to happen. He wants to see who's the best, so they can be the ones who get to stay".

As the news washed over her, Cat couldn't find any words in response, humorous or otherwise.

"Oh is that the time?" Shelley looked at her watch. "I have a telephone interview, must start looking for another job before everyone else does!" Shelley glanced in the mirror and, appearing happy with the reflection that looked back at her, marched out of the toilets.

Cat went back to her desk. For the rest of the day there were whispers around the office of the latent redundancies. Some people actually hoped they would be included in the casualty list. James, who sat across from Cat, mentioned to her that he would welcome being let go. He felt confident his payout would be good, since he had been with the company almost ten years, and had been looking for a new job recently anyway. Cat couldn't share his optimism. Only a SunnySkies employee for a few months, she was sure she would be "last in, first out", as most businesses operate. She was distracted until the clock struck five, and having made no sales that day, she felt thoroughly depressed. There was only one person she could talk to at times like these, so she picked up the phone and called Johnny.

"Hey J! Could we meet for a drink? I've had the week from hell and I need to drown my sorrows in company," Cat asked the receiver.

"Of course! Usual place, in twenty minutes?" came the familiar voice.

"You're an angel."

Cat sat in her damp clothes nursing a beer in front of the fire. Ben, the barman, chatted to her about the weather until Johnny waked in. Wearing a dark blue suit and burnt orange tie, his movie star short blonde hair and fresh face always turned heads, and Cat noticed the few other girls in the room turn to admire the professional-looking man in the doorway. Cat had met Johnny at college, and the two had hit it off almost instantly, principally, to the surprise of both parties, because Cat had found herself immune to his extensive charms. Johnny shook his umbrella and left it dripping at the door. She noticed Ben perk up immediately.

"Hi Ben! Urgh, terrible day, isn't it? Could I get a beer? And better make it another for Cat here!" came the thick Glasgow accent. Johnny pulled a chair around the table to sit next to Cat, and put an arm around her. As their drinks arrived, he nodded at Ben, and watched him go back to serve a fresh group of patrons.

"It doesn't mean it's definitely going to happen, people say these things all the time." Johnny reassured his friend kindly.

"I don't know... it would just be my luck, after leaving a job to come to this one, only to be laid off before the end of my probation!" Cat sighed despairingly, and gulped at her drink.

"It was better money though, the last company didn't value you anyway."

"This company doesn't value me either though - I thought it was a customer service role; instead, they shoved me into cold call sales! You know how that grates against my whole existence!" Cat almost felt like crying.

"I know, I know," her friend murmured in soothing tones. For Johnny, cold calling was no big deal, he thrived off making sales. "Listen, don't get yourself worked up. This news is from a bimbo whose friend is shagging the guy in HR. He could be saying anything; *she* could be saying anything. She probably loves gossip and will spread anything just to feel good about herself!" Johnny spoke so jauntily it made Cat's head spin.

"That's mean, how can you say that about her? She told me because she cares."

"Don't start that Cat, she doesn't care!"

Cat gasped. "You are too blunt sometimes!"

"I know! It's who I am, and that's why I'm your friend. I'll take no shit from anyone, and neither should you! You're too good a person!"

Cat sniffed and gave a chuckle.

"Now, how's that big lump of yours? Has he found a job yet?" Johnny looked at Cat directly and waited for her response.

"...I think I need another drink!" Cat fell into despair again.

"Ben! More drinks please fella!" Ben came promptly with a tray.

"You're a star!" Johnny looked up at Ben "Hey how's your band doing? You guys were great the last time I saw you at The Lime Club".

Cat left Johnny to flirt a little while as she pulled herself together. She couldn't help but feel a little sorry for Ben; if only he knew Johnny was actually married.

After Ben had left them, and Johnny had checked him out again from the table as he sidled up to another table, he pulled his chair in a little, and gave his full attention back to Cat.

"OK where were we? Ah - Dave." Johnny raised his eyebrow.

"Yes..."

"So?"

"So." Cat nodded her head and didn't know what to say. She was pretty sure that everything she said about Dave was negative. She couldn't help it, but at the same time she didn't want her friend to hate her boyfriend.

"Has he found a job yet, or is he still spending all his time shooting zombies from your couch?" Cat could see the annoyance in Johnny; he had found Dave work at his company a couple of months ago, and one day Dave had simply decided not to go in again. He opted to spend his days at home, unaccustomed to the high-shine, high-pressure world of sales and business meetings. Cat had tried to get him to talk to Johnny about it, but the two had not spoken since.

"Well, he said he was going to the Job Centre today. So that's good...". Cat pressed her lips and didn't look at her friend's reaction, aware that Dave had said the same thing the week before but hadn't gone.

"Well, that *is* something." Johnny agreed, and Cat noted it was not in his usual sarcastic way. He sighed and put down his drink on the table. "Cat, I just want you to be happy. If you need a job, please let me know and I'm sure the firm can arrange something-"

"I know that J, and I'm grateful, honestly." Cat was touched, and almost felt the tears begin again. Johnny had offered Cat work many times, but she knew working in offices was not what she wanted with her life. Also the idea of just doing more sales work did not appeal to her. This temp work had been a move which was supposed to give her the free time and the head-space to find the job she really wanted. Trouble was, she didn't know what that was yet. Maybe she should just get another office job with Johnny, but it just would be the same as her last position, wouldn't it?

"Is he treating you right? I mean, you just don't seem happy! I know your job isn't great, but before that you didn't seem happy either." Johnny hesitated. "Do you love him?"

"I'm fine, we're... just going through a rough patch. It's hard when all you think about now is having enough money to pay rent and bills, and it's especially hard that I'm the only one bringing home the bacon. But Dave is looking for work, and once he's found something he'll be happier. I'll be happier." Cat emphasized the last point with a nod and a tap of her beer bottle, and tried to avoid Johnny's question, hoping that this would be enough to satisfy him.

"As I said, I can see if there's work at the company. You just need to say. I just want you to be happy, honey." Johnny put his hand on Cat's, gave her a bright smile, and downed his bottle.

That night Cat went home to an empty flat. A text from Dave told her he was spending the night with a friend. Cat had a sneaky suspicion he was avoiding her, so she poured herself a cup of tea and went to bed. She propped herself on the pillows, staring at the wall and taking sips from the hot brew. It had been so long since they had sex, Cat couldn't quite remember the last time. She knew that they had both had a lot to drink... was it weeks? Months? The costume drama she had watched the night before left her pining for a man who knew what he wanted and made the moves to achieve it. The story of a gentleman who had loved his woman for years, but for whom circumstances made it impossible to declare it. Eventually both threw caution to the wind and made known their feelings. He had kissed her ever so gently, Cat remembered, and then both looking intently into each other's eyes, allowed the passion to take over. She lay on the bed thinking of that moment. Of course, they were actors, but that look of hunger affected her. She was confused, empty, upset and alone in that bed, and as her tea grew cold she fell restlessly asleep.

3

Next day, Cat made the decision to walk down the busy main street on her lunch break; she was determined to be away from the office, and even though her feet ached in her high heels, she continued further and further. Her morning had been terrible, she had a few angry threats over the phone (something of the norm when working at a call centre, but which Cat still had not grown used to). Her boss Adam had been circling almost every twenty minutes, checking whether she had *"made a sale yet*?", which only made Cat feel under even more pressure. Stars galore appeared on the board, one after another, as her colleagues made never-ending sales. Cat had despaired, looking over to Shelley who was smiling chatting on the phone, on a roll with her three sales of the day. Amidst the bustle and throng of the high street, she sighed, and slowed her pace. She knew she needed desperately to make some kind of progress, but every time she spoke to someone on the phone she hated every second of it. It was the complete opposite to how she imagined she'd make money. After her years at art school, she had dreamed that

she would be able to have her own gallery, and create something everyday. Now her concerns revolved around money,
and thoughts of being "let go" from the firm made her palms
sweat. She needed to pay rent, the bills, and buy food. The
art career would need to stay on hold, or maybe it was too
late anyway? She was thirty; so many years had passed since
she had used a paintbrush. Panic rose in her chest at the
thought of her creativity being slowly stifled in the everyday
grind to get by. She took deep breaths as she continued
walking and tried to reassure herself that she would be fine;
she had some savings, they should keep her going until she
found another job. Cat wondered whether to go to the job
centre now herself instead of eating lunch, or would it be
better to just suck it up, go back to the office and make it her
mission to get at least one sale today? That uneasy, stressed
feeling washed over her again like a cold wave, so Cat
continued walking further down the road, leaving her tense
morning behind her, as the dark clouds above loomed over
her. It felt like it forever rained in this city, a dark cloud
permanently overhead, not wanting to share the blue skies
above with anyone. People streamed past Cat as she walked
in a daze, oblivious to her surroundings. Impulsively, she
walked into a corner shop, feeling a strange desire for a
cigarette. She hadn't smoked in years, but she could feel the
grasp of anxiety clenching in her stomach and wanted a
release. Buying the cigarettes at the counter, she waited for
the shop assistant to give her her change, with those few
seconds her eyes drifted to a magazine rack beside the
counter. One of the covers showed a photograph of a man
climbing a cliff stack. She picked up the magazine, and read
the caption under the picture. "Climb the Old Man of Hoy".
She flicked through the magazine to find where this oddly-

named place was, and she at last found more. "Majestic Landscapes, Aurora Borealis, and Grand Cathedrals" captioned under the images, and as Cat took in the green fields and ancient standing stones, she was captivated. A cough came from behind her and Cat realized a small queue had gathered, and the shop assistant was waiting holding out her change. She quickly apologized, bought the magazine and then found a bench outside to look at the article in more detail. Scanning over the words and photographs, something stirred inside her. *Was it excitement?* Emotions fluttered like butterflies wanting to get out of their cage. "The Orkney Isles possess a true unadorned beauty. With an abundance of wildlife and ancient history, they hold an enchantment and romance that is hard to forget." Cat drank in the words, and with wide eyes, the images of standing stones, and of beaches stretching out to a clear blue sea. She shivered, closed the magazine and with electric conviction breathed out quietly: "I'm going to live in Orkney".

~

"What do you mean... it's over? We've been together for years! It can't just end like... like that?" Dave's loud voice carried from the hallway.

"Dave - we aren't happy! We both should admit this, and just call it quits," Cat looked up at him earnestly as he now stood by the bedroom door, pausing for a second in her packing on the bed.

"This is because I haven't found a job isn't it!" Dave yelled defensively, clenching his fists.

"No, it's not." Cat dropped her armful of clothes and turned to him.

"It's because I haven't asked you to marry me, isn't it?" he offered meekly, staring at her intently.

"Dave, I don't think you really know me. I don't think I know myself anymore! You won't acknowledge it, but you know as well as I do.... we're just together for the sake of... being together!" Cat didn't want to say anymore, she shouldn't have to be this mean, but how could he not see?

"That's a lie!" Dave roared, and threw her suitcase on the floor, his face red with fury. Cat sighed and sat down on their small double bed, her energy was beginning to leave her. She closed her eyes and said in a quiet voice:

"Please Dave, please don't make this harder than it needs to be." Looking down at the floor she began to feel the tears starting, blurring her vision. "Dave, you don't love me."

"I.....I..." He stuttered but could not get the words out. He sighed and leaned against the wall.

Cat didn't want to say anymore, but the only person Dave cared about was himself, he didn't think of Cat or her needs. All this time she had fooled herself that they were in love, but Dave was content in just having his own independence, while they both lived like housemates under the same roof. He did not value Cat, and would often make her feel a nag whenever she wanted to do something with him. It suited Dave to have a woman around the house, cooking his meals, paying half the rent, or all of the rent these past few months. There was nothing between them outside of that. Cat had instigated every romantic moment they had over the last year, and their lovemaking had dwindled to non-existence.

Cat went into their kitchen to get a glass of water; Dave followed her and got a beer out of the fridge. He leaned against the door in the cramped space, blocking Cat's exit and took a slug from the bottle. His expression made Cat's heart ache, but she stopped herself from backtracking. She reflected on his handsome profile. They had fancied each other in the beginning; Dave's cheeky smile and blue eyes were irresistible to Cat. But now looking at him, Cat had no real feelings anymore - there was no passion, love or even much heartache over the breakup. Cat watched him: he just leaned there against the fridge, not fighting for her, just giving up.

"Where am I going to go?" he asked forlornly.

"Your parents?" Cat suggested. "This is the right change for us Dave, we weren't a good fit." Cat went to touch his arm. "I'm leaving Glasgow... I'm leaving in a few days. I've paid the rent until the end of the month and spoken to our landlord. You have until then to organise your things."

Dave's face was still in shock. "Well! You've thought of everything haven't you?" he said with a surly expression.

"Look, I'm sorry, I'm not the right girl for you." Cat was surprised at the next words to come from her lips. "Now if you don't mind I have some packing to do!" He drank his beer, as she managed to get out of the kitchen without further debate. She went to her wardrobe and pulled out all the clothes she would be giving to charity. And it was at this very second that Cat started putting herself first.

4

C at had never thought she would be using so many forms of transport to get to her dream destination. As a non-driver, and living in a city, she had never really needed a car. But the epic journey she was undertaking made her realise the perks of being able to drive.

"One step at a time" she said soothingly to herself, feeling her old friend anxiety trickling in at the thought of learning a daunting new skill.

She had bundled all her belongings into two big suitcases that she carted behind her, with a great deal of huffing and puffing. The rest of her things had been given to charity, or to Dave; perhaps the same thing, she thought wryly. She had given away clothes, furniture and a ridiculous number of jewellery boxes which she had collected over the years. She never could quite remember how her jewellery box addiction had started, but once it was out of her hands, and rolling away in the charity pick-up van, she had been glad to get rid of it all. She made a mental note to herself never to purchase any more pointless pieces of junk, ever again. *Clutter in the house, is clutter on the mind!* Even the huge box of home décor from Dave's mum was given to a very happy Shelley, who had trawled excitedly through each item with glee on Cat's last day at work. After that day she had picked up the travel magazine, she did not go back in until the next day, collecting her things in one fell swoop, saying goodbye to a few people, and leaving within the hour. She couldn't believe the lack of attachment she had for the place. Even Adam came over and hugged her goodbye, and she had felt sorry for all the stress they were all going to endure; nobody deserves their job being snatched from them. But Cat finally knew that she would rather make her own way, and take her own chances, than wait to be told what her future would be. She felt rather proud of herself for all her organisation, and her sense of adventure, and she decided to focus on those traits, rather than her being utterly reckless in running away from the life she had in Glasgow to live in the far-flung unknown.

After a jerky taxi ride, she packed her suitcases safely on the bus, and instantly began to feel lighter, as if a heavy blanket over her shoulders had slipped off. The bus was fairly quiet so she stretched out, popped on her head-phones and took in the view. Hours passed with gentle classical music in her ears, but this time instead of city lights, it was hills and lochs that drifted by and after a few hours the bus was threading the winding road on the edge of Loch Ness. Cat looked over the dark murky waters, examining every inch her eyes could cover. The child in her looked for a creature, any creature; maybe the secret of Loch Ness was a giant basking shark or giant eel? Suddenly an image of her mum came to her. She hadn't really thought of her mother as such, just the usual stab-bing pain in her heart which she suppressed, and she quickly willed herself to think of something else. But the vivid memory of her mum tucking her into bed and reading her a book about the Loch Ness monster and a boy who became its friend surfaced again. She remembered a cracked spine, with a beautiful coloured drawing of the green monster smiling down at a red-haired boy in a kilt.

"Mum, does every boy wear a kilt in Scotland?" she had once asked.

"Well no, but maybe in the highlands more people wear them. My dad often wore a kilt as a boy. So much so that his nickname was 'Kilty!'" Cat remembered finding this very funny and they had both shared a giggle. The memory burned and a tear rolled down Cat's cheek as the bus left the dark waters and all its secrets.

Once in Inverness, she dragged her giant suitcases to the next point of call; luckily the train station was beside the bus station, else she would have arrived in a disgusting pool of her own sweat. With only five minutes until her train was due to leave, she couldn't believe her luck, she was just in time. She ran onto the first carriage, and with a little help from a kind train assistant, she got the bulky suitcases on and plonked herself on a seat beside the window. As the train started on its way, she saw the small city of Inverness with its Victorian stone houses fade away and every so often along the way a fishing village or town would appear. Cat marvelled at the beautiful blue sky, which stretched out over the distant sea ahead, and the fields upon fields of promising freedom.

$\approx$

"You've reached Thurso, this is the last stop," came a voice in the distance.

"What?" Cat muttered sleepily to herself and opened her eyes to a big white bearded man with stern blue eyes.

"Time to get off lass, this is the last stop!"

"Am I in Orkney yet?" Cat pleaded in a tired quiet tone.

"Orkney? No no, you have a bit of time before the ferry leaves for the island!"

Cat felt so exhausted from her traveling, her face must have showed her emotions, as the old man's look changed to one of sympathy.

"I might suggest, Miss, that you go into Thurso town and get yourself a cuppa before you take the ferry. It can be a bit rough towards the end, so make sure you get some food and tea in you". The conductor nodded wisely, and helped her off the train with her suitcases. Cat looked at her travel schedule; the sheets of crumpled paper she kept tucked in her handbag showed that she had two hours before the ferry was to leave. She took the conductor's advice and walked into the town of Thurso. She stayed on the straight walk path, and saw the town ahead, which compared to Glasgow looked like a tiny village. The weather had now changed to heavy clouds, and Cat thought of the blue skies and outstretched fields she had left on the east coast. The grey-stone buildings that lined the pathway looked grand, a little like those of Inverness. The odd car passed her by, but other than that Cat saw nobody. She strolled past a church and a school, yet everything was quiet. *Was it a Sunday?* Cat had heard that some Scottish islands closed everything on the Sabbath, and stayed inside. But this was a Wednesday, and not an island? Cat continued on confused, dragging her suitcases behind her until she came upon a little café on the corner of a Victorian terrace. Baskets of brightly-coloured flowers hung on either side of the door, with more pots on the windowsills, making a welcome sight. Cat opened the door and was shocked. So many people were in this large café that Cat thought the whole town must be taking the conductor's advice.

Munching on a scone over a large cup of steaming tea, Cat loosened her shoulders and began to relax her mind, taking in the paintings that hung on the walls. But a voice sounded in the back of her mind, and that old feeling came back to her. *What am I doing? Why did I leave my job, my boyfriend? My life? What do I think will happen here? Why Orkney? This is going to be a terrible mistake and I'll end up asking Dave to take me back in the end...* The anxiety was starting, that feeling began to slowly and ever so gently take hold. Her breathing quickened. *I don't know anybody here. I'm alone.*

"Are you finished?"

"What?" Cat looked up startled.

A plump woman in her fifties with a tea towel on one shoulder, smiled briskly before asking again. "All done? Another cup of tea?" She looked down at Cat's empty cup.

"Oh no thanks, I better be going soon. It's very busy in here, is that usual?"

"The woman looked around and laughed "Oh yes, we have a bit of a clash on Wednesdays, the church committee and the council come in here for their meetings!" She picked up Cat's cup and saucer, "but we don't complain, customers are customers!"

Cat smiled. "I also couldn't help but notice the beautiful paintings. Are they all by the same artist?"

The woman looked to where Cat had indicated; her dark hair was scraped back into a neat bun, and was greying. Her face warmed.

"They surely are, they are my daughter's! They are beautiful aren't they?" Her face shone with pride, the way Cat's mother's once had.

"You have a talented daughter!"

"Thank you, you're very kind. You're not from here are you?"

"Nope, I just arrived. I'm on my way to Orkney to...live..." Cat hesitated with the last word, feeling that there were so many as-yet unknown meanings within it.

"What an adventure!" The woman said in excited hushed tones. "My Jessie lives there, the one whose work you're admiring!" She waved in the direction of canvases on the wall. "She's about your age, I can give you her contact details if you don't know anyone on the island?" She grabbed a pen and pad from her apron pocket and began to write. Cat hesitated a little, thinking she didn't want to bother some girl whose mother was giving out her details on her behalf.

"Thank you," Cat said shyly, "I don't know anyone actually, so this is very nice of you." She didn't know what else to say, but was touched, despite the awkwardness.

"Are you an artist too?" the woman inquired.

"Well not really - I used to be! Feels like a long time ago."

The woman looked up to the clock over the counter.

"If your getting the ferry dear, you better be going...it leaves in thirty minutes!"

The time! I keep losing track of time, where does it go?

"Oh no! Is it just along the road to the ferry?" gasped Cat.

"It's further than that. Don't worry dear I'll call Bill, he's the taxi man around here." She trotted over to the phone and spent some time quietly talking. Cat sat there anxiously waiting, and watched the woman. She asked a few customers how their food was, and took some more orders, then she came back to Cat, whose heart was thumping by this stage, panicking at potentially missing the ferry. "He said he'll be here in five minutes, don't worry, you'll make it in time!" She smiled and then glanced around to see more customers approaching the counter. "I better get back to work, but it was lovely meeting you dear! My name is Barbara, now you make sure you contact Jessie, she's a lovely girl and knows the locals there." She gently patted Cat on the shoulder.

Once safely picked up by the taxi and dropped off at the ferry, Cat marvelled at how big the boat was. It was huge, like a luxury cruise liner. There was a shop, café, cinema and bar on board, and Cat took some time walking around in awe, while the ferry began its journey. Carting her luggage behind her, she decided to sit in the bar area beside the window, and looked out onto the misty sea, though she couldn't see an awful lot, apart from the occasional seagull flying past the window. It was after thirty minutes of gentle gliding that the hell began. The ferry started slowly rocking back and forth, and then waves crashed up all around them and the rocking increased threefold. Cat gritted her teeth, put on her headphones again and tried to imagine she was not on a ship, but in a hammock, with the evening sun drifting over her. As tight as she shut her eyes, she could not keep the tranquil image going. The ferry lunged and shook with force through the wild waves. Cat watched a young couple drinking beer deep in conversation, and a middle-aged man with a pint at the bar watching intently the foot-ball results that flashed and crackled on the TV overhead. No one paid any attention to the sounds of the battering waves or the shaking vessel itself. Cat felt abruptly cold and shaky, and zigzagged her way to the toilet to be sick. As soon as she reappeared at the bar the rocking disappeared, as if by magic. She went back to her seat and curled into a shivering ball.

"Excuse me?" A man with curly dark hair and green eyes placed a glass of water on the table beside Cat. He looked so concerned that Cat almost laughed and began to say that she was OK, but as soon as she moved, she felt the dreaded still-present acid gurgling in the pit of her stomach.

"It's alright there, don't move. I just thought you looked very pale. Drink the water, it should help." His face was still full of sympathy as his large hands presented the glass to her. "Is there anything I can get you?" he asked.

"No I'm fine!" she shakily replied.

"Patrick, another pint when you're ready!" came the football fan at the bar behind them.

"One minute." He knelt down so his head was near hers. "You're not the only one, it's pretty common to feel unwell on the ferry. I did!" He gave her a half smile and stood up again. "Anything you need, just let me know." He turned to go away.

"Thank you," Cat raised the glass a little with a smile, "for the water..", but he had left and was busy serving customers.

The ferry docked and Cat was glad to be on dry land again. She looked at her new home to be, and to her dismay it was cold, windy and raining. Everything was grey; the water, the buildings and the sky. *What have I done? I've come to the edge of the world and there's nothing here!* Cat went immediately to the tourist information centre, hoping she could find accommodation. She berated herself for not sorting out a place to stay earlier; apparently she was not as organised as she imagined. Luckily the centre was across the road from the ferry terminal, but by the time she had reached it she was soaked through. She sighed, and dreamed of a shower and warm dry clothes as she skimmed through the notice-board of holiday houses to rent, calling the few potential places one by one. Each was already booked out. Cat sat down on a dusty chair, and decided the only thing she could realistically do was try and call the local hotels for a room, at least for the night. As she was in a town, she thought, maybe if she walked along the road, perhaps she would come across a hotel.

Cat decided to get the last step over with, grabbed her suitcases and walked back out into the never-ending rain. On the cobbled streets the odd car drove past and a few passersby walked onward with determination, umbrellas up, but threatening to blow away in the now gale force winds that swept through the street. Shop window lights beamed out, spilling onto the road, reminding Cat of old Christmas cards. She peered into some of the windows, seeing a florist, craft shop, clothes shop, fishing shop and café, before she reached her first stop, a small hotel. Stepping into the front porch she was greeted by warmth and several dogs jumping on her. Two big golden retrievers and a Labrador all tried to lick and tackle Cat to the ground.

"Lucky, Terry, Moss! Off!" came a loud voice from a very small woman. Her blonde bobbed hair and big bosom startled Cat. She hadn't envisaged a glamorous woman like this would be living on a remote island. The dogs jumped off, and dashed through another door, to jump on more people, Cat presumed.

The woman, who was in her mid-forties, wore a black round-neck sweater and a burgundy pencil skirt and heels. Her glasses were almost pointed at the corners, to give a 1950s style jaunt, but at the same time she had that secretarial look that would set men panting almost as much as her dogs.

"Hello there, what can I do for you Madam?", the lady asked in a huskier voice. *Is she serious?* Cat thought.

"Er, hello, my... name is Catherine. I've just come to the island, and, I wondered... if you had a room for the night?"

"I do indeed! You're very lucky, a couple just cancelled an hour ago, said they missed the ferry or something, so they're travelling tomorrow, but will skip Stromness and go straight to Kirkwall." She patted her hair and rolled her eyes. "I don't know why they tell me, and as I said to them it's all very well calling, but they should've informed me earlier... this is our busiest time of year and that room was reserved for them for five days!" Cat wondered when the lady would take a breath. "But it was meant to be - you're here and the room is available. That's all that matters." She pointed her finger rigidly upwards as if giving Cat a lecture in the schoolroom. "OK! Follow me," she ordered, and started walking away while Cat grabbed her suitcases. The blonde bob peeped back around the corner, eyes flashing beneath the glasses. "Leave the suitcases darling, my husband will take them up for you. Don't want you sweating any more do we..."

Cat sighed with relief, but was a little offended. Did she smell? She sniffed her underarms, then quickly and obediently followed her hostess.

They ascended a white wooden spiral staircase up three floors, and finally they stopped outside the only door on the top floor. The door was unlocked, and opened to a cosy yet spacious room. A grate fire kindled gently in the corner of the room, welcoming the gloomy light from outside through the window. Cat walked through in exhausted bliss to the adjoining room that had a large bathtub with a long window looking out over the bay, where the notorious ferry was docked for the evening.

The blonde woman fussed about with the fire and looked out the window rubbing her hands together to keep them warm. "I had set the fire already for the couple earlier, just add the logs from the basket to top it up." She indicated the wicker basket next to the mantelpiece. "Everything ok?"

Cat looked at the king-size bed with big fluffy pillows.

"It's perfect!"

5

Her mother cuddled Cat as they both looked out to the water. "Don't worry, there's no monster in there," she said wiping away Cat's tears. The bright light pierced through the clouds, and the sun came out as Cat buried further into her mother's arms.

Cat woke with a start. She still had her clothes on from last night and must have dozed off while reading, going by the magazine sticking to the side of her face. She scrambled off the bed and headed to the bathroom. The mirror presented a woman from a horror film; her makeup was smudged and her eyes blotchy. She glanced at her watch, a silver René Macintosh that her mother had given her on her eighteenth birthday. Swirls of roses were embossed around the outer face, with the message *To my wee one* which Cat cherished so much. She had changed the straps on it several times, but the watch itself remained as beautiful as the day she had received it. She still had a bit of time, it was 7am, and breakfast service would be starting soon. She desperately needed

a wash, so she ran the bath, and poured in some luxurious
bubble bath. She took off last night's clothes, and threw
them in the corner of the room, then put on a face-mask and
stepped into the bath with a sigh of utter pleasure. Sounds
of blowers floated in the distance, chugging boats and men's
voices carried from the bay to the bathroom window. Thirty
minutes in the tub passed by like so many seconds as she
watched the sun rise over the calm water ahead, casting its
flickering golden beams onto the bathroom wall. She could
happily have stayed submerged all day. But her stomach
gurgled loudly; she hadn't eaten since yesterday afternoon.
The ferry trip ended any appetite she may have had. Cat
reluctantly pulled herself up, quickly put on some makeup
and pulled back her wet hair into a ponytail.

Down in the breakfast room, Cat saw an elderly couple
silently sipping tea and munching on toast. They smiled at
her as she bid them good morning, and glided over the deep
blue tartan carpet to the small table at the window.

"Good morning, I trust you had a nice sleep?" Cat was
startled to see the blonde woman from last night standing
over her. Her tailored grey dress clung to her body, highlighting her huge bosom again. Cat found herself thinking,
slightly mesmerised, *those cant be real...?*

"I did, thank you!"

"I'm Monique, by the way. So are you holidaying around
the islands? It's going to be nice weather soon, hopefully
we'll finally get a nice Spring this year!" Monique looked out
at the blue sky.

"Yes I'm here to see the island, though I'm... not too sure
how long I'm here for..."

"Oh really?" She raised an eyebrow "No family here
then?" She arranged Cat's knife and fork, playing for time.

"No, I'm just here to see what it's like. I may stay on for a while."

"Well in that case, we could do a deal for you if you want to stay longer than a week," Monique cut in. "It's a slow start, we wont be getting too many visitors until the festival happens, but that's a wee while away yet. Oh - breakfast! What can I get you?"

"Oh I don't mind, what is there available?" Cat asked with interest.

"Well you could have the usual scotch breakfast, toast, fruit... or my husband does a mean pancake stack?" Monique got out her pen and pad ready to take the order. Cat's stomach gave an alarmingly loud rumble.

"Pancakes and coffee please!"

"Of course, sweetheart." Monique wiggled out of the room and Cat stared after her. She was the sexiest woman Cat had ever seen. She looked at her own reflection in the window, saw her wet, flat hair and pale forehead, and decided she needed to do something different. Her hair was limp and her natural red was hidden under a mousy brown dye that she couldn't quite remove. She had her hair many colours when she was an art student – green, red and blue at times. She had loved matching her outfits with her hair and drawing attention. After college she had looked for work, but offices certainly would not accept anyone that didn't conform to the norm. So the loud locks went, and the brown dye was slapped on. Cat looked again at her boring reflection and sighed.

Monique came out with a large mug of coffee and a plate of toast. "I thought perhaps you might like toast as well, you sound hungry?" She gave a little giggle and Cat couldn't help but feel embarrassed.

"Monique, is there a hairdresser or a beauticians near by?" Cat asked, sipping at the coffee.

"Oh yes, a good friend of mine – Sally Sinclair, she's only down the road. I'll make an appointment for you," Monique said, making her way towards the phone on a side table near the door.

Jeez, Cat thought, *I really must look bad if the landlady is tripping over herself to get me beautified.*

"OK, er, thanks," she smiled.

After the toast and pancakes were devoured, and three cups of coffee swallowed, Cat put on her bright green anorak and small rucksack and ventured out. Walking along the stone flags, she looked again at the small shops along the street. Stopping at a florist, she saw her favourite flowers – bluebells. Deciding to buy some, she gathered a small posy and continued walking to the end of the street to a small jetty. She stood there quiet and still, watching a small fishing boat go past with two fisherman in yellow water-proofs sitting together, smoking, chatting and surrounded by lobster creels. Breathing in and out deeply, she felt light as a feather, and at this moment in time, completely content.

Returning back along the quiet street, she came across a white-lit window with a large painting taking up the whole space. The sign over the white wooden door said "Pier Gallery". It looked rather professional, and slightly out of place in this fishing village. Stepping into the gallery, the bell on the door gave a gentle echoing tinkle and Cat was confronted with a wash of wall-to-wall colour. The space was deceptively large, and the light flooded in from windows all around. She looked at the work on the walls in depth and took in the texture of the waxy paint, the brush strokes and the scenic interpretations of the landscape. The style was very like the pieces that hung in the tearoom; this had to be Barbara the waitress' daughter. Cat was alone in the big room, but she could hear classic rock music somewhere in the distance. The door at the back was ajar and a girl's voice could be heard in time to the music. Cat decided not to intrude, so she gently stepped back to the front door and opened it once more; the music stopped as soon as the bell rang.

"Hello," she heard the voice from the back room, "is anybody there?"

"Erm...yes," Cat said quietly, then spoke up. "Sorry to interrupt you work," she called out.

Out came a petite blonde with her hair up in a polka dot bandanna and paint on her face. Her Bowie t-shirt was ripped at the neck with paint speckled over it. Her fresh face broke into a bright smile, which showed her pale blue eyes to sparkling effect.

"Hello, you're not interrupting! Come in and look around. I always sing to get the creative juices flowing!" She wrinkled her nose slightly and chuckled.

"Thank you; these paintings are beautiful. You are truly gifted." Cat took in the pictures once more and walked over to a portrait of an old man with a pipe in his mouth and smiling. "I love this one, it's amazing you do both portraits and landscapes." She turned around as the blonde came towards her looking at the picture.

"That's old Donald. He worked as a Gardener for the wealthy Power family. He spent almost all his life outside, creating their beautiful garden. You can go and see the little world he cultivated for them. He died last year, but I was able to paint him before he got ill." She smiled sadly. "He was a character though, made me laugh, told me stories of this place from back in the day."

"I can see he's a character!" Cat looked at the portrait

once more, "the mischief shows in his eyes." Both girls smiled at each other and giggled.

"I'm Jessie, but you can call me Jess." She extended her paint-covered hand, looked at it in horror and then decided to wipe it on her already paint-splattered t-shirt.

"I know, I actually met your mum Barbara before I caught the ferry. I'm Cat. I'm over here for some time, I hope, and your mother told me to look you up. I hope you don't mind!"

"Of course not! I need more girls my age around here! Oh bless mum, how is she?"

"Busy I think. That café was packed when I was there. She was lovely, it was really nice of her to tell me about you, just so I had someone I could go to...." Cat suddenly felt strangely upset. *What had she done? She had left everything, she had nothing now – no one in her life, no Johnny, no Dave, no Shelley.*

Jess looked at her intently. "Of course. Well as you can see there are a lot of older people here, not many people our age. What are you doing tonight?"

"I don't know, I haven't made any plans," Cat shrugged a little.

"OK, let's meet tonight! I'll show you what this town has to offer," she said in a mock-American accent. "Oh - and do dress up, it's not every night two gals are on the town!"

Later that evening Cat was in her room getting ready, having stocked the fire with logs and placed the bluebells in a vase by the window, she looked around her space and sighed happily. Her suitcases were unpacked and stowed away under the large bed. She had managed to put all her clothes away in drawers and in the large white wooden wardrobe beside her bed. Cat kept catching her reflection in the wardrobe's mirror; her newly cut and dyed auburn hair had transformed her. Her natural loose curls were cut in a beautiful style that flowed to her shoulder, the colour of the auburn bringing out her green-blue eyes. She was meeting Jess in the hotel bar downstairs in ten minutes and she had changed her outfit five times already. Finally she decided on a knee length fitted black dress that she wore with boots. The weather was cold and windy tonight, and so she thought this attire most suitable in case they ventured into the chilled night sea air.

Jess was at the bar laughing at a punch line of the barman's joke. Her hair was still pinned up, but she was wearing a red ribbon tied over her head. Her lips matched her ribbon, as did the tiny flowers covering her deep blue dress. Cat was aware of a few people turning around and looking in her direction as she timidly walked up to the bar.

"What's it to be Cat?" nudged Jess.

"G and T, please"

"You heard the lady, Jim," Jess said in a silly posh voice.

Jim winked at Cat and set to work.

"Hey, you look beautiful!" Jess looked Cat up and down in awe and gently touched her newly cut hair. "Your hair is stunning, your eyes look so...big!"

"Thanks, I think!" Cat laughed at Jessie's choice of words.

The drink arrived and Jess lifted her glass. "Cheers my darling. May this be a great night, filled with lots of ..." she struggled, bit her lip and giggled. "You know, I don't know a proper toast? At this stage of my life as well!"

Cat cleared her throat dramatically and said in her broadest scotch:

"May the best ye've ever seen,
Be the worst ye'll ever see.
May a moose ne'er leave yer girnal
Wi' a tear drap in his e'e
May ye aye keep hale an' he'rty
Till ye're auld eneuch tae dee
May ye aye be jist as happy
As we wish ye aye tae be"

She raised her glass and drank. Jess stared at her in amazement, then started sniggering as Jim clapped his hands with delight from behind the bar.

Cat blushed but gave a little bow. "When in doubt, Rabbie Burns will help you out." She smiled, but her throat suddenly went dry as she remembered it was her mother who had taught her the famous Baird's toast.

"I'm impressed!" Jess stated heartily, and repeated, "May ye aye be jist as happy, as we wish ye aye tae be!" She raised her glass also and drank.

The two girls enjoyed each other's company for the rest of the evening. After eating a very filling meal in the hotel dining room, they ordered coffees and sat talking about their respective childhoods.

"...I was so bored with the wide open spaces of nothingness; I wanted to see people, see attractive boys! The only boy I fancied in my area was my big brother's friend, and he was married by eighteen! I had to get away, so London called me and I answered with open arms." Jess went on about her college life in London and all the exciting times and creative people she had met there: "Everyone was either successful in fashion, photography or film, it was quite inspiring...but there was a lot of people working so hard all week, that they went crazy at the weekend – taking drugs."

Cat wasn't sure Jess was as hushed as she meant to be, as

two old ladies wearing tweeds looked up unimpressed at the loud gossiping girls. Jess continued paying no attention to their quiet tutting. "There was a fakeness to people there that I hadn't noticed earlier. That lifestyle was not for me, and I was too afraid to stay around in case I became the same! So I packed up my bags, went home to mum, and luckily, found a studio space after much searching. Since it was only a ferry-ride away from mum I took the opportunity. It's the best feeling having my own business. Who knew people wanted to buy art on such a small island!" Jess sighed brightly and drained her coffee. "What about you Cat? Where did you grow up?"

Cat was never any good at talking about herself, she always preferred listening to others, asking them questions. She found strangers much more interesting, and would try to steer the conversation away from herself on most occasions. But she felt perhaps this was not the time to do that.

"Well my father left when I was a little girl, so he's not been in my life at all, really. I don't know anything about him apart from the odd thing or two my mum would say about him. Sometimes she would catch herself, she would be doing something else – like, baking a cake, and she'd smile to herself, saying how my dad used to act like such a kid by eating the cake mixture before she'd put it in the oven." Cat drank her coffee, allowing herself to think of her mum again, the beautiful, caring, kind woman who had always put Cat first.

"Mum and I lived in Glasgow. After my grandparents passed away it was just us two." Cat smiled, and noticed that the tweed ladies had gone, and it was just Jess and her left in the warmly-lit dining room. "She would take me to the beach, to museums... and we would have picnics. She loved the outdoors, so every weekend we would do something together. Then I went to art school. I loved it so much. It made me feel free in a way; I can't explain it. Once I finished my course, things came crashing down on me with mum passing away, so I – well, I needed to get a grown up job." Cat had blinked at the words that came from her mouth. She never shared this much of herself usually, perhaps it was the gin having an effect?

Jessie took Cat's hand. "I'm so sorry Cat, what an awful thing to happen. I don't know how I'd cope if ..." Jessie stuttered a little, and Cat gave her a smile.

"I know, it was a difficult time. But these things happen." Cat played with the corners of her napkin, folding and refolding the edges. "So after that I met Dave, got an office job, paid the bills and thought acceptance was what was expected from me. A normal life." Finishing her coffee, Cat sighed and relaxed a little more. "But then one day I found a magazine article about this place, this remote island, and that night I broke up with my boyfriend, and packed my bags, and the next day made plans to come here! Quite a risk, I've never done anything like it before. To be honest, I don't know how things will turn out, but so far it's the happiest I've been in five years. That stifled feeling I had is gone." Suddenly the words hit her and she began to laugh, "That feeling is gone."

Jessie lightened the mood tactfully. "Perhaps you left it on the ferry!" she giggled quietly.

"Perhaps I did," Cat agreed, and the smallest part of her brought back a thought of the kind barman with green eyes and the glass of water.

6

Cat threw back the curtains and greeted the morning sun. From her window she watched the small fishing boats leave the harbour, with the blue sky highlighting the hills in the distance. The sea looked like a liquid mirror, with the surroundings reflecting on its surface. *What a painting this would make,* thought Cat. She washed her hair, dried it and got ready for breakfast. Grabbing a pen and pad on her way down the stairs, she decided today was going to be productive. Monique came through the swinging kitchen door into the dining room, holding a jug of coffee and went around the few tables of guests. Cat guessed Monique's origins might be American, but couldn't quite identify her accent. The continuous holding of the coffee jug, however, and filling up everyone's cups regularly seemed to Cat a very American-waitress sort of thing to do. She pondered this a moment until Monique came up to her small table at the window.

"Coffee?" she held up the jug with a smile. Wearing a tight skirt and cream silk blouse, Cat was impressed again by her fashion sense.

"Yes please," Cat said as she took out her notepad and pen. "Monique, do you know anywhere I might find work, and also where I might learn to drive?" Cat was a little uneasy thinking of both these things, but there was nothing for it, she had to make a living and learn how to drive. No longer in the city, where she could hop on public transport, at a moment's notice, she needed to finally face up to the dreaded task.

Monique looked up to the ceiling as if there was something of interest there then sighed, "Mrs Hughes is a driving instructor, well at least she used to be. I will check with my husband Iain. As regards to work, well, it just so happens that I have – had - a barmaid who left to go back to Poland last week; the poor love was just too homesick. So you can help behind the bar if you'd like?"

Cat was a little stunned and didn't know what she thought about working in a bar. She had never worked in a pub before. Stopping herself from thinking negatively she accepted immediately before the rational side of her brain had a chance to refuse her timely, and potentially only job offer. "I would love to!"

Monique gave her a pat on the shoulder. "Lovely darling, I'll get Jim to show you the ropes tomorrow night." Cat gulped down her coffee and nodded for another refill.

Standing at the bus stop outside the ferry terminal, Cat wished she had brought her gloves and hat. It was a bit early in the year to wear these, but today's weather had a severe nip in the air. A small empty bus stopped for Cat and took her to the nearest town. On the speeding bus she looked out the window at the outstretched sea meeting the never-ending bright blue sky, while spiralling clouds floated across. Cat lay back, put on her headphones and observed the views to whimsical folk music that swirled intriguingly in her ears.

They arrived at a small group of buses, that Cat could only assume was the terminal. The bus driver had muttered something and left the vehicle, so Cat wandered out into the cool crisp air in search of the shops. After looking at a street map she had found in the hotel, she walked only a few minutes until she came upon a cobbled street lined with shops and cafes. Glancing in the windows, she peered at all sorts different goods on display, and couldn't help but be tempted. She found a sweet shop and selected some toffee for herself, then couldn't resist a paisley embroidered scarf she found in a craft shop. "That's made locally," the large, homely saleswomen said to her as Cat looked in the mirror admiring its rainbow of colours.

"It's beautiful, I think I have too many scarves though," Cat reflected uncertainly.

"Never!" the saleswomen said aloud dramatically, "a person cannot have *enough* scarves". Cat laughed and eventually agreed to buy the item.

After a light lunch in a nearby cafe, she made her way to a very grand ancient cathedral, which loomed over the main street, standing to attention as people walked around it in admiring groups. Cat slipped inside and walked across the very centre of the echoing hall, taking in the beauty of the vaulted structures as different tour guides spoke at length to various huddles of visitors: on old folklore, Viking history, and ancient customs: information that Cat found herself drinking in and wanting to explore further. She overheard one small group of English tourists in particular speaking with their guide. "And there are standing stones here too?" a younger girl in glasses asked an old lady wearing a blue cap and jumper.

"Golly yes! There are standing stones and tombs. Not right here, but they are dotted all over the island, and the smaller isles scattered around us have them too!" She beamed down at the captivated girl, whose eyes widened in anticipation of her next question.

"And are there any stories around the stones? Like, has anyone gone missing?" The girl bit her lip and smiled as a laugh from another visitor echoed in the arching space.

The guide shook her head with a look best described as quiet disappointment. "We have had a lot of visitors recently particularly interested in the stones, and the legends relating to mysterious disappearances, but I'm sorry to say I've never heard of anything personally; maybe it's best we leave all that to Hollywood." She nodded and pressed her lips together. "But that's not to say these stones are not special, either. People would celebrate Beltane; the peak of spring and the welcoming of the summer to come; these sites were seen as powerful places for other reasons, with many tales and histories surrounding them." The lady scratched the side of her throat with a contemplating look on her face and glanced at her watch, but then continued. "If you want to know a special story, then there is one I was told as a girl, of Jimmy Tulloch the shepherd. Jimmy had his own little cottage, right on the edge of the beach, over-looking the wild sea ahead. He cared for his goats and sheep, and lived a quiet, peaceful, but lonely life. Each evening he would lock up the animals safely before the darkness and cold winds set in, but, one night, after returning late from the market on the mainland, he remembered he still had to herd the sheep inside before turning in. Luckily the moon was out, helping him to see the way, because in those days we didn't have electricity. Thankfully, he managed to gather all the sheep away into their pen, but as he was making his way back to the cottage, he saw a figure in the dark water below. The moonlight spilled down over her pale skin, showing him all her beauty, but before he could say a word, she had vanished." The guide snapped her fingers, making some of the listeners jump. "The next night, he went out looking for her, and then the next night, but he saw nothing. Soon he thought he was going mad, but her strange beauty haunted him, and he needed to know if what he had seen was real or not. Slowly growing more obsessed with the girl from the water, he spent each day hungry to see her again, if only for one more time. Then one night, he went to the pub to try to distract himself from his torment, and encountered a storyteller by the smoky fire, who told him a tale of a selkie girl, who came close to shore, to see what it felt like to be human for a night, who then by day would return to the water to become a seal again." The guide continued the story to her quiet group, her words clear and crackling in the thick air around them: "And so it is known that to keep a selkie on dry land, for your own, you must take and hide their sealskin, so that they must live as we do on the shore. Well, the shepherd looked out day and night until the lady returned, and return she did. He found her skipping over the rocks one warm night when the haze of the day's sun was just below the hills. He grabbed the skin, which she had left to dry on a nearby rock, when she wasn't looking, and buried it in the stone circle not too far from his cottage, knowing it would be the last place she would think to go, as stone circles were thought to ward off magical beings. Well, didn't he get his wish: the girl was trapped, as without her skin, she could not return to sea. So he took her into his cottage, and clothed her in soft lamb-skin, and married her. For a time, they seemed happy, and the girl would help with the animals, and keep house. Jimmy thought he was the happiest man in the world, with, as he thought, the most beautiful wife he had ever seen. But as time moved on, the lost selkie girl spent her days more on the rocks than in the cottage, looking sadly out to sea, mourning her lost life. The shepherd dismissed the uneasy feeling he experienced each time he caught sight of his bride depressed, and was not even aware that she often looked high and low for her missing seal skin about the fields and the yard. Years passed, and she birthed him a son, a handsome, inquisitive little thing, who gave his mother no little joy, and the shepherd reassured himself that all was well. But one day the boy went to play around the standing stones, and rolling around in the grass he came across a small wooden stick with a red rag tied around it. He dug with his hands at first, and then with the stick, and was confronted with a sealskin, wrapped in old cotton. He looked at the article, confused, then heard his mother calling him. He ran down the hill, carrying this new strange treasure in his hands. Approaching her, he was met with a madness in her eyes he had never seen before, and without a word, she snatched the skin from his hand and ran out into the water, disappearing completely under the waves. The old shepherd and his boy never saw her again. Father and son lived in that old cottage till the end of their days, vowing never to interfere with spirits, faeries and the like. Even now, it is said that on some winter nights, a woman's shrieking can be heard echoing from the standing stones. People swear it is the selkie girl returning to find she spent too long away in the sea - years pass like mere minutes down there - and has returned to find her child long dead." The guide gave a sad smile. "She haunts the standing stones, hoping they will return her boy like they returned her skin."

Cat smiled to herself at the mystery, but felt the smallest shiver go down her spine. A sad story indeed, but Cat felt it was a warning- for men and women - to not ever fully trust anyone. She stepped away from the mesmerised group, locked in her own thoughts. Like the selkie girl's treasure, waiting at the standing stones, if Cat went there, would she find what *she* was looking for?

Cat walked along the now much quieter street; tourists still meandered glancing down at brochures as they went, as some of the shops began to flip their "closed" signs on doors. Cat made her way home back on the bus. The evening air had begun to blow and Cat could feel the iciness nipping at her, spring had certainly not sprung here, when would the warmth come? She decided she would treat herself to a bath before dinner and heat herself by her fire. When she finally reached her hotel room, she found a note under the door waiting for her.

Only me just thought I'd see if you were here for lunch today. Mon said you went into town today to see the sights, hope you had fun! I opened the studio a bit late today, so feel free to pop into the shop - I may be working there well into the night!
P.S Last night was great by the way!
J x

≈

That night Cat popped next door to the local chip shop and picked up two fish suppers. Walking up the street she saw Jessie's shop-front lit up, but with the blind down. The evening sunlight spilled onto the stone flags, it's last rays soaking everything with a rich gold before it sunk into the sea. Cat waddled with her two heavy bags up to the door and gave the hardest knock she could muster; trying to make a sound over the loud music she could hear within. After a second attempt she went around the back, where the door stood slightly ajar. She soon found Jess bent over and lifting canvases off the floor.

"Hey!" Cat shouted over the music.

Jess screamed and dropped the canvass on the floor hiding her face with both hands.

Cat screamed too in shock, and then dropped her bags. "Jess it's me! You left a note under my door!"

Jess quickly realised and started laughing, leaning hastily over to turn down the music.

"Crazy girl! It's only me, what did you think I was, a ghost?" Cat chuckled after her fright.

"I had no idea! It's an automatic response. You could have been an axe-murderer!"

"Well I don't think covering your face with your hands would have saved much of you!"

"Hmm maybe not!" Jess picked up her canvases and put them to one side as Cat carefully offered up the bags of dinner. "Hey I smell fish and chips! Please tell me I'm not hallucinating from the paint fumes? I'm starving!" Jess stomped her feet eagerly like a little girl.

"OK, OK!" Cat removed the newspaper packages while Jess got together some cushions and blankets and placed them on the floor of her studio. Both sat themselves on the mishmash heap and began eating.

"It's just missing one thing..." Jess said in a silly voice with her finger in the air.

Cat picked up the other bag and brought out two bottles of beer.

"You're a mind-reader! I do declare Miss Cat you are rather fabulous!" Jess giggled and took a bottle.

"I know," Cat agreed; "You just better have a bottle opener!"

"Of course!" Jess jumped up and went in search of the device.

Once seated again the two girls ate their dinner out of newspaper cheerfully. It wasn't long until, surrounded by empty wrappers and bottles abandoned on the ground, the girls were groaning and moaning about being so full.

"I think I'm going to explode... I should not have eaten that much!" Jess grunted.

Cat got up off the floor and stepped over to a collection of similar large canvases. The colours were energetic and intoxicating, prompting Cat to jump right into them. The brush strokes swirled into a deep midnight-blue sky, with standing stones etched out in silhouette below. She thought of the story of the selkie-girl, and gazed more closely at the imposing stones.

"It's just beautiful there at sunset." Jess took down her hair and ran her fingers through it with relief. "Especially on a crystal clear night in the middle of winter when Northern Lights are shimmering above."

"I want this one," Cat said decisively.

"Really?"

"Whatever you're selling it for I'll pay," Cat pursued, determinedly.

"Well I could give it to you for..."

"No," Cat butted in, "I don't want a deal because I'm your friend, this is stunning work, and I could keep looking at it forever." She fell silent a moment. "Although you will need to keep it here for me, for the time being if that's OK? Just until I find my own place."

"Of course!" Jess smiled, happy with her only sale of the day, flopping back down to nurse her full stomach, as Cat gazed in awe at her beautiful new acquisition.

7

M rs Hughes pulled up outside the hotel early the following morning tooting the hooter briskly. Her rattling Skoda made uneasy noises as its engine struggled to stay running. Cat hurried to look out of her bedroom window and ran down the stairs to greet the old lady. Mrs Hughes was squeezed into the driver's seat; a compact arrangement of short grey hair, a wide forehead, and thick glasses perched on top of a winkled nose. Cat noticed the car seats were covered in hair, and distributed an overpowering smell of wet dog.

"Hello, I'm Cat. You must be Mrs Hughes?" Cat asked timidly through the open passenger window.

"I am, I am, come in love, let's get started! I have morning tea in an hour so we better begin pronto!" Mrs Hughes spoke in an authoritative, military tone, which made Cat snap to attention and quickly strap herself in for a ride.

"ON WE GO!" Mrs Hughes cried with vigour, and the clattering car accelerated up the cobbled incline. Cat thanked her lucky stars there wasn't a pedestrian in sight as the old woman swerved the car this way and that. "So are you from the islands?" Mrs Hughes enquired, glancing in her side mirror.

"No I'm not, I'm from Glasgow."

"Very nice, very nice. Well lets stop here and let you take over!" The Skoda stopped abruptly in a lay-by next to the water. Cat began to panic almost immediately.

"But...but I don't- ," she began.

"Enough of that, you want to pass your test, eh?" Her companion examined Cat sternly from beneath her perched spectacles.

"Yes, but I've never been behind a wheel before...?" Cat clasped her now clammy hands and started to feel very nauseous. She'd only ever steered a bike before now, and even on that she had fallen off, and crashed it into her neighbour's garage door.

"Doesn't matter, let's get you started immediately and get you to pass. I have no patience for lesson after lesson, doing baby steps. I'm old and the only local instructor here, so let's get going so I can have my morning tea on time". Mrs Hughes wrestled with her seatbelt and struggled out of the driver's seat. Cat sighed, and resigned herself to the fact that she had no excuses now, and Mrs Hughes was clearly not the kind of person to allow her any either.

Cat stood behind the bar and felt her day had passed by in a whirlwind. Her driving lesson had not been as terrible as she had imagined. She hadn't killed anyone, or crashed Mrs Hughes' Skoda into the sea. All in all, not a bad beginning. But now she had to start learning how to be a barmaid! Fresh feelings of insecurity and shyness bubbled inside her as she waited on Jim to finish talking to a customer and start showing her how to pull a pint. Just as they were bidding farewell, a large group of customers came through the door. The men were all extremely broad-shouldered, and slightly terrifying-looking to Cat. A bald man with missing teeth mumbled a request in her general direction. Horrified, Cat had no idea what the man was saying, and looked over to Jim, who was bent down behind the bar reaching for the peanuts. The man grumbled the order again, but Cat was still none the wiser.

"I'm sorry, sir... is... is it a pint you want?" Cat gave a smile but felt her cheeks starting to burn.

"Yes, eighty!" the man persisted, clearly irritated at not getting his drink.

"You want 80 pints?" Cat asked baffled.

Finally Jim looked her way with a smile and pointed to the draft beside him. "Is it the usual pint of Eighty-Shilling, Terry?"

"Aye!" barked the bald man as Jim coaxed Cat to the pumps. Cat attempted to pull the pint while Jim kept close to her and with an encouraging nod to Cat; she felt that the end result was presentable to the client. After she had worked the till a couple of times, and served several other big men that looked like each other, she began to get into the swing of it; even when Jim went out for a cigarette break she was happy to hold the fort.

As it was during the week and fairly quiet, they closed the bar a bit earlier. Cat watched how Jim politely but firmly told the customers to drink up. Even against protests of the more tipsy drinkers who would remember an unmissable tale they had to tell him, he managed to clear the floor, saying at every turn "you tell me that story tomorrow, fella."

Cat watched how he locked up, counted and ran up the

till money for the night. "Think you'll be here at the weekend?" Jim asked her when switching out the lights.

"I hope so!"

"You did really well tonight, you're good with people - even Terry! I'll see you Saturday night then!" Jim patted her gently on the arm as they both went their separate ways.

Cat walked up the stairs in an energised mood. She was not tired yet and in good spirits after a successful first night as a barmaid. She went into her room and opened her curtains to see the pale moon above and its rippling reflection on the dark waters below. Without a moment's hesitation, she packed a bag with bits and pieces she had bought in the tiny art shop a few days earlier - paper, pencils, along with her little camera and her iPod - locked her room, and went down and out the back entrance of the hotel, her shadowy figure swallowed by the dark silky night.

Dim street lamps highlighting her route, she passed between old, white washed houses which lined both sides of the street. On one side behind the single line of dwellings the sea slapped and slopped close by. Cat found an opening between two houses that led down to the water. She followed the path to a pier where she stood and took in the twinkling lights of Stromness clustered around the rippling water.

Cat zipped up her thick fleece and crouched on a safe spot on the pier. Pulling out pencils and paper, she did what she hadn't done in years, and sketched instinctively. The moon lit up the sky and her view of the horizon. The sky was incredible; she had never seen the same sweep of colours in the city, and she drank it all in, allowing her hand to do what it wanted. In a gentle frenzy she sketched the view before her, and took some photos of the lights with her camera. After a half hour or so, she sighed with pleasant relief, switched her iPod on, letting the music of Debussy swim around her. Leaning her back against thick iron bars of the pier, she sat in tranquility taking in the view.

The next day, Cat had her second driving lesson with Mrs Hughes. This time they were in the car much longer and drove to the next town over the way. At the end of the lesson, Cat had noticed her hands were not clutching the wheel as tightly as they had been at the beginning of the lesson.

"A lot better, lass," Mrs Hughes concluded as Cat parked outside the hotel.

"Tomorrow?" Cat asked, surprising herself.

"I have two lessons in the morning, but I can manage the afternoon." Mrs. Hughes raked in the glove box lifting out all manner of dog related items; but gave up and tapped her head. "I'll store it in here!"

Cat giggled and was left in a cloud of exhaust fumes as Mrs Hughes screeched away along the cobbled street.

Back in her bedroom, Cat took out the sketches from the previous night and wedged them around her dresser table mirror. Standing looking at the drawings, she examined them and picked up her digital camera to browse at the photos she had taken. As she had guessed, the photos where very dark, and a little unclear, but some elements still stood out. The moon was blurry and bright shining out like a headlight from its dusky surroundings. Looking at the dim orb of white light, Cat made up her mind on the spot. Her next shift at the pub wasn't until tomorrow night, so she packed her things, made a list, and caught the bus into Kirkwall.

After a few hours of retail therapy, Cat stocked up on

supplies, had gathered paints, canvases, as well as food and wine to see her through the night. Her backpack was full by the time she had crossed off the final item from her shopping list. On her way back to the small bus station, she was distracted by the sound of a ship's horn blasting close by. She followed the piercing sound, which took her down another cobbled street lined with more shops and people. She continued on through a battered alleyway, which opened up to a sprawling harbour before her. A giant cruise ship slowly glided across the water leaving it's destination, like a slow, graceful whale. A few spectators stood nearby, waving cheerfully to passengers on deck. Smaller yachts and ferries clustered around the bay in pops of colour, dwarfed by their brother ship. The smell of fish and chips drifted past as Cat strolled along the waterfront strip, feeling a buzz in the air, of the energy from people coming and going to and from this lively harbour. She thought of the generations who had passed through here, some leaving for America and beyond during the gold rush, some making their home a stone's throw from the houses in which they had been born. Just then, a small ferryboat swiftly sailed into the harbour bringing in a large party of hooting women. The ladies stepped onto the pier, adjusted their pink sashes and began walking Cat's way. Linking arms and laughing together, the mass of blondes, brunettes and redheads passed her in a perfumed haze, heading purposefully towards the nearest pub. Smiling as the hen party disappeared, Cat stepped into a quiet café. She dropped her heavy bag on the floor and fell into a table seat by a window to watch the lapping water.

Later that evening, a sharp thump at Cat's door startled her; she was deep in a trance painting a midnight sky on canvas. She lay on the floor with sprawled paints and brushes on top of a makeshift carpet of old newspaper and tissues. She had wanted to paint desperately, and thought she could sneakily do it if every part of the carpet was covered. She opened the door a crack, hoping it was not Monique, and saw with some relief a smiling Jess.

"Hey sweety!" Her fresh face beamed.

Cat couldn't help but whisper, "Is it just you?" She glanced down the hallway.

"Of course" Jess looked around, more than happy to be part of any new conspiracy. "Who are you avoiding?" Cat let her friend in and Jess gasped at the mess on the floor.

"What's this?" She tiptoed over the newspapers and gave Cat a quizzical look.

"Oh I'm just experimenting, that's all."

"You paint?" Her eyes fixed on the shapes on the canvas and thick pads of sketches.

"I did, I'm just... I gave it another go the other... Anyway I - I'm not sure where I'm going with it just yet." Cat felt her cheeks grow hot.

"I feel bad interrupting you now," Jess looked a little downcast, "it's just that it's Friday night, and I think we should go out!"

"I had planned to stay in and paint," Cat confessed, looking ruefully at her sketches.

"I'm sorry, I know how important it is to work..." Jess hesitated, "but please...it's Friday night! Look, I received a commission today which will pay me VERY well, and I want to celebrate!" She batted her eyes.

Cat giggled slightly, knowing there was no point in arguing. "That's great, good for you! Anyone I know?"

"He's a tourist... he's American." Jess gave a girlish snigger.

"Yeah...and what else?" Cat knew there was something.

"OK OK - he's really cute! I made him a coffee at the gallery while I got more details on what he was looking for. And, Cat - he's just...dreamy!"

"Tell me more, tell me more did you get very far?" Cat broke into jazz hands and laughed.

"Tell me more, tell me more - like does he have a car?" Jess twirled around on the spot "Oh I totally could sing, if only there was karaoke in the pub tonight!"

"Yes well, thankfully there's not!" Cat hated karaoke, especially after her last work night out where she had tortured Bonny Tyler's "Total Eclipse of the Heart", and one of her colleagues videoed her. She was pretty sure it was still kicking around on the Internet somewhere to this day. Jess's eyes sparkled like a hopeful puppy, and Cat sighed. "OK let's go out!"

"Yes!" Jess screeched at the top of her lungs.

"But, I'll need to borrow an outfit...I've nothing dry to wear." Cat pointed to the stash of dirty clothing in the corner.

"Of course darling," Jess winked, "come to the gallery in an hour, and I'll sort you out".

8

Two hours later, the girls were up in Jess's apartment getting ready for their big night out. Jess had lent Cat a beautiful royal blue dress with a cute set of crimson earrings and choker.

"Those colours go so well together Cat, you really suit blue!" Jess looked her friend up and down. "You're so lucky, I wish I was tall!" She pouted.

"It's not all *that* great, I wish I was smaller most of the time. I hate running the risk of being taller than men!" Cat applied her deep red lipstick and looked herself over in the mirror. She unpinned her hair, letting the deep auburn curls spill onto her shoulders.

"And you have gorgeous curly hair," Jess moaned as she sat cross-legged on the bed teasing her locks with an old pair of tongs.

"Hey, don't start that – we all want what we don't have!" Cat protested, "give me straight luscious blonde hair and I'd be over the moon!" Cat stood up, after crouching before the mirror on the floor and padded over to Jess, who was still pouting under her thick eyelashes and curled-to-perfection bangs. "We can't all look like Marilyn Monroe you know." Cat pecked her on the cheek and chuckled. This statement seemed to please Jess even as she wiped the lipstick off her cheek. After more hair tweaking touchups they finally left the studio and went to celebrate Jess's sale.

Dusk had come upon the village, and with the clear street lamps highlighting their way the girls avoided the cracks with their heels. Linking arms, they passed the bar Cat had just begun work in, and carried along the street a little further. Several people stood outside the pub on the south street corner in a haze of smoke, laughing and chatting amongst themselves, and the girls stepped past their fumes carefully and entered the pub. All down one side of the room was the bar, which was busy with a few members of staff rushing from customer to customer. There was a large fireplace on the other side of the room, with clusters of sofa chairs around a crackling fire. A small two-seater leather couch became free, and Jess wasted no time in dragging Cat by the hand to the available spot. Once she had seated Cat, Jess left in pursuit of drinks. Cat looked around the room to see many age groups crammed into the space: older men stood and sat around the bar, and the younger crowd played the pool table in the far corner. The jukebox started playing a cheesy pop song, to which three young girls near her jumped up from their seats and began performing some rather extreme dance moves. Cat took off her jacket and snuggled down on the sofa, enjoying watching everyone around her as Jess came back, glasses in hand and sat down next to her.

All of a sudden the jukebox was shut off, and an acoustic guitar sounded. Cat squinted and adjusted her eyes to find the culprit, sat in a gloomy corner; a tall man wearing jeans and a green pullover, seated on a threadbare stool and strumming a battered-looking guitar. His voice was deep and gravelly, but very harmonious, and direct, somehow. His singing paused while he strummed, deeply absorbed in his song. His dark curly hair shook as he plucked his guitar faster. Cat was enraptured, and could not look away. There was something hypnotising about the music, and about this man playing before her. She wouldn't have looked away if it were not for Jess's hand pushing her chin up to close her gaping mouth.

"What?" Cat gasped as she snapped out of her daze.

Jess looked round-eyed at Cat. "You literally had your mouth hanging open lusting after that musician!" She laughed teasingly.

"I was not!" Cat snapped her mouth shut, "I was just listening to the song!" she responded defensively.

"Sure you were!" Jess winked.

The girls went back to talking to one another while the music continued. Jess was interested in what Cat was doing with her art, so Cat told her about the night she ventured out and sketched the harbour. Shortly afterwards a couple squeezed in beside them who Jess knew: Kate, who was a plump girl with bobbed mousy brown hair and a bright smile, and Michael, a shy-looking boy in his mid-twenties with tanned skin and glasses taped together at the bridge.

"Kate works in the bank down the road, and Mikey works on a fishing boat," Jess informed Cat, while the couple held hands and grinned at their friend. "Mikey is a good person to know, he gives me the odd lobster or two!" Jess nudged Mikey playfully.

"Only if she's good!" nodded Mikey, chuckling shyly. "But I do the boats just for the time being. I'm also the DJ at Club Blue on Saturday nights and I sing too. I'll be on after Paddy's set, to play a few covers".

"Who's Paddy?" Cat asked.

"He's the guy playing now," Mikey pointed to the musician still singing his deep tones into the microphone. Once the song had ended, Cat started clapping, and whooped louder than anyone else in the room. The man behind the microphone looked her way and smiled, surprised. Something jolted in Cat's stomach as she realised: she had met this man before. He was the kind stranger on the ferry who had given her the glass of water.

"He works on the ferry!" Cat blurted out abruptly.

"He does aye, a good guy. He works on the car ferry every few days, goes to the mainland and back again. He also does a few acoustic nights around the place." Mikey continued speaking to Cat while Kate leaned over to Jess, engrossed in their own conversation.

"No he didn't!" Jess cried out then clasped her hand over her mouth and the two girls giggled.

"Those two love to gossip," Mikey rolled his eyes. "Kate gets all the news before anyone else - since she works in the bank, all the customers chat to her while they sort out their finances".

"How long have you and Kate been together?"

"Oh a few years," Mikey smiled over to Kate affectionately. "Known each other for ages, and our parents are all good friends, so everyone was delighted when we got together!" He took a sip of his drink and got up.

"Sorry, I'm up now. Great talking to you Cat."

Mikey kissed Kate and went off to the stage to set up his guitar. Most people in the pub continued to talk and order drinks without looking at the musicians, or really listening to the songs. Cat looked over to the stage, where both men were talking and laughing while Michael prepared his set. Cat took the opportunity to look a little closer at Paddy while he packed away his guitar. His worn jeans were a little ripped at the knee, and he wore a black plain t-shirt under his green pullover, but he looked clean and smart. Without intending to, Cat thought back to the first time she met Dave. She had been out at a bar with a few friends, and he had been sat in a booth at the back in a group of men. He looked successful, confident and happy, she recalled. He had worn a rather flashy suit, his tie loosened around his neck. Cat must have gone to the ladies toilet about four times that night before he paid her any attention. Her hair had been an electric blue, pinned right back in a high ponytail. Later that night when Dave had approached her, he had informed her she looked like a colourful Lara Croft, which had made Cat laugh, and prompted an exchange of numbers. At that stage in her life, she had been confident; she hadn't cared what people thought of her, as she dyed her hair every colour of the rainbow. Looking back now on her old self, Cat smiled and wondered where the punky girl had disappeared to? Why had she changed? Then an almost forgotten memory popped into her head of the time before Dave's sister's wedding.

"Please, please make the effort Cat!" Dave had said to her over dinner one night.

"I am. I bought a dress and we'll look great for the wedding," she told him.

"Don't you think it's time to become an adult now," he said pressing the subject.

"Look, I'm not dying my hair brown!" Cat insisted.

Dave sighed. "I didn't want to say this. But it will look stupid, especially at a wedding. My family will be there and –"

"Your family know how I look David," interrupted Cat getting more and more irritated.

"Cat please, I just think you need to look a little more... normal. You're not an art student anymore."

"Don't I know it!" Cat snapped at him and played with her food.

"Cat please... It's time," he ended in a condescending tone.

From then on, Cat did not know who she was. She had changed. That feeling of being comfortable in her own skin had disappeared, to be replaced with insecurity and a doubting complex.

While she pondered on this, she did not realize the other girls were trying to get her attention.

"Cat! Cat, another drink?" Jess shook her glass like a bell, with ice cubes rattling together.

"Yes, and I'll get these this time." She jumped up and went over to the bar, while Michael played a Beatles number. The bar was pretty crammed, so it took her a while to get the attention of the bartender to make her order. A man's voice came from behind her just as she reached the front of the jam.

"Hi there, do you remember me? We met on the ferry the other day. Well - I met you!" Green eyes shone down at her as she spun around, accompanied by a beautiful smile..

Cat stammered. "I do! er.. yes, the ferry! I spoke to Mikey...your friend... I thought I recognised you!" Cat extended her hand in a formal manner. "I'm Cat".

He took her hand and laughed. "How do you do Cat, I'm Patrick!" He made a playful bow of his head towards her. "How are you feeling these days? You looked pretty ill the last time I saw you!"

Cat was a little embarrassed thinking how dreadful she must have looked on the ferry, positively green and looking a fright; the thought of it made her cringe.

"Right... Thanks for making sure I was OK. I'm not great with boats, especially ones that rock back and forth like a giant hammock the whole duration of the trip!"

"Yeah, it can get that way some days, it was a windy crossing I remember".

Just at that moment her drinks arrived, and payment was taken, leaving her a little unsure what to say to him. She stood awkwardly with her drinks while he made his own order. Her face began to flush.

"Well it was nice to meet you Patrick, I better get these drinks to the girls over there. Um.. oh - great singing by the way! So...bye!" Cat made her exit feeling like a complete simpleton: *What was wrong with her? Why couldn't she talk like a normal person?*

Once she handed the drinks to Kate and Jess, she slumped herself down on the couch beside them and looked over to Mikey who was now singing Van Morrison.

"What's wrong?" said Kate her big blue eyes showing mild concern.

Cat sighed, and knew she wouldn't be able to lie about this, so she sandwiched between the two girls and unburdened herself.

"I'm just such an eejit! I frustrate myself sometimes, why am I so rigid and clueless about things? I just go through my life being so uptight and formal about everything!" Cat drained her glass and sighed again.

The two girls, on either side of Cat, looked at her with curiosity and caution.

"Love...what are you talking about?" Jess asked, baffled.

"I don't like who I am, this is not me. I feel I've spent so many years a certain way, and it's not... me!" Cat gulped, frustrated.

Jess looked at Kate briefly.

"Love, I'll ask again – what are you talking about?"

Just then Patrick came over to the group and crouched down to speak. He smiled at all three girls, and said a few words to Kate; Cat assumed they knew each other from similar nights out. Jess gawped at Patrick, and then saw the expression on Cat's face. She had Cat's hand in hers, and tightened it reassuringly. Patrick rose to his feet, about to leave, when Jess piped up.

"Hi there!" she spoke clearly, "my name is Jess!"

"Oh, sorry!" Kate bit her lip a little, "this is Paddy, Mikey's mate. I'm usually at pretty much all the gigs on this island, as Mikey - and Paddy - play them all!" she explained. "These are my friends, Jess and Cat." Kate pointed to the girls, while Cat kept her eyes firmly on the ground.

"Very nice to meet you Paddy!" Jess nodded to him, and noticing Cat was saying nothing, she leaned closer and continued: "You were really good tonight, you have a lovely voice!"

"Thanks very much!" Patrick smiled and sipped his beer, appearing a little embarrassed at the compliment.

"I really enjoyed it...but not as much as Cat here! She goes to gigs all the time in Glasgow, and she told me you were the best thing she's seen in ages, quite taken aback really, weren't you Cat?" Jess indiscreetly nudged Cat in the ribs.

"Yes... yes that's right" Cat came to her senses, still unsure how to form complete sentences when it came to engaging with the most beautiful man in the room.

The musician's face broke into a smile, showing off shining eyes. "Really? Thanks Cat. I know it's very different here compared to the big city." He continued smiling her way, and Cat was hypnotised. "What bands have you seen recently?" He sipped his drink and gave his full attention to

Cat as she listed some bands she had seen over the past few months.

Jess quickly got up from her seat. "Listen Paddy, sit here, I've got some gossip to catch up on with Kate." Allowing Patrick to perch on the couch beside Cat, Kate and Jess squished in beside one another with very pleased looks on their faces.

9

The next morning Cat woke up to heavy groans. Beside her lay Jess in the fetal position with her arms over her head. A moment passed and Jess let out another loud groan, so Cat got some water and laid it on the beside table next to the tousled invalid.

"Thank you," croaked Jess, as she gingerly reached for the glass. "Urgh, I swear now I'm thirty the hangovers are much *much* worse..."

"I told you not to take that shot!" Cat sniggered in a high-pitched voice to aggravate her friend.

"Urgh... I don't want to hear it!" Jess dramatically put her hand over her head again. "Thanks for letting me stay though" she opened one eye and looked at Cat.

"Of course!" Cat pulled open the curtains to greet a rather grey morning.

"Urgh! Why are you so happy?" Jess grumbled shielding the light from her eyes.

"What? Have you forgotten? Did you not see me talking to the most gorgeous man in the whole village last night?" Cat beamed at her friend and gave a little hop onto the bed.

"Oh yeah!" Jess perked up and smiled at her friend. "Please do tell more, it might at least make me feel better. Plus, the memories from last night are coming back to me. Och... that American guy!" Another groan.

"What happened? You guys were talking for a while."

"Yeah he's the one who gave me the shots. He turned out to be a dick - and he's married! Bastard."

"Oh hun! So no commission now either?" Cat's hand flew to her mouth.

"By god there's still a commission, he will be paying me for the painting! But the painting is for his wife. Totally led me down the garden path - he was even trying to get a kiss last night! The only place my mouth was going last night was to another drink!"

"Oh darling, I'm sorry!"

"Na it's fine, better to know straight away than wasting any time on mind games." She sniffed and looked back at Cat. "So, back to you and Patrick, tell me the details!"

"If you insist!" She got into bed once more. "After you did your magic trick and got me and Patrick talking, he turned out to be a really nice guy. He's been living here for a while. He's from Ireland! Oh and he plays the guitar and the piano."

"Uh huh... is that it?" Jess laughed aloud. "All that time you spoke to him, that was all you've got?"

"There's more of course!, I'm just a bit hazy of the details." Cat closed her eyes to think. "There was a lot of beer."

"OK wait, is he single?" Jess, the ever practical one, got the most important question in before Cat went floating off to cloud nine.

"Well, erm he didn't say he had a wife or a girlfriend... but I didn't actually ask!" Cat snorted.

"Hey, it's a good question to ask! That's how I found out the American guy was married. He didn't speak of it, didn't even wear a ring, and flirted with me the whole night. It was only when I asked "Are you seeing anyone?" that he confessed.

"Oh no! What if Patrick is with someone? I mean of course he will be... it's a tiny island, and what girl would say no to him?" Cat tried again to tap into the groggy mists of her mind and recollect everything they had talked about.

"Hm...yes this does need to be addressed – oh wait! Kate was there, she never said anything about a girlfriend!" Jess padded the duvet cover with her hands and looked under the bed, then rummaged in her bag until she gave a triumphed laugh when she found her phone and started frantically texting. "Kate will let me know, I'm sure he's single, but best to check before you start to like him!" Jess finished her text and looked at her friend. "You didn't kiss, did you?" she asked suspiciously.

"No way! What kind of girl do you think I am? I just met him!"

"Well if it was me, I would've snogged him all night long, I've done a lot more than that with a man I've just met." Jess raised her eyebrow "But then again that American from last night has put me off for a while..." She sighed. "But let me tell you, I can be a naughty girl! There was one time where -".

"I don't want to know!" Cat pretended to put her fingers in her ears "la la la not listening!"

"Oh Cat, you are a lovely girl, but you're such a prude!" Jess rolled her eyes.

"Hey, just because I don't go around snogging boys! I've only recently split up with my long-term boyfriend!"

"That was two months ago!" Jess cried,

"I know - that's recent!"

"No it's not! It's not like you've been left a widow and loved your husband 'til the end; you told me you'd fallen out of love with Dave a long time before you left. What are you waiting for?" Jess looked wide-eyed.

Cat chewed the inside of her mouth and looked down, unable to meet Jess's gaze. "I don't know".

Just then the phone beeped, making the two girls jump.

"It's fine, whatever the outcome" Cat assured herself loudly.

Jess pressed buttons on her phone, and silently read for what seemed to Cat an eternity.

"You are good to go my friend!" Jess wiggled on the bed and held her phone up to Jess to read "Single!"

The two girls whooped and bounced on the bed.

"You read that for a long time. Jeez, I can't believe how much I wanted him to be single!" Cat screeched, then quickly covered her mouth in surprise and embarrassment.

"Well, the lovely Kate said he was with a girl for a few years. She was local, but she's now living in Australia. They split up, not sure why." Jess re-read the message aloud, and they both settled down on the bed.

"What now?" Cat grinned at her friend.

"Bacon and eggs?" Jess pleaded with big blue eyes.

"I'll get my purse," Cat smiled and for the first time in a long while, thought that life couldn't get any better.

10

Weeks went by in a blink of an eye. Cat couldn't believe how busy she was. Her pub shifts were a comfortable weekly occurrence, and she felt that she was achieving progress with her various endeavours slowly but surely. She had also been given the nickname "Red," after her auburn hair. One of the regular customers started employing it to call for more drinks, and somehow it had spread. People were now saluting her on the street, "Hey Red!", which she was becoming used to hearing, and admitted to Jess one afternoon that secretly she loved it. Her driving lessons had come on too and she felt quietly confident of her imminent driving test. The wait itself however, made her a little giddy and apprehensive the whole day long, so after finishing her afternoon shift in the pub, she grabbed a quick coffee with the other staff members in the kitchen. Another new addition to the workforce was Angie, with whom Cat had recently started to enjoy gossip catch-ups. Cat marvelled at how much Angie knew about everyone and everything on the island.

"Did you see them both drinking at the bar together?"

She held her cup in one hand as she crammed a leftover scone into her mouth. The two girls leaned against the aluminium worktop where the kettle and other biscuits lay. The kitchen was about to start serving dinners, and Jim the barman was chatting to the chef.

"You can't go round saying things like that, lass!" He stopped his conversation and tutted over at Angie.

"I'm not saying anything!" A look of utter disbelief came over her face. "It's over the whole island that they're having an affair, and it must be true if they were drinking together last night!" Angie continued further into another story of two locals who Cat didn't know.

"Come on now, whest your tongue!" Jim shook his head like a disapproving father and started his conversation up again with the chef.

Angie looked at Cat exasperated and shrugged her shoulders.

On her way up the stairs of the hotel, Cat passed Monique, who stopped in front of her. A deep blue dress with black check print clung to her waist and hips, paired with black heels. She looked incredibly smart and sexy. Cat stood back and admired.

"Monique you look amazing!"

Monique put her hands on her hips and looked down. "Oh this old thing? Had it for ages in the cupboard."

Cat was sure that wasn't the case, it looked brand new.

"Anyway - just the girl I was looking for!" Monique announced.

"Oh?" Cat suddenly felt apprehensive.

"Now don't take this personally, we love having you live

here as well as work for us. But the room you're in, well we'll need it soon. It's starting to get busy here."

"Oh... Right! I mean, of course..." Cat bit her lip. *Crap, what was she to do!*

"Cat, honey - do you seriously plan to stay on the island?" Monique asked the question that Cat had been avoiding asking herself since she had arrived. Everyone who came into the pub asked "Are you here on holiday?" or "What brings you to the island?" All these straightforward questions had been uncomfortable for Cat to answer. *What could she say?* "Well, I quit my job, and left my boyfriend after reading a magazine article about The Old Man of Hoy?" She thought not! So she had told people she was here on a holiday exploring. But as she stood in the stairway with Monique's eyes boring into her every cell, she felt speechless, and afraid of what the future might hold. She was beginning to like the freedom of not knowing.

"Erm...I think so. I think I want to stay here. I'm sorry; you've been so good giving me that room for as long as you have. But there's nowhere on the island to rent, I have been looking." Cat swallowed, "within my budget at least. I don't even know where to look for a cheap room."

"Oh darling, that's why I'm coming to you now. You see, a lovely old woman called Margaret, one of our regulars, passed away not too long ago." Monique stopped for a moment, and a tense sadness flickered across her face.

"I'm very sorry for your loss." Cat touched Monique's hand gently.

"Thank you, darling." She sniffed. "It was some months ago now. Marge came to the pub every day at 3pm for her glass of sherry, to read the newspaper, and talk with the staff. She was a gem of a lady, she used to organise our karaoke nights, which were very popular round here. She loved Abba!" She smiled to herself. "Anyway, I'm getting distracted, my point is her family live in London, or France, or something like that, and they've decided to let her old cottage. It will need work, but since I was a good friend of lovely Marge, they've kept me in the loop. And I thought you might want to take it? Or, have a look, and see what you think?" She glanced at her watch not waiting for an answer, "I must dash - just remembered the Chef wanted to talk to me earlier." Monique sashayed away, elegantly distracted.

"Thank you!" Cat called after her.

The next day Jess was locking up the gallery when a beaming Cat appeared, glowing, at the door.

"Hi love, come in!" Jess waved her friend in, who remained on the step, smiling and shaking her head.

"Why not?" Jess looked down the street then back at Cat, bemused.

Cat pulled out a set of car keys and pointed to a bottle green Beetle parked up. "I passed my test!"

"Wow! That's brilliant!"

"I know!" Cat lifted her arms high in the air, completely carefree, and hooted with sheer excitement and relief.

Jess looked again down the quiet road for any disap-proving passers by, but all was quiet and still, apart from her loudly enthusiastic friend.

"OK! Shh there, people might think there's a fire!" Jess laughed.

"Come on, let's get out of here!" Cat threw the keys in the air, tried to catch them but picked them up with a smile.

"You're so daggy my friend," Jess giggled as Cat stuck her

tongue out and walked out to the quirky automobile. "I can't believe it – and, hang on - how did you get such a cool car?"

"I've actually had my eye on it for a while, it was for sale round the back of the chippy. I bought it several weeks ago and told them to hold it for me!" Cat started up the car, which made all manner of noises as they drove off.

"Let's go to those standing stones!" Cat suggested excitedly.

"Oh yah," Jess pouted and dabbed her curls. "Jeremy, *do* take me somewhere nice."

"Jeremy?" Cat laughed while she tried not to run into anybody on the way out of the cobbled street.

"It's a driver's name…I think!"

"You're one strange girl!" Cat concluded.

"And don't you love me for it!" Jess cried in a theatrical manner, and fluttered her eyes in Cat's direction.

Leaving the village and driving past empty fields, Cat leaned her arm on the rolled-down window, and saw in the distance starlings flying in formation, sweeping and darting as one. The view was breathtaking, with the horizon going seemingly on and on, speckled with the tiny spiked arms of the wind farms in the distance. Cat sighed and smiled over to Jess, the feeling of freedom hitting her even more now as she drove her very own car.

"I can't believe how close we were to the standing stones the whole time," Cat said in awe, staring at the ancient boulders on the horizon, as she walked, hypnotized, away from the parked car. "It's just amazing." She strolled up the hill taking in the view while Jess hugged herself, shivering against the cold winds swirling around them.

"It's June!" Jess protested. "Why is it still cold?" she shook her fist at the sky.

"Come on!" Cat took her arm and guided them together up the pathway of green grassland until they reached the standing stones. Cat continued to walk on along from boulder after boulder, and touching each one gently as she passed. Some were covered in emerald moss; others exhibited strange engravings. She closed her eyes and felt a feeling of peace and belonging. Looking out to a loch ahead, she caught sight of two swans gliding across the water. Silence fell over the girls, and the only sounds were from birds on the waterside. Cat's heart felt very big. She didn't know how to put it into words. At that moment she knew instinctively, *this is it*. Zipping up her jacket to her chin, thankful she had taken it, she sat herself down on the grass cross-legged. Time slowed for a moment, and it was only when she felt a poke on her shoulder that she looked up, startled to see Jess standing above her.

"I cant believe you're still sitting here, come back down to the car, before you get a cold! Or even more importantly – before I get a cold!" Jess put out her hand.

"Yes mum!" Cat reached out and grabbed it, steadying herself. "I'm coming back here to paint," Cat said in a wistful way to no one in particular, as they descended the hill.

"I wouldn't have expected anything less," Jess responded, with a fond, knowing look.

11

Early the following morning, Cat packed a picnic and drove to the potential rental property Monique had kindly brought to her attention. She squinted at the inky scribbles that she had been given earlier. Not entirely confident in her interpretation of the instructions, Cat eventually found herself approaching the shadow of a large mansion at the end of an empty road looking out to sea. Here, she pulled into a passing place to consult the cryptic directions. She was to turn up the single lane skirting around the side of the big mansion and go to the end of the road. Cat continued slowly on her way, praying that she wouldn't encounter another car on the narrow lane. On her left, fields of corn swayed gracefully in the wind and to her right were the waves; roaring and crashing gloriously against the rocks. She drove on a little further, noticing a small weatherbeaten church on the hill, blending in almost entirely with the landscape, with its stone roof showing tiles with gaps like a toddler's teeth, and more than a few of the gravestones beneath slanted in different directions. Cat made a mental note to go up there and explore. She found old graveyards fascinating, giving her a glimpse of a life long-past. That was something she would always do when visiting a new city or town, stroll around any cemeteries and read the inscriptions; for some reason it made her happy. Dave had found this pass-time extremely odd: "It's very creepy," he'd inform her on numerous occasions, whenever the subject was broached.

Cat cleared the memory from her head and continued on again, driving down the single-track road until finally she came to a cottage at the very end. It stood nestled between a few sparse bushes and trees, its roof and chimney exposed starkly against the clouds. Cat parked up in a tiny lay-by; she presumed people would usually drive up to this point, realise there was no further road, and out of apparent necessity, reverse to go all the way back to the mansion house crossing. She got out of the car, looked around at the empty scene, but not a soul was in sight. She had never known this particular type of luxury before; it still took time to get used to after living in a city all her life. She went up to the little gate, which was red with rust and already open, then slid through. There was a small over-grown garden, fenced off with bushes and weeds domi-nating the earth. A small shed stood behind the house, sheltering from the wild Atlantic sea out onto which the front of the cottage faced. Rattling in her pockets for the keys that Dominique had given her, she unlocked the back door and stepped into a kitchen. It was cold, that was the first thing that hit Cat, and there were boxes everywhere; it seemed that all Marge's belongings were packed up with nowhere to go. She walked around the icebox to where a wooden table and worktops lay, beside an old Rayburn. The space looked very old, with its traditional oven and stone flags underfoot. She walked into a larger room which had wooden floors exposed and a wood burning stove in the corner. The wall before her had its curtains drawn; she pulled them back and let in some much-needed light. She peered out of the large window and saw bushes blocking the view of the sea ahead; *this woman really enjoyed her privacy*, thought Cat. She went through another door that led her to the side of the house, this had a few more windows than the other rooms, giving it a brighter sunnier quality. She assumed this was where Marge had read her newspapers in the mornings. Cat sighed for a moment, and then retraced her steps. She spent a long time going into rooms over and over again, each time seeing the dormant possibilities within. The two bedrooms upstairs were of a good size, and anyway, she did not need a lot of space; it was only going to be herself here. From the upper floor, Cat could see the view from out over the shrubs. The ocean's grey swells heaved under the moody dark sky, with a distant rumble, and odd flashes of light reflecting off the water. It was breathtaking. Grabbing the piece of paper that had Monique's directions on, Cat scribbled down the equipment and tools she'd need to mend the house. Excitedly, she locked up, and hopped into her car, determined already on an immediate shopping splurge: she would live here, and there was no ifs or buts.

Once parked in her now usual spot in Kirkwall town, Cat walked briskly down the cobbled street in search of supplies. She was peering into a hardware shop window, deciding whether or not to enter, when she felt a tap on her shoulder. Springing around, she gasped softly to find Patrick looking down at her. She had forgotten how tall he was, but not the piercing green eyes, which shone at her, making her skin tingle.

"I, er, didn't mean to scare you!" He had his hands in his jean pockets, looking a little awkward.

"Oh you didn't, it's OK!" she stuttered, "I was in my own world, as usual. How have you been, Patrick?"

"Good, just doing the usual. Bit boring at the moment, been on the ferry back to back shifts, though today I have the day off. Just adjusting my feet to steady ground, you know!"

"That must be so strange. Honestly I think I'd be sick everyday if I worked on a boat!" Cat confided.

"Na you get used to it, trust me. You just need more practice." With this he gave such a small wink that Cat wasn't quite sure if he had in fact winked at her. "So doing some shopping?" He nodded to the goods behind her.

"Well spotted sir! But I have a special reason for this quest – I'm going to be the tenant of a cottage by the sea and need to do a few things to make it more.... habitable!"

"That's great! It's always nice to get new people here. Especially ones I can lure to my gigs!"

"Oh I see!" Cat laughed resisting the urge to look at his lips. "Here was me thinking you like having more people on the island, but really you just want a bigger audience to watch you play!"

Patrick chuckled and looked up the cobbled lane they were both standing.

"Fancy a coffee in there?" He pointed up to the café where Cat had been once before.

"Sounds lovely" she smiled but then looked down at her list, suddenly panicking inside, "but I do need to buy some tools...."

"OK." He scratched his stubbled chin. "Well this is just a

thought; I don't want to take up your time if you have a lot to do. But if we nip in for a coffee - I desperately need, and maybe a bite to eat - then take a look at your list and see if I have anything I can loan to you rather than you having to buy something new."

"Oh yes please!" Cat erupted a little too suddenly with delight, coughed hastily, and stepped sideways away from the hardware shop window.

They stepped into the cozy café, which smelled of cinnamon, as the weather changed to a stormy downpour of rain.

The waitress came over while they both slid into a booth next to the window.

"And this is summertime, can you believe it?" The waitress tutted at the sky outside.

"You'll just need to take a wee trip to some Spanish island, Bernie," Patrick suggested. "You know the true beauty of Orkney lies in the people and the land. Not the weather!"

"Oh yes of course," Bernie scoffed. "But still a little bit of sunshine goes a long way!" She looked Cat up and down, and winked at Patrick. Patrick shook his head, sighing, and introduced Cat to the waitress. "Are you the new barmaid then?" Bernie looked Cat over again appreciatively. "My brother Angus said there was a pretty barmaid, apparently all the boys have been over to the pub to get a look at you."

Cat sat with her mouth open, unsure of what to say.

"If there's an attractive girl around, the boys move fast. I'm surprised you've not been asked out by any of them yet!" Bernie grinned and waved to happy customers leaving the café. "But I see Patrick has beaten them all to it, eh?" Bernie winked at Patrick and Cat was sure he blushed ever so slightly.

"OK, away with you, you stirrer!" Patrick shooed the waitress.

"But you haven't ordered anything yet!" Bernie said with hand on hip.

After their order was taken, she trotted off grinning back at Patrick.

"That one is full of mischief, never you mind her". He ran his fingers through his hair and they both sat in an awkward silence. Outside the rain lashed down. They watched people running quickly down the street, and others hanging about in shop doorways waiting for the onslaught to stop. Their coffees arrived and Cat sipped hers happily while an Ella Fitzgerald record played faintly in the background.

"I love this song..." She relaxed her shoulders and hummed along with the melody.

Patrick watched her with a smile. "It is a classic, her voice is like silk."

"I agree, just pure heaven." Lying back in her seat Cat started to feel a little more comfortable in Patrick's company. "So what's your story Patrick? Why did you come to Orkney?" she folded her hands together, imitating a detective from an American TV show.

"Well, Miss... er what's your surname?"

"It's MacGregor"

"MacGregor, I like that. It's a good strong Scottish name."

"Why thank you, and yours?"

"Flanagan."

"Well, that is the most Irish name I've ever heard!" She clinked her coffee cup with his. "Cheers!"

"You're a little mad, aren't you?" he chuckled while Cat took a big gulp of coffee.

"I have no idea what you mean," she concluded with a pretend-offended air.

He smiled and scratched his stubbly chin again, which Cat found extremely sexy, though she couldn't say why.

"Well as you know, I grew up in Ireland, southern Ireland. Cobh is the name of the town, just outside Cork city." He smiled to himself. "Me and mum lived right beside the water. I never knew my real dad - he died when I was a baba."

"How terrible, I'm sorry." Cat resisted the urge to place her hand on his.

"It's fine, I never knew him. But I think he was a good man, from the stories she told me." Patrick looked down at his coffee. "My mother remarried an Orcadian called Luke when I was older, so he's the only father I've really known. He worked out in Ireland on the boats, that's how he and my mother met. He lived with us until after I left for college. I couldn't wait to go to college, so I left for the student life in Dublin."

"What did you study?"

"Music. I really wanted to be a composer for films!" He chuckled, reminiscing about his younger desires.

"That sounds like an ideal job. I always thought picking songs for films might be a fun way to make a living. Mainly just watching films and thinking, 'Oh I know which song should be played during this bar fight, or, as the hero heads off into the horizon on a horse or -"

"Yeah, it doesn't really work like that, it's mainly dealing with royalties and probably lots of legal issues."

"Not watching films, smoking a pipe and drinking bourbon?"

"You have a very rose-tinted idea there, I'd hate to burst your bubble!"

"Well you have!" Cat gave a slight childish pout.

Patrick stirred his frothy coffee. "Anyway, I loved the music degree, but once it was over I wasn't sure where to go from there on, so I just ended up working in pubs. Making money to pay bills suddenly became kind of important!"

Cat knew that feeling only too well. "Have you ever gone back to music?"

"Well, apart from my acoustic nights and writing my own songs, I play my other instruments from time to time - but nothing more than that."

"What other instruments do you play?"

"Violin, piano, trumpet, flute, harp... but guitar is the easiest one to play in the pubs. Can you imagine me trying to sing, strum on a harp, then play a quick burst of the trumpet in between? It would sound and look a bit mad!"

"Well I don't know, it might be kind of cool! Something different, people always like to be surprised."

He hummed and looked at her with mocking suspicion.

"I'm serious - something to think about! Carry on with your story!" She waved her hand and relaxed into the couch. More people came into the café, shaking their umbrellas and laughing at the crazy storm that was happening outside, to which Cat wasn't paying too much attention at this point.

Patrick scratched his head then leaned back. "So where was I...yes – well while I was working, my mum and dad moved to Orkney, since my dad was from here. They spent a couple of years here, during which I visited them as often as I could. Then mum got ill. I came over and worked here and spent the time with mum at home and in the hospital. The doctors and nurses were just amazing, couldn't do enough for mum. Although in the end, the cancer beat her and she passed." He paused and took a little breath.

Cat still resisted the urge to touch him.

"Anyway, I decided to stay here, I had made friends, and the place felt like home."

Cat didn't know how to react; she couldn't help but feel incredibly sorry for Patrick. *But hadn't she gone through this same thing too with her mother?* Her throat dried and she swallowed, dismissing the familiar sorrow that started to creep in. "Do you see your stepdad much?"

"Oh all the time, maybe twice a week we'll have a drink or he'll make us dinner," he grinned. "Cooking is not my talent, so I leave it to others!"

"Oh don't say that, you're just giving in without trying. Practice makes perfect, or so I have been told!" Cat gave a gentle nod.

"OK OK, maybe you're right." he took a drink of coffee and watched Cat for a moment. "So shall we take a deco at this list then?"

Cat eagerly brought out the scrap piece of paper and smoothed it out on the table.

The car was unpacked and all the borrowed tools from Patrick were safely in the kitchen waiting for tomorrow's epic day of DIY. She stood there in the quiet by herself as the sound of Patrick's van drifted away in the distance. It had only just occurred to her that she had spent most of the day with him. Cat smiled thinking of the fits of laughter she had been in as they packed the car. She certainly liked Patrick, but since she had only just split up from Dave, it was maybe best to just have Patrick as a friend. Cat looked around the house seeing pink light streaming through the window. The sun was beginning to set, making the sky a deep dreamy rose that crept softly into the house. As Cat locked up, and was about to go through the gate she paused for a moment, and noticed lying forgotten on the ground a wooden sign with the very faded words: *Bramble cottage*. Cat turned around to peer up at the house and said to the previous owner, wherever she might be: "I'll look after your house Marge. Thank you." She took a deep breath and sent her wishes to the old lady she had never met, hoping she was in the kind of heaven where an Abba tribute band was performing just for her.

12

"Darling you mustn't do too much, you give me the receipts and I'll see if I can get them to pay for something. These city people in London don't care about anything up here in 'rural-ville'". Monique sat behind the reception desk with papers scattered all across the table. She seemed to be picking up folders and placing them in alternative positions; Cat was not entirely convinced she was organising the clutter. "The more work you do, the easier it is for them to sell the place and make a hefty profit. So we must get what we can from them!" Her face turned a little pink and then she sighed. She stood up, slowly took off her glasses and rubbed the bridge of her nose. "Poor Marge, she loved that house. Those people only care about money, they didn't care about Marge one little bit when she was alive."

Cat gently put her arm around the glamorous woman, feeling a little scared in case she was told off for doing such an informal thing. "I love that house too, and I'll take care of it."

Monique patted her hand with affection. "I know you will darling."

"If the family want the money so much, why haven't they sold it already?"

"That would involve them coming here and getting their hands dirty – or paying someone else to. Besides the market isn't so good at the moment. Different story in London I'd imagine, but not many people are prepared to put their hard-earned cash into a property on a remote island these days." She sighed.

"Would it be possible to stay here two more nights until the house has had a little more work done to it?"

"Of course, you can stay a week if you would like?" Monique's glasses were back on and her sensitive side hidden again.

"Thank you, I don't think I'll need that much time. Just two nights and I'll get a bedroom tidied up".

Monique nodded her approval. "And as a wee favour, could you be in the bar tonight? Poor Jim has flu."

"Just me?" Cat got slightly anxious at the prospect. "It's Saturday night, will I have any help?" Weekends were incredibly busy, and there was usually two people behind the bar.

"Just you I'm afraid darling, I'm sorry, all my staff are unwell!" Monique shook her hands as if wanting to strangle someone, so Cat made her exit quietly and anxiously awaited her shift.

When Cat emerged from the staff door into the bar, she was faced with the three usual customers. She greeted them and received some nods, while one read the newspaper, and the other two watched the TV screen above the bar. *What could go wrong? They order the same drinks all the time, it'll be fine.* She reassured herself.

Five hours later she was not of the same opinion. After
the kitchen staff had gone home, two large parties of men
had entered and soon the bar was full. She ran out of
change first of all, as the tills hadn't been stocked; luckily all
the men had been happy to pay by card so she had quickly
resolved that issue. Then the kegs had needed changed, all
the while men were demanding drinks over the bar with the
jukebox playing in full swing. Cat had scanned the room for
some customers she vaguely knew, and asked them to help
with the kegs while she continued to serve. Just when she
was collecting herself, thinking with relief that now all she
had left to do was call out last drinks; a fight broke out
between the two parties. Fists were flying, and Cat stood
frozen to the spot looking at the scene before her, while the
jukebox blared away merrily. *What should she do? How did
this even happen? They were all laughing just a second ago!* She
shook herself and without further thought, marched up to
the main switchboard, turning off every switch her hand
felt. The result was darkness, and no more music. The
shouting stopped abruptly, the men subsequently unable to
see who they were hitting. Cat clasped her hand around a
broom that lay next to her, and shouted, "OK, EVERYONE
OUT!" A roar of men laughing and shouting met her in the
darkness, so she switched on the light with the bleary eyed
faces looking at her and continued: "I'M CALLING THE
POLICE, GET OUT IF YOU DON'T FEEL LIKE ENDING
THE NIGHT WITH A CHAT AT THE STATION!" She
started to dial digits on the counter phone, and went out the
room to the staff quarters. There she stayed for a few
minutes trying to calm herself a little. After several minutes
had passed, she emerged again to just one man at the bar.
He was one of the old regulars who had sat quietly sipping
his pint all night long.

"Are they are all gone?" Cat asked wearily.

"Yes love, all gone. Thought I'd stay just to make sure." And with that he drained his pint and got up to leave. "I'll be off too, better lock this door after me in case you get anyone else coming in." He slowly put on his waterproof jacket and trudged out.

Cat did as he said and immediately locked up. She took a deep breath and realised she was trembling. She poured herself a dram and knocked it back with a cough. She looked over the mess in the bar and hastily cleared up the broken glass. She put a song on the jukebox, took another dram, which she paid for, and cleaned up a bit more. The cleaning turned into singing, then singing into dancing. After two more songs, she switched everything off for the second time that night, and headed upstairs, realising with surprise she was smiling.

13

The next morning, Cat went down for an early breakfast. Monique wiggled through the door in a tight green dress which looked positively stunning.

"Monique you look gorgeous today, that colour suits you so well!"

Monique graciously took the compliment, never one to shy away from attention, but then she quickly looked around to see if anyone else was listening, and said in hushed tones: "What happened last night?"

"Oh yes, what a night! I can't believe how busy it was!" Cat exclaimed smiling. "Oh, can I have the full fry-up, I'm starving!"

"Yes, yes" Monique said with a slight flick of her hand, eager to get back to the original conversation. "I heard this morning a guy said something rude to you, and you threatened to glass him, and chucked everyone out!"

Cat looked up at Monique in bewilderment. "What, who said that?"

"Oh it's going around the village that you scared a bunch of men away and have quite a temper on you!"

Cat let out a laugh. "Are you serious? It's 8am! How has a rumour like that spread around already?"

"Well you know what village life is like, gossip moves fast and now you're known as a tough-handed woman... did that really happen last night darling?" Monique looked both intrigued and a little scared.

"No it didn't, well not really. Sit down and I'll tell you what happened, so you can set the record straight for me!" Cat told the whole story to Monique, who gratefully lapped up the information with relish. Once every detail was told, Cat let go a big sigh, and asked petulantly: "Now can I have my breakfast? I'm wilting here from hunger!"

"Coming right up!" Monique was clearly impressed, and soon came back with a very large plate of food, and stacks of hot buttered toast. "Cat darling, you are a good barmaid, I hope I can rely on you for a few shifts a week regularly?"

Cat took a gulp of her coffee and got stuck in to her food. "Mmhmm!" and her cup swiftly received a top-up from her admiring waitress.

After breakfast was shovelled down, Cat packed her car with a makeshift lunch and set off to Bramble Cottage in the misty morning. A wall of fog completely covered the sea so much that it was hard to imagine the water that lay outstretched underneath. The cottage came into view at the end of the road looking a little spooky surrounded by the thick murky grey. Cat immediately set to work, cleaning the house of the larger items of rubbish, and clearing the bedroom to paint. Hours passed and Cat continued on, only stopping for a brief sandwich and a swig from her flask of tea. As she was screwing the lid back on, she heard a rumble of a car nearby, and went outside to see who it was. The mist had cleared to expose a beautiful summer's day. Not a cloud in sight, the blue sky reflected in the water as well as the rays of dazzling sun. Cat looked around the back of the cottage and saw Patrick step out from his van. He looked even more handsome today in some paint-splattered jeans and a red shirt. He smiled as he walked towards her, his shirt hugging his broad shoulders, and showing freckled, tanned arms. Cat reflected how Spanish he looked, with his dark features.

"Well hello!" She said smiling with her hands in her pockets and admiring him on the approach.

"Hi!" He came up to her, and both of them stood awkwardly. "I was scared you'd kick my arse around town if I didn't show up willing and put in a bit of time to help you," he winked with a cheeky smile. "You might throw me into the road by my shirt collar next time we meet, followed by a broom and an empty cider keg!"

Cat sighed. "Oh great, you've heard also?"

"News travels fast round here!" He chuckled. "Of course it's all gossip, and I know it won't be true!"

"What makes you think I wouldn't try to beat up some rowdy customers if they asked for it?" she said in an offended manner.

"Oh, you're too nice to do anything like that. Although you are tall and strong-looking, I'd say you could probably win a fight if you wanted to!"

Cat didn't know whether to be offended or flattered, so she just bowed slightly, and escorted Patrick into the house to show him the ever-increasing list of jobs to be accomplished.

"OK, I'll start in the kitchen and repair some of the woodwork, and the window. I'll let you know when I'm done then I'll move on to the bathroom." Cat was utterly impressed by his practical attitude, and left him to it while she continued her own work upstairs.

Cat had finished an undercoat in the main bedroom, mopped down the wooden floors and arranged the wardrobe and cupboards. All she needed now was a mattress, and a couple of rugs for the floor to warm the room up a little and insulate against the cracks. She walked to the bathroom, hearing the sounds of Patrick routing the shower and poked her head around the door. "You want a cuppa?"

Patrick looked up and his lovely green eyes shone back at her. "Yes please, that would be grand." Cat fetched her flask and poured him tea. He took the cup gratefully and stopped to look at his handiwork. "Not bad, if I should say so myself," he nodded.

"It looks great!" Cat wondered to herself how she was ever going to pay Patrick back. "I can't believe what we've done in a day! Thanks so much." She touched his arm affectionately and withdrew her hand immediately, alarmed at her over-friendliness. Cat was quite a touchy person, and always gave her girl-friends hugs whenever she saw them. When it came to guys, she had a little less experience.

"No problem, I'm happy to help," he reassured her "maybe next time we'll get some better tunes on?" He indicated to the old battered radio player in the hallway which played only one radio station.

"Of course, next time I'll hopefully have records and a record player. I've always wanted to play records, and I actually saw an old player in the charity shop in town."

"I'm glad to hear it! It's the only way to listen to music, really!"

They looked at one another with quiet appreciation.

"Right, well I'll need another five minutes here to tidy up, then I'll be finished." He drained his cup and handed it back to Cat.

"Thanks again, Patrick, I really appreciate your help. Anything you need from me, or I can pay you?"

"Get me a pint and we'll call it quits?" he suggested, scratching his stubbly chin.

"Two pints?"

"Done!"

"Give me a shout when you're all packed up and we'll drive back to town for a drink." As Cat left him in the bathroom she couldn't believe how confident she was becoming. She felt a foot taller; as though she could take on anything - even another pub-full of belligerent villagers. *One thing at a time!* she smiled to herself, and picked up the broom with a triumphant flourish.

Once they were back in Stromness, they parked together, and went to a café-come-bar with a terrace overlooking the still water. The afternoon had disappeared and was edging into evening. Patrick and Cat sat with the waning sun beaming down on them as they talked, and drank ice-cold beers.

"I've had such a lovely day with you!" Cat could feel the beer was making her tongue a bit loose. "I mean," she corrected herself, "it's been so productive, I just need to find a mattress, and I can move in tomorrow!" They chimed their glasses together in celebration.

Patrick looked at his watch. "Oh bugger I completely forgot! I'm to play an acoustic set at the club in Kirkwall tonight!"

Cat's smile faded a little and an uneasy feeling swept over her, *was he just making excuses to go?* She nodded to him, trying her very best to look unaffected by his leaving. "Of course, you better go!" The high buzz from earlier quickly diminished.

Patrick looked around distracted. "Jeez what's wrong with me, how could I forget!" He started patting down his pockets, looking for something.

"Hey I've got this remember, beer is on me. If you need to go then go!" Cat ushered him.

"I'm going to have to take the bus as well, I can't risk driving after two pints." He produced his wallet. "Are you sure you want to get the drinks?"

"Of course, please don't get the drinks too - I'd feel bad taking advantage of you!"

He put his wallet back into his pocket. "Damn, that's annoying! I was having a nice time as well." He sighed and stood up. "Well, if you find yourself in Kirkwall tonight feel free to stop in at club48!" He grabbed the empty glasses and gave Cat a kiss on the top of her head, saying as he left, "And Cat, I wouldn't have minded you taking advantage of me." Cat remained in her seat, a little dazed; *did he just do that? Did he mean to do that? Maybe that's how he says goodbye to all his friends who are girls? And what he said - was he just being funny?* Cat stayed sitting in the same spot and watched him return the glasses to the waitress at the bar. The waitress was a young, pretty brunette who clearly knew him, and was giggling, and trying to flirt. As Patrick disappeared, Cat couldn't help but feel a pang of jealousy knowing almost every other girl lusted after him also.

She drained the rest of her drink, utterly conflicted. *Should she go to the gig? She would have to get a bus too, that would seem keen - maybe too keen?* Her mind swam with endless thoughts, and there was only one person who could help.

14

Cat almost ran to Jess's gallery, she tried to calm herself and slow her speed, but something in her kept her going faster. *Perhaps it was that kiss?* Arriving at the back under the eaves, she banged the door behind her.

"Jess!" she yelled, and then realised there was a small woman looking at a painting in the backroom. "Oh! I'm very sorry!" Cat composed herself.

Jess appeared from behind her customer. "If you'd like it in a different frame, I can do that also?" Over her shoulder as she approached Cat, mouthing "Everything OK?"

"I'm fine, I'm sorry. I thought you were closed. Take your time!"

Jess looked straight into Cat's eyes with bemusement, and whispered, "Go upstairs and make us a cuppa, I'll be ten minutes."

Cat went up to Jess's flat, made two cups of tea and sat anticipating her arrival. She fidgeted with her hair, braiding and re-braiding her auburn locks. Time still dragged, so she decided to wash the dishes, and give the kitchen a little tidy as the jittery energy persisted. By the time Jess came up the stairs, the kitchen was spotless. Cat was sat on the couch and had arranged the magazines on the coffee table.

"WOW, what a great sight to come home to! I got a sale *and* my house tidied! Could it get any better?" Jess walked over to the couch and bent down to give Cat a peck on the cheek.

"That's amazing!"

"Yip sold my big oil landscape. The tourists love landscapes, I need to do more!" She fist-pumped the air and did a little dance.

"We should celebrate! Lets go into Kirkwall and dance!" Cat poured fresh tea for Jess and handed it to her with an innocent smile.

"What's going on with you anyway?" Jess squinted suspiciously at her friend and sniffed her tea. After a moment's hesitation she sipped it with pleasure. "Ah! I don't think I've had a cup of tea all day, it's been pretty manic."

"All the more reason to let your hair down!" Cat smiled encouragingly.

"All the more reason to get a fish super from the chippy and have an early night." Jess shoved Cat over to the other side of the couch and sipped her sacred cup of tea.

"Noooooooo!" Cat whined.

"What is wrong with you?" Jess took off her shoes and propped her feet up on the coffee table.

"Patrick is playing in Kirkwall tonight, we spent the day together – you know he's helping me with the house right? And it was just so lovely Jess, we had an excellent day and got all the jobs I wanted done, and then we went for a drink and that was lovely too, then he remembered he was playing a gig tonight and kissed me and left, but then the waitress was flirting with him on his way out and-"

"OK stop!" Jess put her hand up with authority. "Breathe honey, breathe. There's no need to get in a tizzy, he may be a dream-boat but – wait, he kissed you?" Jess quickly put her cup down and faced Cat properly.

"Yes, and it was heavenly!"

"I knew he'd be a good kisser, he's got lovely lips. That's the first thing I noticed - well that and his hair."

"I know I know!" Cat bounced with excitement.

"OK, so: details; was it slow and sexy, or passionate and fast? Jess tapped her friend eagerly for information.

"Neither..." Cat began to feel a little embarrassed.

"Oh I see, was it like a few kisses, gentle and considerate?" Jess's thoughts drifted dreamily away towards the art of kissing.

"No..."

"Oh, was it like-"

"No, he... he kissed me on the head." Cat thought about this statement and lay back on the couch deflated.

Jess was about to ask for further details, then realising what Cat had just said, also sat back and looked at her friend with quiet concern. After some moments of silence, she contributed cheerily: "Well, it's a start!"

"Suddenly I feel depressed - where's your alcohol?"

"Don't drink when you feel down Cat, not a good habit!" Jess put her hand on Cat's shoulder in an authoritative manner.

"OK, miss," Cat said in a low voice.

"Right, I think we need to nut this out. I'm sure there's lots of details you've missed, so let me pop down and get us fish and chips, we'll chat some more on it and see what can be done. Okay?" Jess nudged Cat, but with only receiving a groan in return, she took that as a yes, and went to get their dinner.

.   .   .

The girls had discussed most of the details of the day, had finished their fish suppers and were making themselves comfortable on the couch.

"You know we'll need to go to this club tonight, right?" Jess said, stretching her legs out before her. Her tummy was full; she was sleepy and warm on her comfortable couch, but she walked over to the window and peered out into the darkness, seeing to her dismay that the weather had drastically changed to rain, which streamed down the windowpane. She turned to Cat with a sigh. "But first, I need a strong coffee."

Once the girls had finally opted for casual smart attire, they were lucky to catch a lift by a girlfriend of Jess's who was also going to the gig. The weather was truly the worst Cat had witnessed since living on the island; thunder roared around them, lightning flashed across the blackened sea, and the umbrella the girls had taken between them was already destroyed by the time they had walked briefly to get to the car. The club was dark with red lights highlighting the bar and seating booths, elegantly mirroring the ominous weather. Cat looked to the lit stage at the far end of the room and saw Patrick singing steadily into the microphone, the guitar echoing as his hands glided over the strings. *Strumming my pain with his fingers*, thought Cat wryly. He wore a simple white t-shirt, and his hair looked wet from the rain outside. "*Killing me softly*," she murmured, smiling to herself.

"I'll get the drinks, off you go!" Jess whispered into Cat's ear, and coaxed her in the direction of the music.

Cat walked towards the small stage lulled by the music, there were several people dotted around the dance floor drinking and watching the performance. The guitar gently echoed as his deep voice sang slowly;

Your kiss your touch
sends me over
I fell under your spell
Take me lover?
Carry me away
The fire's in your heart, the fires in my heart.

The guitar suddenly stopped, and out of nowhere came drums from behind him, the beat suggestive of an army standing to attention. White light poured over the drummer as he continued the beat, then another instrument sprung up next to him; a long-haired man playing electric guitar to a trance-like rhythm. Cat stood transfixed, letting the sounds wash over her, and take her to another place. Patrick joined in again with his acoustic guitar, and the sounds blended together to bring the room closer, tying them all tightly into the moment.

Cat stood mesmerised until Patrick finished his set, and loud music came over the speakers to fill the interim for the next band. Patrick chatted and laughed with the other band members who came on stage and started to prepare their set. Cat cast her eye around the room, there were a few girls lurking around looking up at the stage – *like she was*, she thought glumly. *He must get groupies. How can a guy like that not have girls falling at his feet every weekend?* Then she felt a sharp prod in her side, breaking into her jealous reverie.

"Hey!" She turned around to Jess, who had drinks in her hands.

"You don't want to look like a stalker!" Jess said loudly over the music. Cat was about to retort, but realised her friend was right. It was one thing to come to a friend's gig, but quite another to be staring at him open-mouthed when the rest of the audience had gone back to the bar.

"I had to take a shot of tequila with Stephanie," Jess indicated to their driver earlier who was at the bar making up for lost time. "I feel a hell of a lot more perky than I did after those chips!"

Cat laughed, and then her laugh turned into a strangled cough as she saw Patrick approaching with his guitar case. "Hey, you came!"

"Jess... wanted to come out... She just made a big sale!" She nudged Jess, beside her who raised her glass to Patrick and drained its contents.

"Of course, Jess is not one to refuse a night out!' He laughed and took Jess's empty glass. "I'll get you both a drink, same again?"

The two girls smiled and watched him go to the bar.

"I never noticed before... but Patrick does have a rather fine arse!" Jess remarked, with her finger tapping her chin.

"Hey!" Cat playfully shoved her friend and they both giggled. They watched a few younger girls approach Patrick at the bar, which Cat tried hard not to notice.

"You'll need to contend with all those groupies!" Jess laughed, ruining her friend's good intentions. "That's why I never was interested in band boys, I want to be the one who's admired!"

"Well you are admired, you're a talented artist!"

Jess looked taken back by the compliment. "Aw thank

you honey!" She rubbed Cat's arm affectionately, and Patrick approached them both again, this time with glasses.

"Great set Paddy!" Jess took her glass and raised it as a toast, which encouraged them all to do so.

"Thanks, it was alright. The sound tech wasn't the best, but their PA equipment is old."

"I thought you sounded beautiful," Cat stuttered. "I mean really great, I loved your last song. I don't remember you playing it the other night?"

"OK!" Jess interrupted, "so, don't mind me, but I see some people over there I know - thanks for the drink Paddy!" She winked at Cat and sauntered off with a grin.

Cat giggled a little.

"That girl gets odder and odder!" Patrick mused while Jess joined the rather loud group in the corner.

"I think she's incredible," Cat smiled to herself, realising suddenly that she couldn't imagine not having the effervescent little artist in her life.

They walked over to an empty booth and sat inside. The bar started to get busier as more people came in for the next band to play. Patrick sat on the opposite side to Cat and nursed his pint.

"I actually can't drink much tonight, I decided to drive after all."

"Yeah we got a lift, though I don't know if our driver is intending to go home!" She glanced over at the bar where Stephanie their driver sat drinking and laughing with friends. "It's so insane out there tonight! I've never seen weather like it – and that's coming from a Glaswegian, rain for us is pretty much a daily occurrence!"

"Orkney weather is the best. I love it when it's stormy, I'm quite happy to go out on nights like these – getting blown about, it sets the creative juices going!" He said with a cheeky glint in his eye.

"Well I'll let you go out on your own, I'm happy staying inside warm and dry!" Cat laughed.

They both went a bit quiet for a few moments, Cat suddenly felt awkward and very shy. Just looking at Patrick's lovely warm open face, his glowing eyes and those lips, Cat felt her cheeks flush, then felt a pang of relief at the fact that they were in a dark club.

"I did really like the last song you sang, is it new?" Cat inquired. It was something to talk about, anything to talk about to stop her face going luminescent.

"It is actually. I wrote it only a week ago. It just sorta poured out of me. I never write songs that quickly. I've wrote a couple recently. There's something really therapeutic about writing down your thoughts, especially if they can rhyme!"

"I wish I could be like that."

"But you are, you paint. It's in you. And your work is beautiful and intriguing-" He looked a little uneasy at what he'd just said.

"But I haven't shown you my work"

"OK a little confession," he scratched his jaw. "I saw your sketch pad when I was helping you with the house today. Cat you have a talent." He looked directly into her eyes. Cat felt a little woozy and didn't know if it was her drink or Patrick.

"Oh god, I'm so embarrassed." She cringed and buried her head in her hands.

Patrick touched her hands. "Don't be, I'm sorry I looked. Although I'm glad I did, you need to show people your work". Patrick's hand stayed on Cat's, then went up to caress her cheek. Cat felt completely weak. His hand went to a stray hair and tucked it behind her ear. The moment between them lasted forever, both staring into each other's eyes under some spell and unable to look away. But the spell broke when the next band finally appeared on stage and played rock music. Patrick looked around and everyone had crowded around the stage on the other side of the room. He slid out of his side of the booth and came over to Cat's side. He gently moved towards her and sat next to her, all the while looking intently into her eyes. Cat sat motionless waiting for him. His hand went to her mouth and she could hardly bear the sensations she felt. She wanted to kiss him but at the same time felt utterly paralysed. Patrick moved his finger across her jawline and leaned in to kiss her. Deliciously soft at first and then with hard passion. He enveloped her in his arms and Cat was in heaven.

15

*S*he felt the sun on her skin and giggled, her heart felt full. Her mother stood above her and scooped her up into her arms, tickling her until she couldn't take it anymore. She wriggled free, and padded clumsily across the sand, squealing with delight as her mother ran after her. The beach went on forever; to her left was a building not quite in focus, and on her right; the water. She tripped suddenly, but her mother caught up, took her quickly into her arms again and cuddled her there on the sand, rocking her, and taking her tears away before they had even started to fall. She was safe.

Cat spent the next few days painting and settling into the cottage. She felt invigorated walking along the nearby shoreline, sitting on the pebbled beach and gazing up at her new home. She thought of Patrick. She hadn't heard anything from him since he dropped her off at Jess's after the gig. They had shared another kiss before Cat tucked into bed a very drunk and merry Jess. The last few days of solitude had, however, given Cat the chance to get bits and bobs organised for the house. She had put up Jess's vibrant painting of the standing stones on the bare wall in her living room. It hung above her newly-delivered sofa, which sat perfectly up against a wall between the stairs and the door to the kitchen. Sitting on the sofa, she could look out the large window on the opposite side of the room to the sea ahead; she just needed to trim back those bushes that clustered around the house outside and the view would almost be a painting itself.

She couldn't believe the generosity of the locals. News got around at the pub that she was moving into an empty house. Subsequently Monique had given her the sofa, and also a bed which she had 'in the garage and needed a home'. Then some kitchen appliances appeared from Angie, and Jim delivered a wardrobe for the bedroom. Cat was truly touched by everyone's well-wishes.

"I better not leave now!" she joked with Monique who helped her one night in the busy pub.

"Don't you dare!" Monique wagged her finger. "We want you to stay, it's lovely having another young girl around I can chat to!"

Monique wasn't exactly a spring chicken, but she certainly did put Cat to shame with her sense of style and energy. The younger woman squeezed her arm, and smiled warmly.

The rain had started, so Cat walked briskly back to the cottage, casting her eye down to the sea before her. The dark clouds spilled a shadow over the water, and as Cat drank it all in, its beauty was so magnificent, she knew she had to paint. She quickly ran to the house and picked up her sketchbook and pencils, before returning back to the same spot to find that the view had completely changed again. Sunlight burst through the clouds, streaming more bright light over the dark sea. She sighed with pleasure and gave in; allowing herself not to think, and just to sketch, letting her hands do all the work. She stood there for what felt like only minutes then fumbling for more paper, saw that she had sketched several pieces already. Pages had been torn out of her book and lay on the rocks around her, remnants of her creative fury. She smiled in her state of relief and calmness, the rain had completely passed, but the clouds still lingered. Cat breathed in the salty air; she decided to get her paints and settle for the day, putting colour to the outlines she had started.

Cat poured herself another cup of coffee and stood in her living room with her paintings covering the floor. Sheets of rough sketches and vibrant landscapes looked up at her. She walked around them, feeling cleansed, free and elated. All the time she'd spent in Glasgow, all those years, and no creativity had come to her. It was like it had been locked in a box, she had known she needed to open it but she had been unable to find the key. Since living in Orkney she couldn't help *but* be creative. *Is it here or is it me? Have I changed?* Cat felt she had to do something that very second to let off more energy. She rummaged through her bags and found some old CD's she'd brought with her. She put on a classic Rolling Stones album. Singing out as loud as she could, she turned up the volume and danced around the room, singing along with Mick Jagger. *What utter bliss to be on your own with no neighbours!*

~

Cat was woken up in the early hours by her phone ringing loudly. She cursed it, switched on the light and tried to find the offending item. Standing on wobbly legs, tripping up half asleep, she stood on her hairbrush, and she was very grumpy by the time she answered the phone.

"What?" she snapped

"Hey, sorry I know it's late," came a male's voice.

Cat lay on her bed confused. "Who is this?"

"It's Johnny... long time no speak!" came the voice. Cat almost had to ask *Johnny who?* This person certainly didn't sound like her old friend.

"Johnny, is that really you? I haven't heard from you in ages!" Cat looked bleary-eyed at her bedside clock; it was 3am.

"Yeah, I know... It's been crazy busy here. You know marketing duties are always on the move." Johnny's usually fun, friendly aura did not shine though the small-deflated voice on the other side of the line.

Cat sighed, put her dressing gown on and made her way down to the kitchen. "What happened?" she asked in a gentle tone.

"Oh you know, parties, people and more parties..." The faded voice joked on the phone.

Cat pressed further "Johnny, is everything ok?"

The sound of a grown man crying choked out over the phone.

"J... do you want to come and stay?"

The ferry arrived smoothly at the pier. The size of the vessel still amazed Cat, it towered above the buildings as it crept into the small village harbour. Cat thought of Patrick, despite herself: *would he be on the ferry today*?

Johnny was one of the last to leave the ferry; Cat stood waiting for him by her own rickety vehicle. Johnny had always dressed immaculately, and today was no exception; he wore a smart white shirt, jeans and a tailored jacket. Johnny beamed at Cat, ran up to her and twirled her around. Cat laughed. She had no idea why her old friend was here, but she knew he needed her.

"Hey gorgeous, it's been too long!" he kissed her on the cheek.

"Yes, ages! I haven't heard from you – have you been receiving my voice messages and texts?" Cat reflected that she had heard nothing from Johnny after she left Glasgow.

"So - look at this quaint place!" Johnny interrupted. "How did you end up here?" He briefly glanced around, then opened her car boot, and placed his small suitcase in between drills, screwdrivers and various other tools. Johnny looked down at the clutter, one eyebrow raised. "Are you opening a hardware store?" He chuckled and closed the car boot.

Cat ignored this last comment. "I did say about all this in messages to you, but maybe my phone isn't working?" Cat thought of the messages she sent to Jess and Monique, which were always received promptly, and wondered how bad a time of it Johnny had really been having. "Anyway, it's kind of a strange story, the place just sort of... spoke to me." Cat started the car and waited for Johnny to put his seatbelt on.

"Strange, but of course – it's so you darling!" He kissed her again on the cheek. Cat rolled her eyes; she knew Johnny well, and she knew the face he put on for the outside world was that of a happy-go-lucky guy, who thought everything was fabulous. Well, everything was clearly not fabulous, and that's why he had reached out to her. She would soon find out why.

"Coffee!" Cat announced firmly, and they headed for the nearest café, while a downcast Irishman with sad green eyes watched from the ferry behind them, hands clenched in his pockets.

~

After they were seated comfortably in the café that Cat had begun to love, the waitress Bernie took their order. "Here again Cat?" The short dark-haired girl said with pen and paper in hand, and smiled at Johnny. "And with a new fella?"

Cat gritted her teeth slightly at the girl's remark.

"No Patrick today?" Bernie giggled, making Johnny look up.

"Oh Cat, do you have a young man?" he said, with an air of someone far older. As they were in fact the same age, she'd be damned if he was going to embarrass her after only just arriving, Cat interposed quickly.

"Yes – I mean, no! Patrick, he's just a friend I've made on the island. This is my friend Johnny; Johnny, this is Bernie." She introduced the two mischief-makers and noted to herself to keep a closer eye on Bernie in future.

"A pleasure, always nice to meet beautiful local ladies," he remarked to Bernie, and Cat cringed at his flirting.

Bernie tucked her hair behind her ear and beamed at Johnny. "What can I get you both?"

Cat looked over to the cake stand. "Caramel slice please!" She couldn't help herself, their cakes were to die for, although at the same moment, she thought to herself, maybe a break from the café might be a good idea; her jeans were growing more tight on her waistline by the day.

"Make that two!" Johnny nodded to the waitress and winked, making Bernie giggle as she sauntered off.

Cat decided now was as good a time as any to ask Johnny what was going on. "Johnny, love - is everything ok?"

"Of course!" Johnny smiled, but his usually bright blue eyes looked the complete opposite.

"I think we both know that's not true." Cat waited for his response. He was quiet for some moments, and looked out the window.

"Can't a man visit a friend?" he murmured sadly.

"Of course," Cat continued to look at him as he watched the street outside. "Only I've not heard from you at all until now."

"I know." His body language softened a little as he sighed. "I just got caught up with work, and before I knew it time had passed, and - "

"I understand that, Johnny. But didn't you get my messages? Even if you had just contacted me once to say you were OK?"

He looked down at the coffee Bernie had quickly placed down in front of him. "Thank you, dear," he said with a small smile. Bernie, confused by the very different reception she had received this time round, discreetly left them to their serious conversation. He looked up at Cat. "I could never hide anything from you, could I?" he sighed.

"How is Mark?" Cat asked and stirred her cappuccino.

"OK" Johnny sighed again. "Actually, I don't know, he... he's left me."

Cat had suspected this might be the case. "I'm so sorry, Johnny... what happened?" She put her hand on his.

"Turns out you're not the only one I've been neglecting.

Work took over my life. After getting made partner at the firm I thought things would be easier. But with that responsibility I had to be a part of landing big clients, taking them out to dinner, entertaining. I was hardly at home." He fiddled with his teaspoon.

"Do you still love him?"

"Of course I do!"

"But you're here!" Cat said, confused.

"I needed a break..." Johnny put his head in his hands.

"I'm sure you do, love, but you need to talk to Mark too."

"I don't know what to say!"

Cat looked at her old friend, he sat looking utterly miserable, and utterly exhausted. Cat bit into the buttery caramel shortbread and savoured the sweetness on her tongue.

"How's your shortbread?" she asked through a full mouth.

Johnny quietly followed her lead and a flicker of light came into his eyes. "It's really good!"

16

Cat had a busy shift at the pub that day. There were divers, fishermen and tourists all crowding up the restaurant, and she was run off her feet trying to keep up. She managed to pop into the gallery for a quick lunch, where she found Jess positively ecstatic after selling two of her paintings that morning.

"It's all these rich Americans we're getting to the island!" Jess had laughed as she poured a hot steaming coffee for them both. She had put a lunch break sign over the gallery door and the two girls enjoyed some moments relaxing on the sofa upstairs. Cat bit into a cheese sandwich and rifled through a magazine.

"Have you seen Patrick recently?" Jess pushed out her lips and glanced over to Cat innocently.

"Not since *the kiss*, I've been crazy busy." She flicked over to another page of a skinny model seductively holding a watch. "We never exchanged numbers, but we both know where the other works.... so we'll see, I suppose!" Cat didn't really have a plan when it came to Patrick. She realised, however, that deep inside her, she had been waiting for him to get in touch. He knew where she worked; he even knew where she lived, after all. It had been a long time since she had dated anyone, and the thought of letting herself be vulnerable with another person again made her palms sweaty.

"How's Johnny?" Jess sipped her coffee and kicked her feet out.

"He's OK, though I'm not sure how long he plans to stay for." Cat had explained the situation to her friend previously, as Jess had heard reports that a handsome stranger had arrived on the island, and had immediately phoned Cat to investigate.

Jess sighed. "Such a sad thing, I hope they make up." She took a deep sip from her cup. "I've had so many people ask who Johnny is".

"I hope you haven't been gossiping about us?" Cat looked up in alarm.

"No! I've not said a thing - it's none of their business about Johnny. I've been very good at changing the subject, you'd be proud of me!" Jess nodded with satisfaction.

"Good." Cat relaxed a little, hoping the locals wouldn't pay too much attention to her new guest. "I'm just giving him space, and if he needs me then I'm there."

After Cat's shift at the pub had finished, she came home to find Johnny drinking wine and going through photos.

"Where did you find those?" Cat dropped her bag and marched over to the coffee table where several black and white pictures lay.

"I'm sorry, you know I'm nosy." Johnny certainly didn't seem remotely sorry as he picked up another old box from under the table and started rummaging through more photos. "I gathered they weren't yours, but they're so interesting - look!" He turned over a photo and read out the writing on the back: *Catherine and Celia* at the beach - 1935 - weird that she had the same name as you!"

"Catherine is a common name," Cat remarked, as she picked up Johnny's glass of wine and took a sip.

"Hey! that's mine!"

"Mine now!" She took another sip. "So where did you get these, were they along with the other old boxes in the shed?" Cat had amassed a few things that had been collecting dust in the house, and made room for them in the shed. She'd only seen old furniture, and the odd bit of faded homeware, nothing that looked particularly important.

"Yes! I thought I'd stumbled across some priceless antiques, but these are almost as interesting. Now - I thought I'd do a bit of gardening this evening." Johnny took back the wine glass from Cat in such a casual way that Cat didn't even notice the glass leave her hands. "It was a gorgeous evening, I can't believe how late it stays bright up here!"

"Yip, the other night I came home from the pub and the sun was only just behind the hill – that was 2am!"

Johnny tucked his hair behind his ear; his usually slicked-back look had disappeared since the first day he had stayed on the island. His thick dark blonde hair now flopped over his eyes as he squinted at a photo before him. "Anyway, I actually wasn't being entirely nosy - I went looking for something to dig up the weeds. And once I saw a few old dusty boxes I couldn't help myself." Johnny pulled out his glasses from his hoodie pocket, and put them on to examine the photos closer. The old Johnny would never have been seen dead in glasses, stating on many occasions that they made him look boring and approaching retirement, so had settled for contacts most of his life. Looking at him now, Cat couldn't help but admire him; the glasses gave him an air of relaxed intelligence, and made him look even more handsome.

"Make yourself useful and get me a glass then!" Cat made herself comfortable on the couch and browsed through the old photographs.

She picked up a coloured photo of a woman about her own age. She was surrounded by flowers and greenery and was laughing shyly at the camera. On the back read "Me in the garden - June 1975". Cat looked at the young woman, who seemed so content and happy perched on a bench next to the stone archway.

"Oh Margaret," Cat said warmly, and smiled at the pretty girl.

"Who's that?" Johnny came in with a large glass of red.

"That's Margaret, or Marge, as her friend's knew her. This was her house."

"She was beautiful," Johnny said as they both relaxed on the couch, chatting like old friends again and looking happily through boxes of kept memories.

17

The next morning Cat decided to make a picnic, and take Johnny out to the nearby island. She was eager to see the Old Man of Hoy stone stack, famous in her own remembrance for that fateful, magnetic magazine cover, and today was her day off, so they rented a couple of bikes and set off. Cat was delighted she had a basket at the front of hers; she had often loved the idea of having a pretty bike with a basket full of flowers, gliding through quiet country lanes with her dress floating in the spring air. Luckily the day was forecast to be sunny, so Cat wore a dress, and brought a jacket just in case. With food and provisions packed away in backpacks, they both peddled down to the harbour where the small ferry was scheduled to leave. Unlike the large car ferry that came to Orkney, this little boat could only hold about twenty people. They were helped on with their bikes and the boat set off shortly after. Cat looked back at the island they were leaving, its grey buildings set amongst the small hill looked as though they had sprung up there as naturally as the gorse and the scrubby grass. She was really starting to feel at home here. She had never really had this feeling before, of course, with her mum most definitely, but never about a place. Johnny was chatting to one of the ferrymen with interest. Cat smiled; she loved that most about Johnny. He was incredibly social and could talk to anyone. It was one of his best qualities. Cat mused awhile as she watched the waves billow from the back of the boat. Her mind wandered onto Patrick; his smile, and his kiss. She thought of his last song at the gig, and how it had transported her. Goosebumps prickled up and down her arms. She hoped, in a small hidden corner of her chest, that he thought of her the way she thought of him.

The sailing was short and choppy, this time Cat enjoyed the rough sea, being outside in the salty air helped. *Maybe Patrick was right, you just needed practice?* The ferryboat eased into the harbour of the island of Hoy, the anchor was thrown, and the people jumped onto the pier, assisted by the ferrymen.

"This is so rustic, I love it," Johnny said with quiet excitement before it was his turn to hop off, with a helping hand from the young man he had chatted to earlier.

Without any dilly-dallying, they quickly mounted their bikes and headed into the glen that loomed before them. The sun, high in the blue cloudless sky, shone so brightly that Cat and Johnny gladly took off their jumpers and glided through quiet roads that lead them through an empty landscape.

Another mile or so passed and Cat spotted with relief a place they could take a breather. They laid down their bikes at the side of the road, and walked out to a very large boulder set in the heather.

"It's a stone...?" Johnny stated gingerly.

"Johnny this is incredible!" Cat enthused while she walked around the impressive boulder. "It's more than a stone, it's a tomb! Look how smooth the surface is." She peered into the centre of the rock, which was hollowed out. "Just think - this was done before the Iron Age, before machinery or modern equipment existed. How did they do it?" She had read up on the local folklore; legends of dwarves and giants on the island, all connected to this rock. She stood still and looked up at the stone in wonder. "It's just magical".

Johnny couldn't help but be charmed by Cat's love of the world. She had a childlike innocence sometimes that he loved about her. She always saw beauty, even at times, and within things, where others didn't. He rubbed her shoulder affectionately, and smiled at her gently.

After they enjoyed a brief cup of tea and a biscuit, Cat pulled out her old camera and started taking photos. Johnny groaned inwardly as he waited until Cat had captured the many variations of the stone that she alone could see, including a photo of her beside the stone, and finally one of Johnny. To Johnny's relief they then returned to their bikes and continued on their journey until they came into a village, or rather more of a hamlet - several houses dotted in a straggling cluster on the hillside. They could see the ocean at the end of the road, and a pathway leading up the hill, winding around the little cottages and moving upwards and further beyond.

"That's our path!" Cat pointed breathlessly, and they made their way up the steep hillside.

Cat stood near the cliff edge, overlooking the wild sea and the Old Man of Hoy sea stack, which stood majestically with the waves crashing against it down below. She breathed in deeply and began to feel emotional. If it hadn't been for the Old Man of Hoy on the front cover of that magazine, in the dreary newsagents in Glasgow, she might still be scraping by with Dave, and Sunnyskies, and no paints or sketchbooks in sight. Something had captured her imagination seeing the ancient sea stack. She had never heard of it before that day, but looking at it now conjured up familiar feelings; there was something about it that seemed so well-known...

"You really shouldn't stand that close to the edge!" Johnny called from an overly-safe distance.

"I'm hardly near the edge Johnny! I think you're being a bit dramatic!" Cat dismissed her friend and returned back to the spectacular view before her. She opened up her bag and rooted around for her camera again; turning to Johnny to get him to take a photo she suddenly lost her footing and stood on some uneven rocks. Cat gasped, and in a split second she lost her balance and fell to the ground. Her ankle gave a crunching noise as she collapsed onto her arms, trying to protect herself from the fall. She lay there for a few seconds until the stabbing pain in her right ankle throbbed too intensely to ignore.

"Ow!" she yelped, as Johnny reached her.

"You silly girl, what were you doing?"

Tears sprang uncontrollably to Cat's eyes. "I'm hurt, I don't need you to call me stupid too!"

"I didn't call you stupid, I said silly!" Johnny protested.

"Ow!"

"Well, if you'd been any closer to the edge you would've

fallen into the ocean!" Johnny berated Cat once more, then looking at her trembling lip, stopped himself from saying anything more. "I'm sorry, you just don't listen sometimes Cat!"

"Ow!" came the cry again as Johnny touched her ankle.

"Jesus Christ, Cat!" Johnny looked around wildly for anybody or anything nearby. Except from the one mountain hare they saw earlier, however, they were completely alone. What was more, the clouds above them had turned an oppressive dark hue that didn't fill Johnny with much optimism. He packed their bags and slung them over his shoulders before lifting up Cat in his arms.

"Jesus, Cat! How much do you weigh?" Johnny almost buckled under her weight.

"Hey! I'm not overweight, I've been busy... and... not eating right!" Cat cursed the caramel slices at the café, and shed a few more tears at the thought of being fat and a cripple.

"You're lucky I lift weights at the gym," Johnny joked but it was lost on Cat who looked at the path downhill before them. Johnny looked in the same direction. "I could roll you down hill if that suits you better?"

Cat couldn't help but give the tiniest laugh through her tears. "You bastard... just start walking!"

Wobbling down the steep hill to the sparsely dotted houses, Cat yelped along the way distracted by her pain. She had not noticed that a man was approaching them with his walking stick.

"Are you alright?" came a loud voice to their left. The man appeared to be in his sixties, in a yellow waterproof jacket, and sporting a scraggly white mop of hair and a white beard. He appraised them with a wild look in his eyes, or so Cat thought.

"She took a fall up the hill," Johnny yelled out over the wind that had now picked up.

"Come down to my house", called the newcomer, and he gestured towards a grass roof house near the beach ahead.

"Oh I don't know -" Cat started to protest, unsure of what to do. Every horror film she had ever seen started like this.

"Great, I'm not sure how long I can carry her!" Johnny rejoiced, and Cat kept grumpily quiet whilst they edged towards the small dwelling.

They descended the hill and arrived at the house in no time. The man grunted to Johnny to make his way to the living room and lay the invalid on the couch. They hobbled through to the back of the house, and gasped at the giant window in front of the couch, looking out onto a deserted white beach, and the moody Atlantic sea. The house couldn't have been in a more spectacular spot, its windows positioned perfectly to create an immersion in the landscape circling around.

"Wow..." Johnny gaped, quickly running to the couch before he collapsed under the weight of his friend.

"Ow!" Cat cried as her foot banged the corner of the couch.

"I'll never lift a weight as beautiful as you again, Catherine..." Johnny gave her a dry smirk, and massaged his biceps, gazing out of the window.

"Hey!" was all Cat could say, feeling huffy after Johnny had made such a fuss. She knew she really didn't weigh that much, but made a note to herself that if she did see a gym in Orkney, perhaps joining it might be worth consideration.

The old man came in wearing a ripped red jumper and carrying a bag. Cat was still somewhat wary, and tried to move, but couldn't for the searing pain that persisted.

"It's peas." He held up the bag. "For the ankle?"

He placed the frozen bag of peas on Cat's ankle and stuffed two pillows underneath, propping up her leg.

"Thank so much for you help, sir," Johnny offered in a formal tone.

"Billy." The man removed Cat's shoe and sock, which rendered Cat speechless, unaccustomed to having a stranger touch her bare skin. She felt like a heroine in a Jane Austen novel having been rescued by a handsome man, but instead of the dashing love interest tenderly caressing her leg, it was an old, brusque villager. He tutted, eyeing her ankle. "Looks like a bad sprain, but it should be better tomorrow."

"Tomorrow?" Cat gasped, "but I have work tonight!" She felt like a wounded animal, and hated being at the mercy of others.

"It's better you stay the night," the man announced, with some authority. "If we put you in a car, that won't do - you need to keep this ankle upright, and there's the ferry too, getting on and off that wouldn't be too comfortable, lass."

"Oh dear," Cat muttered.

"Just call Monique and tell her what's happened - they can't expect you to work on a sprained ankle," Johnny said, making himself comfortable on a soft chair beside her.

"Give me my phone," Cat extended her hand, and waited for Johnny to root around her backpack before giving her the device. "Damn, as I thought, no reception!" Cat looked over to Johnny concerned. "Oh dear, I need to let Monique know!" She bit her lip hating the idea of letting people down.

"Monique? From the pub?" Billy asked.

"Yes, I work there".

Billy got up and went to another room, then a few minutes later re-emerged with the phone at his ear. "Hi Monique, it's Billy here from Hoy. Are you well? I have someone here who wishes to speak with you." Billy held out the land-phone for Cat who took it gratefully. "I'll be putting the tea on then," Billy said to Johnny with a smile.

~

"Aw! I love him!" Johnny whispered to Cat as their host left the room. They had all enjoyed a meal cooked by Billy; his specialty spaghetti bolognese was a hit, with both guests accepting second helpings. The day passed into early evening, the rain had stopped, and bright pink skies outside shed their vibrant colours through the window before them. Cat lay on the couch with her foot still raised, a glass of wine in her hand, feeling blissfully content and relaxed. After her initial reservations, she had warmed to the gruff Billy greatly. The old man had told them over dinner that he was a retired fisherman who had owned his own boat at one stage and did very well. He was able to put his money into his home, for the benefit of himself and his wife.

Billy lit the fire in the large living room area and brought out a bottle of bourbon, placing down glass tumblers on the coffee table in front of them all. He poured the dark liquid into the glasses and handed them out. "I hope you like Bourbon, I can't drink whisky." He gestured towards the bottle and took a sip.

"I've never heard of such a thing, a Scotsman not liking whisky!" Johnny exclaimed in mock outrage.

Billy gave a curt chuckle. "I'm a terrible excuse for a Scotsman. But when you try bourbon first it's hard to go back. I drank it when I worked on a boat off the coast of Maine".

Cat drank in his words as well as the bourbon.

"I did a spell out there, and loved it. But home called me

back after a while. It's not the most happening place, or the best weather. But I'm glad I came back when I did; I think it would've been harder to leave if I had stayed longer. And thank god I did, as I met Effie when I came back." He nodded confidently. "Meant to be, we were." He took a sip again. "Enough of me talking your ears off. Tell me about you two. Have you been together long?" Cat and Johnny gazed at each other for a moment then burst out laughing.

"No, we're not together!" they both protested quickly.

"We're just friends, we've known each other forever!" Cat insisted, trying not to move her raised ankle through laughing.

"You clearly get on well!" Billy seemed almost put out to have misjudged the situation.

"We do get on, really well!" Johnny smiled at Cat, then took a breath. "I'm actually married. His name is Mark." Johnny still felt occasionally unsure about telling some people that he was gay, but there was no denying it here. Cat saw a softening in Johnny's eyes as he spoke the words, and hoped it was reflective of a desire to call his husband, and talk things through.

Billy took a moment to digest the information, looked at them both, and guffawed out loud, slapping his thigh, then poured them all another dram.

Cat spent some time chatting to Billy about Effie, while Johnny was in the kitchen at Billy's insistence to phone Mark.

"Married long?" Billy quietly asked, as he gestured to the kitchen doorway, where soft sounds of talking were issuing.

"They met at college, but married a few years ago." Cat

reflected. "Mark is a sweet guy and very patient. Johnny is the outgoing one, but Mark keeps him grounded. I hope they'll be OK."

"Aye, well, I'm sure things will work out." Billy stretched out on his chair and rubbed his eyes, then gave a long yawn. "Right I'll get you a blanket, I'm knackered – it's not everyday I'm entertaining two young things and drinking bourbon into the early hours!" Billy shook his head with a small smile and went to get bedding.

The next morning they all suffered from sore heads. Cat woke to find the swelling in her ankle had gone down, and that she could put her foot gently on the floor.

Johnny had prepared bacon sandwiches and coffee for them all, and then ventured up the hill back to the scene of the crime, returning with the two bikes they had left the day before. Cat still was unsteady on her feet, so Billy had loaned her one of his walking sticks for the journey back and drove them both to the ferry, with the bikes piled in the back of his van. They stood at the pier leaning against the van and watched the ferry glide into the harbour. The same ferrymen from yesterday leaped off the boat and secured the ropes, then began to help people on board. Johnny organised the bikes onto the ferry while Cat edged closer to the boat, her arm linked with Billy's.

"Billy - you've been so kind, I left my phone number on your kitchen table. I'd love to repay the favour and have you come to mine for dinner one day?"

Billy looked away stolidly. "You're welcome, lass." He coughed. "Lovely having the company."

"Don't be a stranger, give me a call and we can have dinner next week sometime!"

"Thanks... aye, thanks." Billy smiled a little awkwardly and Cat gave him a quick hug.

In no time they had boarded, and the ferry began its return journey. The two friends waved to Billy in his bright yellow raincoat until he became a tiny dot in the distance; *but not for too long*, Cat hoped with a smile, wondering where in the locality she might procure some Bourbon.

18

Autumn had started to set in and the days were getting shorter. Cat decided to practice a bit of self-care, and treated herself to hot steaming baths and good wholesome food. She had always loved baking and cooking, and the autumn season in particular was the time of year she took most delight in homemade food. Johnny had left the house for a ramble along the seafront, taking a picnic with him; "I'll be gone all day, I'm going to find myself!" He announced thespian-like as he walked out the door. Himself and Mark were chatting regularly on the phone, but Johnny had said nothing to Cat about any reconciliation, so she avoided pressing him on the subject.

Cat decided to pop into Kirkwall to stock up on food shopping and buy various local ingredients for soups, stews and pies. Kirkwall was the quietest she had seen it since moving to the island; no tourists could be found mooching around the shops or strolling around the cathedral. Cat relished the quiet, and popped into the deli, bakery and the grocers without having to queue. She strolled along the cobbled street, feeling now for the first time, like a local.

Once her car was packed with fresh produce, she made her way back to her little cottage. The familiar journey back showed changes in the rugged landscape; the colours of the hills and the drop in temperature whispered to her that autumn was coming. Autumn was Cat's favourite time of year. She loved the change in the air, and stepping out into the crisp mornings, when the mist was just starting to clear and the birds were happily tweeting in the sparse city bushes, made her heart sing. There were very few trees on the island, something Cat missed greatly, especially at this time, when the trees were dressed in a fiery mantle. Back in Glasgow the parks would be glowing with red and orange tones; how she would love to see those now. Cat parked the car at the old gate and smiled to herself. Despite missing the urban autumn of old the cottage gave her a warm fuzzy feeling every time she came home. *Perhaps she could plant her own trees in the garden?* Rowan, oak and beech would make a beautiful sight, and protect the house from the sea winds. She walked around the cottage grounds, admiring her tidy work cutting back the bushes, and the other little touches she had made to really make this cottage her own.

Over the next few mornings Cat went out to forage for berries. With Johnny's help, she collected bucketful's of brambles found in bushes around the house, and used them in muffins, cakes and jam. She immersed herself in cooking and baking, which soon started spiralling out of control. Cakes and jam jars flooded the kitchen worktops as Cat tried to make more room for even more baking.

"Are you OK?" Johnny popped his head round the kitchen door as Cat put two bramble and rhubarb crumbles into the oven.

"Of course, why?" She turned around, her face covered in flour.

Johnny sniggered. "You have a *tiny* bit of flour on your face."

She wiped her cheek with the back of her hand, only to spread even more flour towards her ear.

"It's been a while since you were with a man, eh love?" Johnny leaned against the door, with a look of pity on his face.

Cat stared at Johnny in disbelief, taking off her apron and casting it on the kitchen table in irritation. "Johnny for Christ's sake, I'm baking. I'm doing fine without a boyfriend. I don't need one. I just need some time to myself. Jesus! As if you're one to advise!" Cat's temper flared.

Johnny put up his hands "OK, OK, I'm sorry. It just looks a bit excessive, all this cooking!" He grabbed a muffin from the plate on the kitchen table and exited the room quietly with a cheeky smile on his face.

"It's called baking. And I don't hear you complaining!" Cat shouted after him. Johnny would always provoke her; he couldn't help it. But she did have to admit secretly that she had been distracting herself. She hadn't heard anything from Patrick since their kiss, and thought, or rather hoped, he had been trying to reach her. *Maybe he had called over to the house a few times when no one was there, or maybe he went to the pub to see her when she hadn't been on her shift?*

Cat decided that rather than encourage her and Johnny to gain any further weight, she had best give away the rest of her treats, before it was too late. She drove into the nearby village and delivered two big pies to the ferry men – one for them, and one to be dropped off to Billy. She took a box of muffins into the pub for her colleagues to eat, which Jim ended up consuming almost in its entirety in front of her, whilst she chatted to Angie. Finally, Cat went to see Jess in the gallery with some rhubarb crumble.

"My favourite!" Jess grinned and took the plate. She rummaged around her work desk and pulled out a fork, and without ceremony started eating the crumble there among the paintings.

"Do you not want some custard with that?" Cat laughed.

"It's been busy here, I haven't had time to eat!" Jess said in between mouthfuls. She sat down at her front desk and stretched her legs. "How's Johnny settling in?"

"He's good, loving the fresh air here. He's enjoying the island way of living." Cat leaned on the desk.

"What? Drinking tea and pottering around"

"Yes!"

"Well, quite - who wouldn't love that?" Jess scoffed.

"I'm just letting him relax, he needs a break to think."

"Such a shame he's gay..." Jess grimaced. "He is seriously hot. Hey speaking of hot men, how's Patrick? Have you seen his flute yet?"

"He plays guitar!" Cat rolled her eyes to Jess's taunts. Just then two ladies came in and asked to look around.

Cat smiled and invited them in, thankful for the distraction from the subject of men. She glanced at her silver watch. "OK, I'm taking over."

Jess looked at her with an open mouth "What?"

"You go upstairs and relax. Or go for a walk. Anything. I'll mind the gallery until closing."

"Cat you don't need to - "

"I want to, not another word!" Cat pointed to the door with a matronly air.

"You're very bossy, aren't you!" Jess walked away slowly, appearing both scared and pleased at the same time.

After the door had closed, Cat looked around the gallery.

"Well, it shouldn't be so difficult, I've watched Jess do it time and again," she said to herself reassuringly. Romantic, slow music from the 1940s played throughout the gallery and Cat looked around the spacious room, admiring the pieces on display. Jess mostly painted women, each with a dreamy quality, yet with bold, vivid outlines, which reminded Cat of the Pre-Raphaelite artist William Waterhouse. Cat truly admired Jess's exquisite compositions, and understood why so many others did too. She went to the back of the room, which was cut off by a Chinese room divider. Behind that lay Jess's studio, which to Cat's surprise was for once pretty spotless. Canvases of works in progress and sketches lay on the table as Cat took in the shading and textures. Some sketches were of local people, including, to her surprise, a very scantily clad Monique. Cat looked away, feeling that she had seen something she shouldn't. She made her way back to the doorway of the studio, and suddenly in the corner of her vision, she saw herself looking back. Up on a shelf beside the door was her own face, staring out at her. Her red hair loosely fell over her shoulders, as she looked at the viewer with a quiet sadness, shrouded in a green textured fabric not unlike seaweed, which covered her body. Cat stared at the piece, feeling strange emotions stir within. *Is this how people saw her? Did she look really like this?* The painting was beautiful, such skill inherent within, but Cat couldn't look at her own sadness any longer.

The hours disappeared quickly. Cat welcomed in a few customers, and enjoyed talking about art. She almost sold a painting, but the client decided to come back with her husband to view a certain piece one final time the next day. She felt satisfied as she closed up the gallery and ascended the stairs to find Jess sleeping soundly on her sofa. A half-eaten plate of pie lay on the dining table, and a dreadful reality show was booming loudly on the TV - families going on holiday together with one member voted off each week. *What rubbish will they think of next?* Cat turned off the TV. She wrote a note to Jess of the afternoon's highlights, and quietly stuck it to the fridge.

Cat walked out into the evening air, and strolled around in the gloomy light to the pier she had once sketched before. Admiring the twinkling lights that now flickered on, she sat there with her legs hanging off the pier. The water was low tonight and it lapped gently against the wooden landing; it was the only sound that was heard in the silent evening air. Cat walked back to her car and opened her car boot. She picked up the last cake, wrapped in tinfoil, and summoned up all her courage to face Patrick. She knew they hadn't really talked in a while, but hoped she could start the conversation again with cake. She bit her lip and willed herself onward. Walking up the street, she came across stray cats along the road. Two large tabbies lay on top of a very nice BMW, and on her approach sat up and looked at her, meowing gently. Cat could never help herself when it came to cats, and petted the two tabbies that jumped down to walk around her legs. It wasn't long before they smelled the cake and their inquisitive noses went to it. Cat tore herself and the cake away from the all-too-easy distraction, and turned off to the avenue where Patrick lived. She strolled along the terrace of houses, and stopped. She stared at the door before her, with the number seven over a brass horse-shoe. She was sure this was the door, Patrick had casually mentioned his address on the night of their kiss. *This must be it.* Her heart thumped hard in her chest, she was terrified. *What would she even say to him?* Before she could talk herself out of her nervous gift, she knocked on the door, hoping to god he wasn't home.

She heard a laugh from within, and a girl with long wavy brown hair opened the door. She was dressed only in a t-shirt that was far too big for her, her long golden brown legs on display.

"Hi!" Her full lips showed pearly white teeth. "Can I help you?"

"Oh, erm.." Cat felt her face grow hot, and her chest grow cold. "I...er.. does Patrick live here?"

"Yes, he does," she smiled.

Patrick's voice came from out back. "Who's at the door?"

"I don't know," she shouted, and turned back to Cat, who stood there frozen slightly.

"He's in the shower" The girl nodded and waited for Cat to say something.

"I'm....I'm... sorry - never mind, I've just remembered I have to meet someone." Cat turned to go and said over her shoulder, "I'll call him, it was nothing important..." and sped back to her car. She threw the cake in a bin on the way, feeling sick at the thought of the redundant gesture.

Of course he has a girlfriend. How could a musician go that long without having a girl hanging off him? Why did I wait so long to get in touch with him? But he never got in touch with me! Maybe she was always there, and I was just another groupie? Oh god, am I a groupie?

Cat fretted these thoughts over and over in her car until she reached home. She got out of the car and slammed the door. She felt humiliated, angry and hurt. *Patrick was having sex with as many girls as he liked, pretty girls who answered his door and wore his t-shirt. How could I be such a fool?* Cat quietly let herself in her cottage, aware Johnny would be fast asleep upstairs, and threw her keys onto the kitchen table. She marched around downstairs, unable to sit still. She really wanted to talk to Johnny, but what would she say? *A guy she'd met a couple of times and had kissed was now sleeping with other girls?* Cat bit her lip and listened for any movement upstairs, but there was only silence. It would be better not to bother him with her small stupid problems. What could he do anyway? It was down to herself to fix things, just like the last time.

All her emotions pent up inside, she suddenly knew she needed a release. She dragged out some paints and canvas from a cupboard, and laid them on the living room floor. Then going to her kitchen, brought out a bottle of whisky and took a large gulp, before slapping paint to canvas in hot, rueful anger.

19

Her mum tied up her dark hair, her curls tightly bound up as she sat on the sand beside Cat. The water crept up to their toes, sliding back at a hair's breadth away. Cat drew swirls on her mother's hands, following the lines and creases around her thumb and fingers. She took Cat's little hand in hers and sighed laying back in the sun. Time stood still as they lay there, happy; together.

The morning came and Cat woke to find sketches and graphic, kaleidoscopic canvases sprawled on the living room floor. She looked at the shining paintings, and was truly stunned at what she had produced. They exploded with a passion that Cat hadn't realised she had in her; paintings of trees with faces showing in the gnarled wood, and others with shapes that formed hands and eyes. She examined the composition, unsure what was deep within her to produce such work. Then a feeling of satisfaction washed over here, a calming reassurance that made her feel she was finally unlocking what was inside of her, piece by piece. One by one, Cat leaned her paintings against the walls to let them dry. Her larger canvas was an abstract, like sea waves, evoking a sense of loss. A shiver went down her back. *What had been holding her back all this time?*

"Really?" Jess was wide-eyed, with her hands on her hips. "You want to do a show?"

"Why not?" Cat laughed feeling dizzy with courage. "That is, if you like my work?"

Cat had driven to the gallery with a couple of her still very wet oil canvases; she had not been able to wait to show her friend, and inspiration had come to her on the way.

"I love them! I see lots of influences here, Jackson Pollock, Gerhard Richter and even Monet."

"Maybe! Yes! All I can say is it just flowed through me, and all I want to do is paint!"

"But a show Cat?" A look of concern flickered on Jess's face. "Are you sure it's the right time, I mean - I love your work. But maybe it's all a bit rushed?"

"It is, you're right, I know that," Cat agreed. "But this feels so right, it's time".

The two girls agreed to collaborate together; Cat would have a show at the gallery and give a cut of the profits to Jess if she sold anything. She would also help out with marketing and general cover at the gallery.

"I want you to include some of your work too, I think both our styles would compliment each other," Cat insisted, and Jess nodded her acceptance as they shook hands with a grin.

The next week was a blur for Cat; each day rolled into the next, bringing colours, darkness and new feelings. Whatever she felt, she let it flow through her and onto canvas. Each morning she would have breakfast and plunge straight into painting. She had never felt more alive or more in control of her life. She had had enough of being unsure of herself, and once again she had known instinctively to take action. She thought of Patrick occasionally, and painted with him in mind at times. She had come to the conclusion that it was better this way, apart; she did not want to be dragged down by another man. He would probably have ended up the same way as Dave; it would just have been a matter of time.

The next week, the girls met up for coffee at a favourite café in Kirkwall. Cat suggested the meeting, and was relieved to have some time away from her house after hours of intensive painting.

"What you need is a studio," Jess said in a motherly tone, placing a notepad and pen on the coffee table. "Trust me, you need a space to work that's not in your house."

"You're right, it's just easy at the moment. But I might clear all Marge's boxes out of the shed and start working there, while it's still warm. I just don't know where to put everything."

"Good problems to have, how exciting you're painting for a show!" Jess cheerily whooped, "It's all happening darling!"

"I don't know how" Cat reflected. "It's incredible, I would never have imagined I'd be in this position this time last year. I feel so free."

Jess patted her notepad with authority. "OK! Now let's start planning, it's only a couple of weeks to go!"

With that, the girls discussed jobs to be done for the exhibition, starting with the wines to be served.

"Shiraz and Chardonnay," Jess stipulated, and Cat agreed; happy to have any wine as long as people drank it in front of her paintings. They also discussed more integral details; to which magazines they should send press releases, and the other different ways they should promote the event.

"Social media of course," Jess mumbled, the pen hanging from the corner of her mouth, "and maybe some country style and art magazines?"

They made notes, decided on which tasks each one would undertake, and ate several slices of much-deserved cake.

The local press soon got wind that a new exciting exhibition was on at the art gallery. Cat found the whole experience very surreal, but a piece of her was enjoying talking about her work, something she thought would never be possible. The two girls had appeared on the local radio station, chatting with the presenter, who had flirted shamelessly with Jess on-air.

"Well, what can I play for *you* beautiful lady?" he asked Jess quietly off air as the first song was playing. "Any requests?"

Jess and Cat wasted no time in making a long list of songs to play as their interview commenced, to the presenter's dismay. "I only meant one song..." he grunted.

"Oh come on, why not a few? We could make this interview last a little longer!" Jess smiled back at him, which appeared to make all the difference.

"So tell us about the exhibition?" The clammy-faced presenter gazed at Jess eagerly.

"Well Darren, the show is named, "On the Edge", and it

showcases work from the talented Catherine MacGregor here, and a few other local artists. It's all about the stormy dramatic landscape that inspires us, and the way it mirrors the strong feelings that we deal with within ourselves - all of us. Catherine will have her solo show on in the front gallery, and the other artists will be in the studio area behind." Jess winked at Cat, looking calm and cool under the immense pressure of engaging the small number of Orcadians who would be listening to the show on their daily work commute.

"Well that's just lovely, isn't it?" Darren had his head resting on his hand, staring directly at Jess. "Where will your work be Jess? What about the landscape truly stimulates you most?" He swooned.

"Well of course, for me, it's hard not to be inspired by the sea!" Jess smiled, then looked over to Cat. "But it's Catherine's show, so why don't we ask her?" she encouraged Darren, who looked over to Cat with as much interest as watching paint dry.

"Catherine MacGregor, then - what is it that inspires you about our little island?" He spoke in a slightly condescending manner that Cat couldn't help but notice. "As I believe you're not from here originally, but from Glasgow?" he added, on a superior note.

"Yes, um, I am from Glasgow, yeah," Cat stuttered. She took a moment to think of what to say. *I'm on radio and I don't know what to say?* was all she could think.

"Yes - so Glasgow, why come here?"

Cat just sat there with that anxious uncertainty feeling rising in her again. She gave herself a moment to breathe out, and to let go of the doubting voice within her head. *Relax, you've got this!* And words just started coming out of her mouth: "This part of the world truly moves me; so much that I left my life in Glasgow to come here. It's been such an incredible experience that I find it hard to put into words. Each day triggers feelings in me that I didn't know I could have. There's something about the light; it changes constantly, making me want to capture every moment before it's lost. Also, capturing how it effects me too, is a constant magnetic pull on my creativity." She let out another breath and looked over to Jess, who grinned widely back at her. "I think in some ways I was meant to come here, I feel such a connection to the landscape. It's strange, but familiar to me at the same time. I try to understand these surroundings, and myself within them. This land holds ancient secrets, and I'm trying to unlock them, in the best way I can - through my art."

"Well, yes, wow – that's... amazing..." Darren sat taken aback.

"The show will open at the end of September, and runs until November. Come along on our opening night, there will be wine and nibbles for everyone. It will be the artistic *and* social event of the season!" Jess gave a dramatic hand gesture as though she were a Spanish dancer, which left Darren all the more transfixed.

"Thank you, girls – I'm certainly convinced! Right, we have one final song that Cat has selected. It's by local musician Patrick Flanagan, called "From the Word Goodbye".

"Patrick is an amazing musician," Cat butted in. "I really think he's one to look out for, especially as he lives on Orkney. He's playing the Club48 soon, so get tickets quick – for the show and for Patrick - before they both sell out!" Cat had tried to block Patrick from her mind as much she could. The image of the girl in the t-shirt still came to her, and as much as she wanted to never see him again, it would be unlikely, given that she had decided to stay. There was, in addition, no denying that he was a good songwriter, and deep down Cat couldn't have forgiven herself for letting an opportunity pass to help someone else who needed it.

"Thanks for that, Cat..." Darren looked at Cat over the microphone, clearly unimpressed with her blatant free-promoting.

∾

Once the girls had returned back to the gallery, Cat called up a couple of art magazines to check whether they were advertising the exhibition in their next issues. Meanwhile Jess opened up the premises for business as usual.

Monique wiggled into the gallery holding a tray, and wearing a dramatic long, black woollen coat. "Ladies: I thought perhaps you would appreciate some coffee and a sandwich. I got the chef to rustle up bacon and eggs for you both, I hope you both are looking after yourselves?" She placed the tray on the front desk and cast her eyes around the room. "Things still going to plan?" she asked, gently smoothing her blonde hair and looking the epitome of elegance.

"Oh yes we're fine!" Jess grabbed her sandwich and bit into the fluffy white bread with relish. "Lots to do, but we're getting there. Aren't we Cat?" She asked, her mouth stuffed.

"Yes, things are going well!" replied Cat, pen in hand, crossing off tasks. "I've called all the local avenues of press, scheduled in some interviews, spoken with international magazines too, oh - and I've been keeping things updated on social media... did you hear our interview today?"

"I didn't I'm afraid," drawled Monique sweetly. "We had a bit of a busy morning at the hotel, very unusual for this time of year. How did it go with Darren - that creep...?"

The two girls laughed in response and drank their coffee.

"The interview went well I think," Cat speculated. "I'm just amazed that Jess somehow wangled it that the radio station would mention the exhibition every day until opening night!"

"Well, I did say for Darren to come to the opening night... and that I would have a glass of wine with him." Jess grimaced. "What I do in the name of art!"

"Make sure it's a quick glass of wine, darling," Monique suggested, "else he will be keeping you talking to him all night!"

Monique had asked Jess if they could talk about her commission. So they went to the back of the gallery and into the workshop, leaving Cat a moment to order banners and invitations for the exhibition.

"We need more post-its!" announced Jess, as she said goodbye to Monique.

"We always need more post-its!" Cat smiled. "I'm happy to get some tomorrow before I come in. Perhaps make a list of any other stationery, and I'll make a dash to the shops for office equipment."

"Excellent!" Jess grabbed a pad and pen then looked over to Cat who was making her lists of things to do for the week. "Is Monique OK with my stealing you?"

"What do you mean?" Cat asked.

"You should be working at the pub, but you've been here everyday helping me plan the exhibition".

"Oh of course," Cat waved her hand. "We chatted, and she's cut my hours for the next month so I can help out here."

"Is that OK?" Jess bit her lip "I mean, I know you'll need

the money? I would pay you if I could, but I'm not sure I'm able to."

"Jess, don't worry about it, I'm looking on this as an investment. I have some savings still so a month away from my salary is fine,"

"OK!" Jess nodded. "If you're sure!"

"I am." Cat went back to her notebook. "Now, start writing that list so I know what to buy tomorrow!"

20

The autumn season grew colder with each passing day. The sea winds whirled around Cat's cottage, stripping away any warmth inside, forcing her to have her little fire on at all times. She had raided her cupboards for warm woollen jumpers and to her dismay, had given away most of her warm clothes to charity back in Glasgow. Luckily there was a local knitwear designer on the cobbled street near Jess's gallery, that Cat passed often and would peer at their beautiful window displays. This month's offering had scattered autumn leaves, with manikins placed on either side, elegantly dressed in draped wool coats, with quirky hats and scarves. Overhead, fairy lights and lanterns bathed the window in a warm bright light. The scene was very autumnal, with burnt amber, deep yellows and rich reds. She decided she would treat herself to a couple of new pieces and mentioned the decision to Johnny, who immediately jumped into the Beetle to help.

"Shopping for you Cat - well, you don't do it very often! In your best interests, I need to be with you." He strapped in his seat-belt joyfully. "Come on!"

"Hey, give me a second!" Cat could never keep up with Johnny when he was in this kind of mood. She rummaged her bag for her car keys, all the while barking back at Johnny's taunts of: "Faffer MacGregor."

Johnny was right; she did need him. Not only did he encourage her to purchase some styles she might not usually pick, but also he bargained with the shop owner.

The large lady stood with mouth open. "I don't haggle on a price, this is not a market stall, or eBay!"

"Come on now, Laura. It's Laura right?" Johnny leaned against the till desk seductively.

Oh wow, he really does want me to buy these things. Cat looked back at herself in the mirror in a very chic grey shirt-dress.

Laura flashed a scrutinising look over Cat.

"She looks fab right? She'll be in the art gallery, day and night, wearing all these beautiful clothes of yours, and people won't be able to help but ask where she got them! And of course, Cat will tell them all about the fabulous Laura, and her fabulous shop - and you'll get an influx of artistically-minded customers." He punched the air. "Then – bang! More sales!"

Cat wondered if this was the way Johnny did business back in Glasgow. *Heaven help them while he's gone*, she thought fondly.

Laura threw up her hands. "OK OK, it's a deal!"

Johnny turned round to Cat, glowing with triumph, as Laura started folding the clothes in dusky tissue paper, and gently placing the items into their bags.

∿

"Woot woo!" Jess catcalled from the back of the gallery when Cat entered in her new long wool coat, grey dress, and red beret. Johnny led her in on his arm and Cat strutted in to the centre of the room and gave her best model pose. She twirled on the spot, only then realising that there was a lady in the corner of the room smiling at her.

"Hello dear," the old lady smiled. "Very nice."

"Oh, ah, thanks!" Cat said colouring a little.

Jess circled around her friend. "Now Mrs White, wouldn't you think this stunning lady before us was a French model?"

The old lady smiled again warmly. "Oh yes, she's a beautiful girl."

Jess winked at Johnny. "And with her model boyfriend too!" Johnny waved his hand like the Queen and graciously took the compliment.

"They make a very handsome couple," The old lady chirped in.

At this stage Cat's cheeks were turning a deep shade of pink, and was too embarrassed to correct the woman of her incorrect assumption.

"Thank you..." Cat mumbled. "May I get you a drink while you look at the artwork?"

"Thank you dear, but I won't." Mrs White clutched her shoulder bag and looked around. She had short wavy white hair, her kind face was rosy and void of wrinkles. "Jess knows I can never afford one of these paintings, but I like to pop in from time to time".

Johnny piped in: "Art is in the eye of the beholder. We all need it in our lives no matter your salary."

"Well I'm pretty sure managing directors of successful marketing companies should put their money where their mouth is and perhaps have some art on their own walls...!"

Jess gave Johnny a pointed look then went to the old lady and put her arm around her. "I love having you as my biggest fan. Go on, stay for a cup of tea?"

The old lady looked unsure. "Well.... OK thank you".

"Mrs White teaches in the local school," Jess filled in the pair as she walked off to make tea.

"Oh really, how lovely?" Cat said, "How old are the children who you teach?"

"They are primary, so aged five to twelve years old. They are all darlings. I'm very fortunate; it's a good school, and I love my job. Been at it for thirty years now!" The old lady looked surprised as she spoke the words.

"My mum is a teacher," Johnny said. "High school though. I'm not sure I could do teenagers, very hard work!"

"The little ones can be too!"

"But a lot cuter!" Johnny countered.

"Well that's true, they can get away with an awful lot more if they're loveable with it!" Mrs White smiled then shook her head. "They're actually all very good children I love seeing them grow and learn day by day!"

Cat took off her beret and coat. "So thirty years teaching, I'm sure you know a lot of people here!"

"Oh yes!" Mrs White chuckled. "I still see my old students, some with children of their own now, and those children I teach."

"That's incredible." Johnny smiled. "I think teaching is one of the most worthwhile jobs out there, and to be part of the community here must be special?"

"Oh yes," She took the cup of tea that Jess presented her with. "I've lived here all my life, well apart from a brief period living in Australia for a few years. I knew it was here that I belong, and I haven't looked back since.

Cat thought of Billy, and how he had moved halfway

across the world too, still returning home eventually. "Wow Australia to Orkney, what a change!" Cat said, "What made you go to Australia?"

"Oh it was the sixties," Mrs White glowed. "I decided I wanted an adventure, so I saved some money working in the local bank and went over on the ship. They called it a 'ten pound pom' in those days."

The two girls and Johnny were enraptured, and listened to Mrs White talk of her travels in the quiet echoing gallery. Cat was fascinated; she missed that about not having any family – the stories, and the advice. When she was younger she would daydream about having a grandmother to take her out on picnics and trips out to museums. Her mother's parents had passed when she was very young, so she had few memories of them. It was just her mum and her growing up. The vision of having grandparents tucking her in bed at night and telling her stories had been a fond thought.

"If it would be alright with you, may I take the children next time? I think they would love it, and I'd make sure they were on their best behaviour."

"Of course!" Jess exclaimed. "We'd be happy to see them, wouldn't we Cat?"

"I'd love to meet the class!" Cat enthused, looking over to Johnny. "Maybe we could talk about different styles of art, techniques and maybe some information on our artists. Oh - and give them a questionnaire to do too?"

"I'll let you take care of that, my friend!" laughed Jess.

"I'd like to help too," Johnny said.

Mrs White excitedly invited them all to the school for a visit in the near future, and left the gallery, putting on her blue hat and gloves as she walked out the door into the cold.

"Oh, she's so sweet!" Cat went up to the window to wave

the old lady goodbye as a few other islanders strolled past carrying bags of shopping.

"She's a darling," Jess agreed. "She's in here every month to see what new pieces I have on display. She's an art lover." She picked up a box under the front desk. "Johnny, could you help a girl?" Johnny who was also looking out the window, came out of his daydream and marched up to help Jess with a couple of small boxes.

Cat continued to look out the window, and in a trance, watched people go about their daily life. An older man in a red scarf and black wool coat stood and talked with a younger man, with his dog on a lead. The dog looked around, straining madly to get away, while his owner talked in the cold. The two men laughed like old friends and Cat's eyes drifted over to a tall figure coming into view. It was Patrick. He was talking on the phone, eyes down, his expression one that Cat hadn't seen before. He paced back and forth, preoccupied with his conversation, as he ran an agitated hand through his hair. Then he froze still, his face pale. He looked at his phone momentarily, then held it back up to his ear again; the caller must have hung up. He kicked a loose stone on the ground and glanced around, before his eyes met hers, Cat broke out of her trance immediately.

"Are you OK?" Jess asked, seeing her stiffen.

"Yeah," came a small voice, with a sigh. "Now, what can I do for the exhibition?"

21

J ohnny stood washing the dishes as Cat came in wearing another new outfit, this time in a deep red wool dress and a black cardigan. She popped on her heels and scraped up her hair into a bun all the while drinking a quick coffee and munching on a slice of toast. Johnny leaned against the kitchen basin wearing rubber gloves and an apron, looking over Cat like a proud mother.

"You look good, girl!"

Cat gulped down the last dregs of coffee and fiddled with her keys. "All thanks to you for styling me!" she went to kiss him on the cheek.

"It's a joy to dress a beautiful red head with long legs, every man's fantasy!" he laughed, turning back to the dishes.

Cat stood in the doorway eating her marmalade on toast. "What're your plans today?"

"Well I thought I might pay Mrs White a visit. Maybe see what the school looks like."

"Really? I thought you'd find all that boring?"

"What makes you think that?" Johnny looked back with hands still submerged in the soapy water.

"Kids, Johnny? You've never liked them!" Cat recalled all the nights out with other friends who had children, and how every time they were mentioned, Johnny would get bored and change the subject.

"People change," he murmured, looking distantly out the window, as Cat left in a hurry, distracted. Johnny remained, quietly washing the dishes, and thought of the many application forms he had previously printed and half-filled out. He knew something needed to change in his life, and those possibilities lay on his bed upstairs. The question was, could he make his idea work?.

Cat parked a little outside the village, as her usual parking spots were all taken up.

"Jesus!" She muttered to herself as she walked in her heels up the street. She thought uncomfortably of the last thing she had said to Johnny; had she been unfeeling to him without knowing it? Maybe she was a terrible friend, and didn't give people enough time to be themselves? Johnny was going through a crisis in love and here she was making all sorts of assumptions about what he wanted from life. She stepped out into the road and at that moment her stiletto heel caught in the cat's-eye in the middle of the road, making her trip and fall. It was at that exact moment a van turned the corner, speeding towards her. Cat stared help-lessly at the fast-approaching vehicle; it was too late for her to move, and she closed her eyes thinking this was the moment she would die. Her mum's eyes flashed in her mind and then... no pain came. The van had stopped, just in time, right in front of a cowering Cat who looked up at it, terrified. Patrick got out of the driver's side.

"Cat...! Are you OK?"

Cat got to her knees and couldn't help the rage from building inside her. "What is the matter with you, you could've killed me?" She pressed her hands onto the cold tarmac road and slowly got up.

"I'm sorry..." Patrick tried to help her up but she shrugged him off. "I didn't expect to see someone lying in the middle of the road...?" He put his hands up letting her compose herself.

"You were driving really fast!" Cat looked at her bleeding knees and wanted to cry. But she was determined not to cry in front of *this* individual, that was all she needed. Cars started to block the road, and Cat hobbled off to the pavement in the direction of the gallery. Before she knew it Patrick's van was slowly crawling beside her.

"Let me give you a ride!" came the Irish accent. Cat couldn't look at his face, she felt angry and sad all at the same time. These feelings she couldn't push away, they were always hiding in the depths of her, no matter how many landscapes she painted. *Derek was right to be skeptical*, she thought glumly.

"Leave me alone Patrick, I'm fine."

"You're clearly not fine, you're in shock!" He stopped the van next to her and got out again. "Let me help you fix your knees at least?"

"I need to get to work, we're opening the show tomorrow, I don't have time!" Cat started to walk on again.

"OK, well let me give you a ride to the gallery" Patrick blocked Cat's path. "Cat, please!"

She stood on the spot, and looked at the cars Patrick was holding up on the road.

"OK then!" she said huffily.

They drove down the main street, and Patrick continued on, driving past the gallery.

"Where are you going?" Cat protested, "I need to get to the gallery!"

"We're taking a detour, we'll fix your knees first, thank you very much." Patrick drove the car at a slower speed through the cobbled lanes and shortly after parked at the end of the dreaded avenue. They went up to the familiar door at which Cat had met the lovely tanned girl in what she assumed was Patrick's t-shirt. He opened the door and let her in, leading her through a long hallway to a bathroom.

"Now - sit up on there." He pointed to a washing machine in the corner of the room.

Cat did as she was told, and sat down showing her scraped, cut and very sore knees. The blood dripped down her leg and she almost gagged at the sight of it. She hadn't realised she was squeamish until now. Patrick came back into the room with a stool and sat across from her. He tutted at the knees and rinsed some towels under the tap before gently dabbing the red-raw cuts. Cat could not work out what had happened here, she was crossing the road, then the next minute she was on the brink of becoming a pancake under a speeding van... ? And now here was Patrick in front of her, holding her ankles gently in his warm firm hands as he cleaned her cuts?

"This might sting a bit," he said as he dabbed a little more.

"Ouch!" she moved her knees a little at the biting medicine he dabbed. She looked down at his curly head of hair, as he examined her cuts like an attentive nurse. More antiseptic lotion went on, and then he lightly placed a bandage round each knee. He looked up at her with an uncertain smile.

"Done." He held out his hand to help her down from the washing machine.

"Thanks. Look, I'm sorry I snapped at you, Patrick, I- "

"I'm sorry I almost killed you!"

"I was in the middle of the road, and that was nothing to do with the van."

"But I wasn't looking where I was going!"

"We could be here all day trying to apologise to each other," Cat interrupted, and let him lead her gingerly back through the hallway.

"You're still shaken Cat, sit here and I'll get you a cup of tea." Cat let him make her a drink, and wondered to herself if her trembling really was from shock, or as a result of being touched by this heartbreaker-come-musician?

They both sat at the kitchen table with their tea. The window beside them looked right out onto the water, over the harbour.

"Wow, you must see all the boats go past from this window?" She looked out at seabirds swimming on the water.

"Yeah, it's pretty close to things, it can be quite wild though being this nearby on a stormy night!"

Cat gulped her sweet tea and felt it heat her all the way to her toes. She looked around the room and saw a simple, tidy kitchen, with nothing much on display apart from an abstract photo of Jimmy Hendrix on the wall.

"I love Hendrix."

Patrick followed her gaze. "Aw, he's a legend! I saw a cover band recently. They're from London and they actually played in Orkney. It was incredible."

"I'm sorry I missed it." She sipped her tea, feeling better with each mouthful.

He scratched a clean-shaven chin. "Well, maybe next time I'll take you?"

"I'd like that." The words came out of Cat's mouth without a second thought. *But what's the point if he's with someone else? Do I really want a best friend I'm insanely attracted to?*

Patrick's phone abruptly buzzed making them both jump. He pulled it from his inner jacket pocket, glanced at it, then placed the still-vibrating device back in his pocket.

"You can answer that, I don't mind," Cat said quickly, in her most convincing encouraging tones.

Patrick shook his head. "Nah, it's... not important."

She watched him, unable to work him out, and a different kind of silence fell between them. Cat handed back the cup and got up to leave. Still feeling a little woozy, she took her time as Patrick led her down the hallway to the door. Only then did she catch sight of a few telltale items: ladies hairbrush lay on the hall table, with some bright hair-clips, and a beautiful red coat was draped on a hook by the door. *Yes, a woman lives here all right.* Cat smiled at Patrick briefly and walked out into the pale daylight.

22

The gallery looked every bit as worthy as any venue in London catering to the uptown boroughs. There was a banner outside announcing the exhibition, and inside at the front desk were laid flyers, and booklets for the clients to peruse. The gallery opened to Cat's biggest painting on the far wall, and her other canvases lined the lateral space, bringing into focus stormy scenes and abstract faces. The colours flowed from dark greys to cool blues, drawing the viewer into the storm themselves. Cat continued walking through to the next room to see the other artists' work. Landscapes and still lifes greeted her admiring eyes, which then fell on Jess's familiar work, and in particular, the painting of herself. Cat moved closer and scrutinised herself.

"Is it a true likeness?" Jess had appeared in the doorway of the back workshop.

"I don't know..." Cat continued to study the painting. "It's a bizarre feeling seeing yourself on a wall. It is beautiful though, Jess."

"I hope you don't mind?" Jess stood beside Cat to look at

the piece also. "I couldn't help myself, there was just one night I saw your eyes and your hair do something enchanting, and I wanted to capture it. I felt like I could see you drifting in water, like a mermaid or like Ophelia floating in the weeds."

"That's sad" Cat shivered, thinking again of the selkie girl story near the standing stones.

Jess put a hand lightly on Cat's shoulder, "you have been sad".

Cat was taken aback by Jess's statement. *Was she sad?* A quiet moment fell between them and she shrugged off negative thoughts. "I'm just a bit embarrassed, what will people think when they come to the show?"

"That an artist painted a portrait of their model?" Jess nudged Cat's shoulder and looked proudly around the room. "Now, I think everything is organised. All the paintings are labeled, the wine is chilling, and everything else is as ready as we'll ever be." Jess clapped her hands, looking satisfied and pleasantly nervous.

"An hour till everyone arrives," Cat looked at her watch. "Let's have a glass of wine to cool our nerves!"

The guests started to arrive slightly earlier than planned, but the girls were highly organised, and allowed them to take a glass of wine and look around. The first to arrive were American tourists Jess had spoken to earlier in the week.

"We wanted to get here before everyone, before anyone buys a piece we like!" The lady said flamboyantly, and walked determinedly into the gallery, examining all the paintings.

"Now remember," Jess whispered, "sold pieces are to

have red dots, and the red dots are..." Jess spun around about to look.

"I know!" Cat caught her arm. "Under the desk is where the red dots are! You know I *have* been working here for a few weeks now!"

"How *did* I rope you into doing that, I wonder...?"

"I think it may have been me who roped you into making me work here!" Cat laughed, and ushered Jess away to talk to the American couple examining her work. Meanwhile, Cat welcomed the steady influx of newcomers, and invited them to take a glass and brochure before they started viewing the pieces. Cat recognised a few faces, and smiled at everyone, feeling the happiest she'd ever felt in a job before. Monique came in with her husband, both of whom were dressed in beautifully tailored formal wear.

"You both look wonderful!" Cat said warmly as they entered.

"Oh, thanks darling!" Monique patted her hair as usual. "Iain is taking me for a meal in Kirkwall tonight." Iain took her hand in his, and smiled proudly down at his wife. Cat felt a pang of longing, and then a familiar touch on her shoulder, turning to find Johnny and Mrs White smiling at her with linked arms.

"Place looks great, gorgeous." Johnny kissed her on the cheeks in the manner of his usual social ritual.

"I can't wait to have a look around." Mrs White almost bounced on the spot, full of youthful energy. Cat noticed a change in the woman from the first time they met. The shyness and uncertainty was no longer present, she looked at ease as she glanced up at Johnny. "Don't let this man go, my dear. We must make him stay on the island."

"If Johnny wants to stay, I'd love him to!" She nudged his shoulder affectionately.

"Well we'll see, but we're having a jolly good time so far, right Florence?" Johnny started to lead the old lady away, and she whispered quickly to Cat: "He's been amazing with the children, such a natural teacher!"

More people trickled in, and Cat welcomed them all. Seeing that the wine needed topping up, she turned to check if the coast was clear for a supplies run, and saw Billy, striding through the door, looking very handsome in a kilt and a black shirt. He smiled, and looked around with one eyebrow raised. "Very posh!" He shook Cat's hand, but she pulled him in for a hug and the old man gave in.

"It's so lovely to see you Billy! Did you come on the ferry? Was it rough out there? Do you need somewhere to sleep?"

"Steady lass," he shook his head, "one question at a time!"

"Did you come here just to see our little show?"

"I did, certainly!" Billy said "And there's nothing little about it - looks very professional."

"Uncle Billy!" Jess came up to them both and gave the old man a hug.

"Uncle?" Cat gawped at the pair as Jess put her head against his shoulder affectionately. The old man chuckled at Cat's confused face.

"Well, not *exactly* my uncle. But you and mum are good friends aren't you?" She looked up at him beaming proudly, and then back to Cat. "He helped me get set up on the island."

Billy sighed, and rolled his eyes. "I didn't do a thing! I just knew a fella who had a shop he wasn't using, that's all!" Billy went pink as Jess described how he had gone out of his way to get the flat and shop fixed up for her.

"Billy helped me too - when I hurt my ankle on the hill

over in Hoy!" Cat was delighted that she had become a part
of the unexplained system whereby everyone knew
everyone else on the island.

"Oh yes, you said you stayed with someone that night.
Now that I think of it, of course it would've been uncle Billy
that helped you!"

Billy waved his hand, dismissing the praise. "Come on
now lass, you're embarrassing me!"

Jess laughed at his objections. "Fair enough, well I'm
glad you already know each other. Right - I better go talk to
some more attendees!" She squeezed his shoulder gently
and wandered off.

Billy and Cat walked around the exhibition together and
to Cat's surprise Billy gave each painting his full attention.
"What's this one?" He pointed to a modest watercolour of a
copse of trees.

Cat followed his gaze. "This is about life's voices. How,
well - you think you are on the right path, sometimes, but
you can still get caught up in thinking, am I doing this right?
Should I be making different choices? It's about the whispers in your ear that make you doubt yourself. Self-doubt, in
other words!" She chuckled at her ramblings.

"I love the different faces you see in the trees,"
commented Billy. "More and more keep appearing the
longer you look."

"Yes, you're right." Cat replied, encouraged. "And they all
seem to be looking in the same direction, to the tree over
here." She pointed to a smaller tree from left-of-centre.

"And this tree, is it you?" Billy asked, earnestly.

"Yes." Cat gave a small smile, at the same time feeling
very exposed, showing her self, and her inner workings to
the world.

Cat left Billy to walk around while she went back to the

entrance again to welcome people. Jess was there, grinning widely and talking to a few others, she had gathered a small crowd around her, and looked very much in her element. The small crowd was listening to her artistic process, and theories on method, smiling and nodding in agreement at what she thought of Cat's half of the exhibition. Cat moved closer to listen, but she was stopped in her tracks by Patrick, who emerged through the door and smiled at her. Her heart fluttered like a small bird waiting for release. She took in his appearance shyly; he was wearing a suit jacket, blue scarf and jeans; certainly more of an effort than his usual performance gear. His hair looked a little wild, with his curls standing up from the wind outside. She couldn't help but giggle.

"What?" he asked, patting down his hair. "Have you not been out there, it's gale-force winds!" He smiled again, and Cat melted a little more.

"Fancy seeing you here!"

"Yeah, I thought it would be a good idea to make sure I don't have a court case ahead of me!"

"What? By coming and drinking all our wine?"

"That, I will be yes, and obviously checking up on the invalid!" He put his hands in his pockets, and nodded at her knees.

"Well, thanks to your administering, I'm fine." She glanced down at the bandages just peeping out from underneath the hem of her dress. "You took good care of me!"

He looked away for a few moments and sighed. "I just feel so bad about it, and, well... you must think I'm like that."

Cat wasn't really sure what he meant; to her, Patrick was many things, and she couldn't work any of them out. Which, unfortunately, both attracted her and warned her to back away. She smiled reassuringly at him. "Look, you may as well know: I'm a bit of a clumsy person. I'm always hurting myself, so this was just another weekly occurrence for me. So far this month I've already burnt myself, scalded my arm, scratched my back picking brambles, oh and catching my heel on the road and falling over – I mean who catches their shoe in the middle of the road?" She laughed.

"You're accident prone? Well, I'd better watch out in case something like that happens again!"

"I mean, hopefully it wont, but you *were* going pretty fast out there!" Cat giggled.

"So coming tonight and making sure there's no court case might have been a good idea?"

"Perhaps, maybe buying a painting might help too?"

Patrick laughed, and his green eyes glowed, then looked quickly at her mouth – *she was sure he just looked at her mouth?*

"Can you show me around?" he asked hastily. "It's not everyday you know the artist of such a high-flying exhibition!"

"Sure!" Cat downed the last dregs of her glass of red, and filled another for her and Patrick, then escorted him around the room. "How is your music going? Played any more gigs since I last saw you?"

"Yeah, a few." Patrick ruffled his hair, and Cat couldn't help but feel drawn to him. His face was open, and his green eyes looked directly into her own every time he spoke, making her melt with delicious ease. "Oh hey - I forgot to say, thanks for what you did on the radio!"

"Oh it was nothing." She shook her head.

"No, it helped. That Darren has never played anything of mine before. And the next show has sold out in tickets advance – that's never happened before!"

"That's great news!"

"Yeah, I couldn't believe it! I've never played to a sell-out gig!" Patrick laughed. She listened to him speak with that lovely, twisting Irish lilt, which had the slightest Scottish undertone, his lips soft as he spoke slowly, explaining some of the new songs he had written. Cat remembered kissing those lips that stormy evening in the dingy quayside night-club; now all she wanted to do was reach for his hand and kiss those lips again. She was so overcome with sensations running up and down her body that she felt sure if she didn't get away that minute, she would kiss him there and then in front of everyone. *Did he feel this chemistry? Maybe it was all completely one sided on her part? Where was his girl-friend anyway? Remember he has a girlfriend!* After a few moments, Cat excused herself and went through the back door to cool off in the workshop. She stood still on the spot taking deep breaths. *Why must she feel this way? If only she could completely shut herself off from men and just focus on her life. Why couldn't she be attracted to a normal guy who didn't have girls drooling over him? This was really her big night, and all she could think of was Patrick!* Cat peered out of the work-shop door to see even more people admiring the artwork. *Get a grip Catherine, be proud of what you've achieved; don't wait for his approval to enjoy the moment!* Patrick came into view and stood in front of Jess's painting of Cat. She felt her face heat up all over again. *I am a strong independent woman, and I don't need anyone but myself to be seen; to be wanted !* With a sigh she gave herself a few more minutes in the welcome, anonymous cool air, before stepping out into the gallery once more with a smile on her face.

23

J ess rushed into the gallery waving a newspaper "We made front cover!", which made Cat wake up immediately, after a rather groggy start recovering from the many glasses of wine she had drunk the previous night. The opening had gone extremely well. Cat had sold her largest piece to a couple who were staying with local friends, and she had another two potential commissions, including one from Monique to hang in the hotel. Jess had also sold a small canvas sketch and the large piece of Cat, to Cat's embarrassment, both to a buyer who was on holiday. Jess spread the newspaper on the front desk before them and read aloud as a customer was viewing the exhibition.

"Talent comes to Orkney: Meet the two young entrepreneur artists Catherine MacGregor and Jessica Morgan; each bringing their own unique style, wowing the locals with art that stands up against the modern-day greats. Opening night showcased work from the two ladies, alongside other local artists, which proved a resounding success on all counts. Exhibition runs until November."

Jess continued reading the smaller font, as Cat looked at the photo of them both standing in-front of her large canvas.

"I'm amazed it's out so quickly!" Cat read over the article again unable to stop beaming at the words 'talent' and 'unique'.

"Oh they don't mess about here!" Jess laughed. "This is awesome, I'm going to have it framed!"

Cat stipulated that the good news called for a bacon sandwich, and she popped out to the local café to procure some. She walked with confidence, passing by friendly locals en-route who congratulated her on the article. *News gets about town quickly!* She grinned all the way back, with a spring in her step. Walking up the cobbled street, passing the white harbour cottages, she felt at home. The local cats roamed around in their usual spot, and Cat stopped to pet them. "Hello wee guy!" she said to the tabby cat she had seen the day before, who meowed gently and frolicked indolently in front of her. Within moments more cats were wandering around her, emerging from under cars and leaping down from the stonewall to greet her. Cat was a little concerned at the spectacle, only then realising that she had a bag of bacon sandwiches on her, and jogged laughing back the rest of the way, lest she be carried away by the hungry mob.

Over the next few days, Cat returned to her normal shift pattern at the pub and every morning Johnny would walk to the school and help Mrs White in class. Whenever he saw Cat, he would chat about the kids and his lunch breaks hanging out with the other teachers. Each night Johnny cooked, and with every meal surpassing the previous one, Cat relished the task of being his taster.

"I could get used to this," she said, as Johnny handed her a glass of wine on her arrival home from the pub early one evening.

"I know darling!" He smiled, the smell of roast chicken wafted out from the kitchen and Cat's mouth watered. "It's been heavenly here. I hadn't read a full book in years, and since I've been here I've already read three!" He beamed with pride, and took a hearty gulp from his own glass.

Cat laughed. "Well that's what happens when the WiFi is so crap it's basically non-existent!

"I've also had a lot of time to think too, of what I want to do with my life, and I've been speaking to Mark about it the last few days too." He bit his lip a little. "I don't want to be one of those people who die and regret not spending enough time with their loved ones. I see how much I was working, instead of living, and it affected my relationship." He gestured for Cat to sit on the sofa as he sat down on the other side. "I've loved it here, Cat."

"I've loved having you here J!" Cat went to pat his hand and he took it in a firm clasp.

"You've helped me so much, I don't think you realise just how much."

They both sat in a comfortable silence for a few moments.

"I'm leaving tomorrow." Johnny looked over to her, his eyes serious.

"Oh.... so soon!" Cat was taken aback, she loved having the company of such a charismatic friend, and had been sure Johnny would stay longer.

"Yes, I'm meeting Mark in Inverness. We're going to

spend a couple of nights there and see what our next steps could be."

"Oh. That's wonderful, J." Cat paused and realised this was good news; she had to get on with her own life, and really learn to stand on her own two feet. "How do you feel about things?" She asked, a hint of concern in her voice.

"I feel sad to leave you to be honest. We have a good time together, eh?"

"The best." Cat felt tears wanting to surface but suppressed them.

"You've always been there for me, no matter what, and I feel stronger for it. You're a gift, Cat!" He took a sip from his wine and looked down at their intertwined hands. "But I feel cleansed, rejuvenated, I feel as though I can think clearly again, and I realise now how badly I treated Mark. I want more from my life than just work. It's not about that really, is it? Life is not about making money, working all the hours that are humanely possible just to be successful. I mean what even is success?" He took off his glasses and rubbed his eyes. "Life is to be appreciated, to gain experiences, and be surrounded by friends, family, love..." He trailed off, running out of ways to put his feelings into words.

"Oh Johnny, I'm so happy for you!" Cat cried aloud, and hugged her friend.

They both enjoyed their last night together, watching movies, drinking wine and gradually packing Johnny's things for his journey back home.

The next morning was full of mixed emotions for Cat. She was happy to see Johnny so excited, and his determination made her swell with pride. But she was also devastated to see her old friend go – the one person on the island who knew her inside out.

"Come back soon, and bring Mark next time!"

Johnny laughed. "Definitely. Mark would love it here. I can just see him joining committees and baking in the village fetes!"

"Then come really really soon!" She smiled inwardly at the idea of having them both live nearby.

"I'll be in touch".

Cat cleared her throat. "You better contact me soon, I won't be impressed if you go back to your old ways and screen my calls!"

Johnny raised his hands in a mea culpa gesture. "That won't happen again, you'll hear from me, I promise." He put a hand on Cat's shoulder. "Now remember you always have a spare room in Glasgow."

"Thanks, I think I'm happy to be away from there for the time being. But I will need to go down there at some stage to see mum." Cat gave a grim smile.

"Let me know when - I'd like to come to her grave too. Sheila was so good to me, such a beautiful woman." He stroked Cat's hair affectionately. "You know, you look more and more like her." And with those final words, he kissed Cat on the cheek, squeezed her hand and left. As he boarded, Johnny looked back at Cat and smiled, his bag thrown casually over his shoulder. His immaculate clothes were now creased, and along with his messy hair gave him the look of a wandering poet, rather than the successful businessman he was. *What a change*, thought Cat, smiling. And then: *I wonder... have I changed as much too?*

Cat stood watching the ferry leave, and couldn't help it; she cried uncontrollably and continued to do so for the rest of the afternoon, thinking of both her friend and her mother leaving her. She drove back to her cottage with tears streaming down her face. She rushed inside its comforting walls, locked her door and grieved for the rest of the day. She spent the vanishing hours looking at photos of her mother and her childhood, wishing she had a family again, and wondering, her heart aching, of what the next few months on the island would bring.

24

S *he lay on the sand with her mother in the warm breeze.*
Her mum opened the palm of her hand to Cat. "White
heather, these are lucky, baby." She put the weeds into
Cat's little hands. "May you always have luck, my wee Cather-
ine." Distant shouts sounded behind them, as a figure waved,
calling them....

A loud thud on the back door woke Cat from a deep sleep. She woke to find that she must have passed out on the sofa, surrounded by photos. She had smoked an alarming number of cigarettes too, after resorting to her hidden emergency stash. The room was dark, with shards of white light piercing through the gap between the curtains.

"Are you in there?" came Jess's voice from outside.

"Yes!" Cat croaked, and summoned herself from the sofa. Tripping up on various objects sprawled across the floor, she made her way slowly to the door. She opened it to find Jess looking fresh faced but with a concerned countenance.

Her hair was tied back in a tight bun and she appeared to be wearing a wetsuit with a baggy jumper over the top.

"I called, I texted, why didn't you answer?" Jess barged through the door and saw the mess strewn across the floor – photographs, tissues, bottles of wine and cigarette butts.

"What's going on?" She looked around and then back to Cat. "Are you OK?" She squeezed Cat's shoulder, which made the tears start once again.

"I don't know why I'm feeling like this," she blurted out with a shaky voice. Jess stroked Cat's hair, then gave her a long hug to let her friend cry some more on her shoulder. "I mean it's just my friend going back home, why do I feel this awful?" She blew her nose with a tissue that Jess quietly gave her.

"Look, I can't imagine how you feel. Your mum passed away and left you on your own; it's something that will always be there deep inside. These things come to the surface when we least expect it and it's important to grieve, let it out. Don't lock it away." They both sat down on the sofa and Jess stroked Cat's hair again and spoke in soothing tones: "But you're not alone, I'm here." Jess let Cat blow her nose again and they both sat in the quiet for some moments. "I have come here to rope you into something too, so you go upstairs and wash your face."

"I hope it's nothing to do with that wetsuit you're wearing...?" Cat smiled and looked her friend straight in the eye.

"Never mind that just now, I'll make you a quick cup of tea".

Cat did as she was told, and felt a lot more herself once she had washed her face and changed her clothes. Upon her return downstairs, the living room area was cleaned from all the mess, and the curtains pulled back to bright midday light outside. Jess had a cup of tea waiting for her on the coffee table, and was busy lighting the fire.

"Thank you, you didn't need to do all this." Cat took in the clean surfaces and smelled the forest air freshener she had bought from the local shop.

"Don't sweat it, lovely!" Jess had managed to get the flames to a satisfactory level, and she put a small log on top of the pile to keep the fire going.

"How's the tea?" Jess said with a gleeful smile.

"It's good," Cat commented after she gulped down most of it. "What are you up to?" She looked at her friend with suspicion.

"Well as you can see, I am wearing a wet suit!" Jess spread out her hands and turned around like a model from a 1950s photo-shoot.

"Yeah..." Cat did not like where this conversation was going. Her friend merrily skipped to the kitchen where she pulled out another wetsuit.

"I thought a swim would be a great idea!"

"Oh no!" Cat protested, "I'll get hypothermia!"

"No you won't!"

Cat tried to think of reasons not to.

"The sea is just out there, we're metres away from it, plus I have a fire on, see!" She pointed to the flames in the grate with a playful smile.

Cat resigned herself, her heart sinking. "Oh... ok!" She knew her friend would get her in the water one way or another, and she felt too feeble to protest much today. "How do you have two wetsuits anyway?"

"Oh, I know a guy at the diving centre in Stromness," Jess winked, and handed over the wetsuit.

"Of course you do!" Cat grabbed the wetsuit and went upstairs to change.

In a chorus of yelps and screams, the girls ran out of the house in the direction of the water. It was a cold but sunny day with blue skies overhead. Cat had never really been in water like this before. She recalled her mum took her to the beach once near Loch Lomond, but that was a loch...not the ocean. She walked carefully across the stony beach and dipped her toe cautiously into the edge of the water.

"It's freezing!" Cat moaned, as she saw Jess already wadding through the water and easing her whole body under it.

"Come on, wimp!" Jess laughed which spurred Cat on, grumpily. Cat hated to admit it but she did have a slight competitive streak.

Stepping from stone to stone, the water gradually got higher and higher until Cat lunged into the dark liquid hoping to god there were no sharks in the Orkneys. The cold spread all over her body like very tiny knives.

"*Holy shit!*" Cat yelled, to hear a chorus of giggles erupt nearby.

"Ye better harden up lassie, ye aint a townie no more!" Jess called out in a thick Scots language.

It took a few minutes but the coldness subsided, and Cat found herself gliding through the crisp water. Swimming came naturally for her, her teenage years spent in the enormous local swimming pool prepared her for this, although being in the sea was much more intense. She flipped onto her back and looked up to the blue skies where a low flying flock of geese passed by, squawking noisily.

The two girls emerged from the sea and ran into the house giggling. They both quickly showered and settled themselves beside the crackling fire with two large hot chocolates.

"Thank you." Cat looked over to Jess who was wrapped up to the chin in a tartan blanket.

"For what?"

"You know." Cat smiled and felt content staring into the crackling flames.

25

Cat had suggested to Jess to use her house over the next couple of days, while Cat worked at the gallery. Jess relaxed away from the gallery and used Cat's small studio space to sketch out some new ideas. Cat didn't really know if she was allowing Jess to stay for selfless, or selfish reasons. After Johnny had gone she began to feel so lonely that having someone in the house made her happier, and more confident. Meanwhile the gallery had been hectic, she spoke with newspapers and clients almost every day, promoting their work. Thinking of her ever-busy days, she scolded herself for not asking Johnny to help while he had been staying. On top of everything, she had chosen for some reason to wear the most impractical shoes she owned, the pair that had tripped her up on the road that day Patrick had almost driven over her. At each moment she could, she would slip them off and walk barefoot around the gallery, which never proved long enough, as there were always people coming in. Cat decided she'd be putting the heels in the bin once she got back to her cottage. She made a plan to have a bath, smother herself in jasmine body butter, and wrap herself tightly in her dressing robe by the fire. To her relief, she was not working at the gallery or the pub over the next few days, making tomorrow her first day off in weeks. Cat looked out her windowpane at the darkness that had fallen on the village; seeing her reflection looking back at her, she self-consciously wiped away the flecks of mascara from underneath her eyes, and let down her hair with relief. The street was quiet; as the days grew shorter, it seemed everyone was deciding to stay at home of an evening. She glanced at her watch, and decided to lock up a few minutes early - no-one would be passing now tonight. She went around the gallery, switching off the lights, locking the till and making sure everything was as it should be. Just as she approached the door, she noticed in the gloomy light that the label accompanying her tree painting had been blacked out. She flicked on the closest light and saw what looked like traces of a biro-pen, scribbling out her artistic process and the description of the painting. Cat took down the label and sighed. Possibly some teenagers had come in while she had been momentarily distracted, and thought it funny to leave a pathetic little mark. Luckily, the painting looked untouched. Cat cast the cardboard piece onto the front desk, deciding it could be easily retyped by Jess tomorrow. She collected her bags and locked up, finding the street was still deathly quiet; no passing car or dog walker roaming the road, as was usual at this time. A strange eerie feeling came over Cat as she walked to her car, as if she were being watched. She shook off the notion dismissively, before her imagination could take over, and left quickly, eager for home, and her fire.

Upon her return to the cottage, she immediately went to run the long-anticipated bath, wanting to forget her fatigue, and the strange end to her day. It was only while she poured bath salts into the water and began to undress that she heard Jess downstairs.

"Only me!" Came the cheery voice from the bottom of the stairs. "I didn't hear you drive up!" Jess went through to the kitchen rattling about pots and pans. "Oh my god I'm feeling good, did so much work in that shed of yours today!" Jess merrily sang and shouted. Cat put on her dressing robe and wandered down.

"Hi Jess!" Cat looked at her friend in the promising act of pulling out pasta from the cupboard and vegetables from the fridge.

"Hey you, I'm just going to make us dinner, then I thought we might go out," Jess said breezily while she opened a plastic bag and brought out a bottle of wine.

"Oh hun..." whined Cat, "I have no energy, I'm only able for bed!"

"Nonsense" Jess shook her head grinning, "You want to go out, you just don't know it yet".

Cat sighed and looked unimpressed, while Jess poured out a glass of wine and gave it to Cat. "I will cook, you just toddle upstairs and enjoy your bath!"

"I can't promise I won't fall asleep in there!" Cat grumbled, crossly.

"Well, maybe a fifteen minute snooze will make you fresh as a daisy!" Jess shooed her friend up the stairs.

Jess promised she'd drive them both in, and they would get a lift back from one of her sober friends nice and early, telling her it was all planned, so Cat sighed, and looked out clothes to wear. Jess put on a sparkly black dress and heels, looking very sophisticated, while Cat couldn't bring herself to wear anything other than her jeans.

"You're not going out like that!" Jess had insisted Cat

should at the very least wear a "dressy top", and sent her friend back upstairs. Finally, after much trying on and throwing multiple options onto her bed, she settled for her comfy jeans, and a silk black halter-neck. Once she had achieved Jess's grudging approval they drove off into the cold night to the nearest pub.

"Oh I forgot!" Jess squealed.

"What? Did you leave the cooker on?"

"No, no not that!" Jess calmed down slightly. "I remembered that tonight is the ceilidh, so - we have a change of plan!"

"Oh great, I thought the pub was going to be hard work. Now I have the prospect of being flung across the room by a string of big burly guys!" Cat sniffed, and suppressed a yawn that had caught in her throat. The last time she had found herself at a ceilidh, was back when she went to one a few years ago at Dave's sister's wedding. Dave had spent most of the evening drinking at the bar while she had danced various highland flings and every other dance going. Most of the steps she had no idea of, but she had found you could get away with improvising if your partner knew them well enough. She lay still in the car, dreaming of disco lights and whirling tartan pleats, while Jess drove steadily in the darkness, the car gently rocking...

"Wake up, sleepy head!" Jess shook Cat by the shoulders.

"Oh sorry..." Cat murmured, and readjusted her eyes to find Jess staring at her. "Um, did I just-"

"Yes, you fell asleep!" Jess flipped the car mirror and applied red lipstick. "OK, ready?"

Cat stumbled from the car in the direction of the illuminated village hall. Music, and the sound of laughter, grew louder the closer they drew. Jess linked her arm through Cat's, and guided her in.

People stood outside smoking, and saluted the girls as they passed. They walked into the hall to see a band at the far end playing a jig, with various couples stepping in time and spinning to the beat. Kilts swung, people laughed and drinks were gulped. The hall was dimly lit making it hard to make out people. Cat snapped out of her trance at Jess's stiff poke in her ribs. "Drinks!" she ordered, and led Cat to the bar in a smaller adjoining room, which held just as much people, crammed into the smaller space and even louder in voice. Cat smiled at a couple of familiar faces while Jess ordered the drinks.

Cat received two plastic cups, one in each hand, and looked at Jess, confused.

"You need a boost, so drink one now and we'll head back into the hall."

Cat did as she was told, and the feeling of fatigue left her body to be replaced with a warm adrenaline. As soon as the girls joined the groups of people in the hall the band finished and took a few moments to take a drink, and mutter companionably between themselves. The fiddler stepped forward and announced with a boom into the microphone, "Take your partners please for: *Strip the Willow*!"

"Oh I love this one!" Jess cried, and was approached almost instantly by a very handsome broad-shouldered man "Well, how about a dance then?" he asked.

"Hell yeah!" Jess gave her drink to Cat. "Oh sorry, is that OK?

"Of course!" The music began and the dancers lined up before launching into a wildly coordinated spin. Cat watched Jess laugh and glide with elegance, her gaze moving outward to follow the movement of the people around the room, enjoying the energy and the music, until her eyes fell on the dark curls of Patrick. He was laughing and watching the dancers, and the pretty girl who had opened the door to his house that evening, and whose red coat hung on the back of that very door, was beside him, talking in his ear. Cat gulped down both drinks, and headed for the toilets to compose herself.

She gazed at herself in the mirror. *Now, stop it Cat. He's out of your league. What happened was a bit of fun, but now it's time to move on. He has.* She wiped her eyes, fearing the tears might make her face blotchy, and quickly reapplied makeup before anybody else came in. After a few minutes the alcohol began to take effect, and she felt surprisingly better. She went back to the bar, ordered more drinks, and went back into the dance hall where she soon found Jess.

"Oh Cat, there you are!" Jess took one of the drinks. "This is Andrew!"

Cat was very impressed. Andrew looked smart, strong, and was clearly already very fond of Jess. He smiled at Cat, and asked her if she wanted to dance.

"Take your partners for the Gay Gordons!" announced the fiddler and plunged immediately into playing a fast-paced jig.

Cat agreed, and left a smiling Jess to her top-up. The dance was simple, and Andrew guided her with strong hands, so that it was impossible for her to get the steps wrong. The beat became quicker and quicker, and Cat lost herself in the movement. Then as abruptly as it had begun, the dance came to a trumpeting end. Everyone applauded, and scrambled to find their drinks as the musicians drank away their sweat, and chatted amongst themselves once again.

"Great, eh?" said Andrew, breathlessly. "You're a good dancer!"

"Yes!" Cat, exhausted from the dance, could hardly form words through her dry lips. "I need a drink though!"

Before they made their way back, Andrew asked if Jess was single. Cat was thrilled for her friend, and confirmed that she was. Cat had hoped that Jess would find someone special. *Maybe, just maybe this was him?* Before Cat could grasp her drink, she was approached by a younger man who looked a little nervous.

"Would you like to dance?" With his open, earnest baby-face, Cat put him at about eighteen, and was flattered.

"Yes, why not!" She fanned her face, trying to recover from the previous dance, ready to launch into another. This one was different, still with a deal of twirling, but with variations involving kicks and a burst of graceful hopping. Cat laughed as she missed a few steps, trying to keep up both with the music and her partner. She loved the movement and the strength of the steps; they made her feel so alive, like her stint swimming in the sea earlier that month. Her partner spun her around one last time, and the music stopped suddenly, and everyone clapped again. The fiddler started playing on his own, a much slower waltz to which Cat was about to start gliding with her partner, until a cough came from behind them.

"May I interrupt?" Patrick smiled, and looked down at them both.

"We're just about to dance!" the boy said "Go find your own partner Paddy!"

"Come on now, Archie!" laughed Patrick, "you know I'm only good at the slow dances and there's lots of girls lined up by the wall over there just waiting for you to ask them!"

The boy looked at Cat, then at Patrick, considering his prospects for a few moments. "OK then," he finished reluctantly, handing his partner over without any more complaint, heading quickly in the direction of the waiting girls. Patrick took Cat's hand in his and held her against him, leading her further onto the floor. The guitar and accordion joined in to bring the sweet sad song echoing out over the dim, crowded floor. Cat was now so close to Patrick, that she could hear him humming along to the music under his breath, and smell a warm, woody musk on his clothing.

"You know this dance?" he asked gently in her ear, making her body stand to attention.

"No, of course not!" she laughed. "Can't you tell? I'm stepping on your feet!"

"I hadn't noticed..." he muttered in sarcastic tones.

Cat pinched him on the shoulder.

"Oi!"

"Well I'm trying my hardest!" she defended. "And it's not getting any easier, with the drinks I've had!"

He laughed and held onto her tightly as they moved to the notes of the swaying fiddler. Cat was now so totally confused of what there was between her and Patrick, her mind seemed to be on pause, hearing only the music, and feeling Patrick's hand on the small of her back. She looked over to Jess, who was sitting in deep conversation with Andrew.

"You look very pretty tonight," Patrick offered with an awkward air, making Cat unsure of what to say.

"Oh, erm thanks?" Cat looked down at her attire. "I actually didn't plan on coming out..."

"What made you?"

"Or who made me?" Cat laughed, "That wee blonde over there who's now getting chatted up!" Patrick followed her gaze to see the couple giggling, then all of a sudden kissing enthusiastically before the entire room.

"I call that shifting!" Patrick nodded with a glint in his eye.

"Eh?" Cat couldn't take her eyes off the happy couple.

"Shifting, snogging, kissing, all that good stuff. That's what they'll be doing the rest of the night," he explained, in a matter of fact way.

"I'm sure *you'd* know..." Cat muttered bitterly.

"What?" Patrick squinted at her for a moment, then carried on dancing.

The music had stopped and Cat excused herself. She had said something about getting more drinks, but on making her way to the bar she felt the dizzy effects of the alcohol already consumed, and decided some air would be a better option.

She walked out into the chilly evening air, welcoming the cold that surrounded her. As usual, it brought everything into focus again. She headed down onto the main village street, with a few street lamps above lighting the way. Continuing walking past the cars that lined the road, she adjusted her eyes and could soon see all around her almost as clear as day, the moonlight was so bright and the sky so clear.

She realised she was very close to a few small local standing stones, and decided to walk on further to see the Neolithic monuments, passing by a church and a small field. Six large standing stones stood in the middle, outlined in a hazy silver light. She strode up to them, pressing her hand tipsily on the cold stone to see if she might feel something from those people, thousands of years before her doing this exact thing, or if, even better, she might be transported to another time, like shows she had seen on television. It was only then that she heard someone approaching.

"Hey, lassie! You cannae be out here all alone at this time

o' the night!" came the deep voice, putting on a terribly dated Scottish accent.

"I think I can defend myself... also, I imagine that the most crime this place has ever seen in the last decade is a twelve year old stealing a pack of cigarettes from the local supermarket!" she countered, trying to not sound annoyed at Patrick, or give away how much she had actually drunk.

Gentle sounds of water lapped near them, the night was still and quiet. Even the ceilidh in the distance could not be heard.

"No, I meant from the Fae!"

"The Fae?"

"Yes, the Fae. Mostly in Scottish and Irish folklore - the bad fairies; brownies; little people that cause disappearances and ill-doing. They might take you away to their realm."

"Frankly, living in a magical world would currently be a lot more fun to me than the real one."

"Yes, but you'd never be one of them, Cat, you'd never understand them. It would be the life of a prisoner."

"So you're superstitious then?" Cat scoffed.

"I'm Irish, of course I am!" Patrick laughed and walked right up to Cat. His hand reached out and touched the stone too. "I wonder how many people have come to see these things, can you imagine? Going back through the centuries, to the very day this stone was placed here; from the folk who put it here, to us – here, now. Thousands of years of history," He mused for a moment, then looked down at Cat. "Sorry, I love old things. I geek out a little about this sort of thing."

Cat looked at his face, the pale moonlight hitting the side of his cheek. "I'm the same, I find history fascinating. Though it's the people I find the most fascinating. Like, why did anyone want to erect a stone here in the first place?" Cat wandered dreamily further into the field to the next stone, feeling Patrick close behind her.

"It's quite cold Cat, should we not be going back in?"

"I feel good..." Cat sighed, and stumbled a little on the uneven grass. The copious amount of alcohol she was carrying made her giddy. "Come here." She leaned up against the second stone. Her back pushed up against the cold bumpy surface, with the moon shining on her pale face, she untied her halter neck, looking steadily at Patrick. Then very slowly pulled down the silk, to expose her black lace bra.

Patrick stood in front of her and looked around, perhaps checking for anyone watching. He went up to Cat and kissed her softly, tenderly on the lips. She could feel him taking off his jacket. She felt the dizzy deliciousness of the alcohol calming her mind and lubricating her limbs, only to open her eyes and see Patrick was trying to put the jacket over her shoulders.

"No Cat," Patrick said in a small voice. "I can't".

Cat stood still; paralysed by the unexpected rejection of the man that stood before her.

"Cat, you're shaking!" He wrapped the jacket tightly over her then rubbed her arms.

They walked back to the hall, Cat adjusting her top before they greeted people again. The walk was quiet, with a painful tension between them. Cat felt humiliated, and couldn't quite believe what she had done. *She had thrown herself at him, and he didn't want her.*

"Look, Cat- " Patrick started, as they approached the music and passed the people smoking outside.

Cat just carried on walking, feeling the most unattractive

she had ever felt, and that was after having virtually no sex with Dave for the last year they were together. She could not even look at Patrick, whatever he was going to say, his actions spoke far louder than any words could. She walked through the mass of people, then up to Jess who gave her one look and said gently, "Let's get you home".

26

Cat lay in bed for most of the next day, stirring only to get a cup of tea from time to time. She had no appetite; whenever she cast her mind back to the night before, she cringed, and her stomach lurched. She spoke to Jess briefly on the phone, reassuring her friend that she only felt unwell from drinking last night. After many suggestions that perhaps Jess should come over, Cat insisted all she really wanted to do was sleep and have a quiet detox. She watched a string of romantic comedies, where the leads would declare their love for one another in the rain, or at an airport. *Why was it always the same? Who had time at an airport, and who wouldn't wait until they were inside, dry from the rain?* Cat thought bitterly of her own two failed attempts at falling in love, and cried into her pillow. *Was she always going to be unloved? But then, Patrick had women all over him - did she really want to be just another? Was she that eager to have sex, that she was happy to have it with someone who would pick her up and put her down whenever he felt so inclined? Who already had a girlfriend?*

By the next morning, Cat had made up her mind. She

packed her small backpack and set off for Glasgow. She had a few days off work, and had seen on her calendar that it would have been her mother's birthday. The same deep instinct that had taken her to Orkney was now taking her back to Glasgow.

The sun spilled out over the water before her. She twirled on the spot, her new flowery dress billowing in the breeze. She held onto the strands of white heather and tied them together, trying to make a bracelet like her mum had done many times before with daisies. But her hands were too small and cumbersome. She turned around and saw the two women in front of a house on the outskirts of the beach, talking to one another and looking back at Cat. She knew they were watching her, loving her, but still she felt as free as a bird.

Cat woke as the plane landed heavily on the tarmac. The familiar, almost comforting grey skies greeted her as she made her way deeper into the city. Seeing her home again, where she had grown up, where her mother had raised her, was now a welcome sight. The liveliness, the friendly people, the old buildings that lined the streets and towered higher than any standing stone, was something Cat never really acknowledged before. She was from this place; it was a part of her.

Cat had not mentioned to Johnny that she was visiting Glasgow. She assumed he might be still in the highlands with Mark, trying to build on their marriage together. So, she booked herself into a hotel and organised to have dinner that evening with someone she knew well. She wore a plain black dress and her woollen coat, feeling comfortable in her new style; she placed her red beret on her auburn waves and headed outside.

A short walk in the cool air brought her to the restaurant. She looked at her silver Macintosh watch and saw she was a little early, no matter; maybe it was best to arrive in advance and compose herself before dinner. She entered the busy candle-lit room, and scanned around for a familiar face. To her surprise he was already sitting by the window, looking out, deep in thought. Dave glanced over in her direction suddenly, and his bright blue eyes lit up as he flashed a warm smile.

"Cat, you look amazing!" He came up to her and hugged her.

"So do you!" He smelled good too; Dave had never worn aftershave before, this was a change. His hair was smartly cut, and he wore a very tailored suit. *Was this really Dave?* His greeting was so comfortable and familiar, and she had always loved his hugs. He enveloped her in his strong arms, making her feel small and protected again, just like he used to.

They sat at the table and spoke with ease, to Cat's amazement. The awkwardness that she had feared was not there. He spoke of his new office job, and how he was aiming to be a team leader.

"That's really great Dave." She touched his hand. "I'm so happy for you."

The dinner went well, and they spoke about people they both knew. The glass of wine turned into a bottle of wine, which turned into a dram or two of whisky afterwards, and still Cat was enjoying the company. She knew Dave, but at the same time he was different. Good-different. They paid for their food and made their way out onto the street. Cat stopped short in the doorway of a closed shop.

"I'm sorry for everything, Dave," she blurted, "I was so impulsive in breaking us up."

Dave took some moments to reply; he kicked the outside wall gently. The lights of the city around them were energetic, constantly moving in their peripheral as they stood still, and looked at one another. He gave her a smile. "I'm glad you did. Cat."

"But I loved you!" Cat placed her hand on his arm and felt the familiar muscles underneath. "I've felt so lost." She moved closer.

"I loved you too." He took a step back. "But I think that in some ways I never really knew you. I loved what I thought you were." He looked at her with kindness in his eyes.

Cat waited, unsure of what he was saying.

"Oh man, I never had your way with words, Cat." He rubbed his eyes.

"What are you trying to tell me?"

"We weren't right for each other. Remember, you said that?" He folded his arms steadying himself. "And you were right," he sighed.

"...There's more, I think?" Cat blinked, waiting.

"I think we were good, once. I know I didn't get a job as soon as I should have, and maybe I wasn't attentive to your needs either."

"You barely touched me!"

"Yes but Cat, you never really let me in to begin with. I thought I knew you, but you kept things from me, you wouldn't talk to me. After your mum died, I don't think you wanted to trust anyone... in case you lost them too."

"You're blaming me for all of this?" Cat could feel anger building up inside her.

"No, but I'm trying to show you. I may have given up on us," he swallowed, "but you didn't even give us a chance."

Cat couldn't believe her ears. All the times she had helped him. Was affectionate to him. Wanted him in her bed.

"I wanted you"

"You never told me that. You never told me anything," Dave said quietly. "Look Cat, I care about you. You helped me realise that we would do better apart, and you were right. I feel so happy right now, the happiest I've ever been. I met someone. I want to marry her-"

Cat walked off. She couldn't listen anymore. She was so angry; with Dave, with everyone, but mainly with herself. Dave called after her, but she just walked faster into the darkness. *What was she thinking? She'd thrown herself at Patrick, now she was throwing herself at Dave? Could she not bear to be on her own? Whatever Dave claimed, she did let him in, of course she did! She spent so much time trying to help him get on his feet again!* Cat continued walking down the busy dark street. *Perhaps it is better to be on your own; everybody lets you down eventually. Patrick, Dave, and her mum. They all leave eventually, is it worth even starting anything when you'll be hurt in the end?* Cat breathed in thinking of Dave's last words. *Had she really not let in anyone? Who was she?* She stopped walking and hesitated taking another step. Maybe she didn't share her emotions with Dave when she'd had sad days, thinking of her mother. *But what was the point in telling people you're upset and grieving? They can't do anything!* Cat swallowed hard, and that anxious feeling crept up, grasping at her. Her throat felt tight, and she breathed in and out, trying to shake off the sensation.

She turned around and traced her steps back as quickly as she could, suddenly eager to find Dave. Walking turned into running, and she reached the restaurant once again, but Dave was not there, so she continued down the next street hoping he'd walked back the same way. She was about to phone him, until she saw a figure standing at the bus stop. It was getting late and people were emerging from the pubs that lined the street. Dave was leaning against the bus stop post with his arms crossed, staring down at the ground.

"Dave!" Cat gasped with relief at finding him.

"Cat, are you OK?" Dave came out of his deep trance and stared at her in disbelief.

"I'm sorry Dave!" Cat breathed out shakily. "You're right. I'm sorry for what I did." She walked up to him.

"I'm sorry too, Cat." He gave her a hug, and Cat felt the tightness leave her body for the last time.

27

She held her mother's hand in hers. Her appearance was so different now, at the end. Her healthy, pale Celtic skin was now tinted a dull yellow, like marzipan. Her skin clung to bones, she had lost so much weight as the cancer ravished her body. Her breathing grew raspy, but her body tried to take in the oxygen, determined to continue living for as long as possible. Cat held onto her mother's hand, the one thing that remained familiar. Those hands had held her as a child, made jam with her on late summer afternoons, and cradled her face when she was upset. Those freckled hands were the last thing Cat remembered of her mother as she held onto them tightly, until the end, until there was no more of her left to hold onto.

Cat bought some flowers, and made her way to the grave-yard that morning. She had no idea where her head had been at yesterday, coming down and secretly having dinner with Dave. She hated to think that, for a moment, she had wanted him back. She hadn't been in her right mind. Thank god Dave saw she had been in a low place. He had protected her. And after leaving on good terms, she felt at peace, and what was more, happy for him. He had told her a little about Louise, and how they had met. Cat could see how different they both were now to when Dave first knew her. It was meant to be; Dave had found his path, but Cat knew she was still to find hers.

The sun cast its warm morning light onto the icy grave-yard, bringing another new day to that place of constant death. Cat walked by the familiar graves until she came to her mother's:

Here rests Mary MacGregor
Loving daughter, and beloved mother
Dearly missed

Cat thought of all the words she had wanted to say to capture her mother's life, much more than what had ended up on that small gravestone. It hurt her still that her mum would never see certain moments of her life. If she ever got married, had a baby, none of them would know her mother, Mary. Cat cleaned the grave a little, lay down the fresh flow-ers, and rubbed away the moss that was starting to grow on the stone edges. She cried for her mother in that quiet tran-quil space, breathing deeply, and allowing the sorrow to seep in.

A hand touched her shoulder, accompanied by a familiar voice: "I'm sure she's proud of you, lass," said Billy. "Anyone would be proud to have you as a daughter."

Cat turned around to see Billy and Jess each holding a bunch of flowers. Cat cried harder, too much in pain to be surprised, and let them take her heavy burden.

"It's OK," Billy murmured, gently hugging her. "We're here. We've got you."

Jess rubbed her friend's back, until Cat's sobs steadied, and gradually her breathing slowed.

Billy and Jess laid a large bouquet of lilies, and one of daises next to the flowers Cat had brought. Billy wore a smart tweed suit, and Jess had her hair tied up in her usual 1950s flowery scarf, above a long black coat.

"Daises were her favourite...?" Cat said to Billy, confused.

"I know, you told me." He smiled.

Cat couldn't remember any discussion of her mother's favourite flowers.

"You speak of her often." Billy patted her hand gently as Jess nodded.

"Oh..." Cat was lost for words. "I didn't realise I really spoke of her at all."

Jess smiled at her "Of course you do, and so you should. She was your mother." Jess looked sadly on the grave. "I wish I had met her. She sounded very interested in art and I think she would be so happy for you and the life you've created, Cat."

Cat looked down at the small chipped words on the grave that summed up her mum's life of fifty short years.

"I just don't want to leave her here," she breathed, "If I move on, then she gets lost, or left behind."

Jess handed her another tissue. "But she's with you Cat. That's what I believe anyway. She may have gone from this world, but she's in a happy place – just, somewhere else now. And a part of her will always be with you. I'm sure she wouldn't want you to feel stuck because of her."

Cat couldn't put into words how she felt, but standing there with the people that she loved, opening her heart to them and letting them love her, helped more than she could have imagined, and she felt stronger for it.

They stood there for a time, Cat relaxing and

consciously speaking more of her mother than she ever had done before. She adjusted the flowers on the grave. "I love you, mum." She sighed with a deep feeling of gratitude as she looked at her friends standing either side of her around the grave. "Thank you both for coming. But how did you know where I was, I never told anyone?" Billy and Jess looked at each other sheepishly.

"Well, the postwoman said you weren't in your cottage. She told Monique, who told a few people at the bakery, which included Mrs White. Then Mrs. White came into the gallery and mentioned it to me..." Jess ran through the subsequent events at rapid speed.

"Jeez, that bloody island! Nothing is a secret!" Cat shook her head in amazement.

"But you love it!" Jess chimed in.

"I do!"

That afternoon they planned to go for a coffee; Cat took them to her old haunt, the Irish pub, which was warm and welcoming. She waved to the barman who recognised her.

"Well well! How are you, haven't seen you in ages!"

"Yes, I kind of escaped to an island!" Cat chuckled.

"Did your boyfriend enjoy it too?" he gestured behind Cat. She spun around to find Dave at a table with a girl. Dave noticed Cat too and stopped talking; the girl with straight silky brown hair cast her eyes over Cat in a questioning way as Cat approached them.

"Hi Dave." She smiled awkwardly and extended her hand to the girl. "Hi there, I'm Cat."

"Cat, Hi!" Dave looked over to his companion. "This is Louise."

Cat shook the girl's hand, Louise looking her up and down, trying to work out who she was to Dave.

"It's nice to meet you Louise. Dave's told me all about you. I just want to offer my congratulations to you both." She gave Dave a smile. "I think you'll both make each other very happy."

The girl still looked confused.

"I'm an old friend of Dave's by the way," she clarified quickly. "It's good to see you Dave, and so nice to meet you, Louise." She smiled at them both and walked back to her table.

"Who's that?" Jess scrutinised Dave from the table. "And where's our drinks?"

Cat glanced over once more to Dave and gave him an apologetic smile. "Yeah, I'll tell you about that soon, but I think we should go – I may have just accidentally spoiled a marriage proposal!"

That evening they landed back on the island, and as their plane touched down, Jess mentioned her friend Andrew would be picking them up from the airport.

"Oh Andrew, is it?" Cat mocked as Jess's cheeks turned pink.

"Shut up!" Jess folded her arms.

Cat nudged her friend. "Jess and Andrew up a tree, K-I-S-S-I-N-G!"

"Shut up!" this time face turned crimson. "He's just a friend!"

"What are you waiting for Jess? I know from personal experience. Don't wait, if you like him, and he likes you; go for it!"

Cat spent the next few days at the gallery, and gave Jess time off to spend with Andrew. Andrew worked at the diving centre and took Jess out along with his groups; each day he'd pop into the gallery looking for her, and Cat would roll her eyes. "You again, Andrew! Can you not leave each other alone for five minutes?!"

Andrew's cheeky smile was however irresistible, and she could never make fun of him for long.

The pair spent the days together, and the nights also.

"Oh my god, Cat," Jess swooned one afternoon, recounting all the moments spent with her new man, "he's a diver in more ways than one!" Jess laughed as Cat covered her ears.

"Please...don't say anymore!" Cat cried. "If you tell me all your sex stories I won't be able to look him in the face!"

"But he does this amazing thing with his-"

"NO!" Cat walked out of the quiet gallery leaving her friend giggling with unashamed pleasure.

28

Cat got into a routine of swimming in the mornings, and splitting her shifts between the pub and the art gallery. It turned out her old friend Angie, who had helped show her the ropes at the bar, had changed jobs, and was now her local postwoman. Which made complete sense, as Jess had told her it was because of the postwoman that Jess found out Cat had left for Glasgow. Cat couldn't be annoyed at Angie; there was something innocent and friendly about her that she found extremely likeable. Angie called in everyday with her post, and stayed for a cuppa even if she had none to deliver.

"Got anything for me today Ange?" Cat opened the door to the postwoman, who was wrapped up in a high-vis water-proof jacket and wellies, her dark hair messy and wild from the wind.

Angie nodded, her hands full with packages, and stepped into the warm cottage.

"I'll get the tea on!" Cat trotted through to the kitchen and Angie followed, taking off her jacket and sitting at the kitchen table. She looked tired.

"Make mine a coffee, Cat," she sighed.

The packages were left on the table while the two women gossiped.

"The old house at Errols place has been sold" Angie said as she took a sip of her strong hot coffee "Oh that's good Cat, you're good at the old coffee. I went into the tearoom the other day and asked for a coffee – they turned around and said "Well that's fine but just so you know it'll be instant!"

Cat laughed at her friends animated description of the ensuing scene.

Angie took another sip at her own coffee looking at Cat with approval. "So how is the famous artist? Still painting?"

Cat hadn't been painting since she had run into Patrick at the ceilidh dance.

"Oh not right now, but I will. Just waiting for another bout of inspiration." Cat flicked through her packages on the table and found a large envelope from London.

"Well if you need me to model, I'm sure I could be very inspiring. I've been told I have good bone structure." Angie pouted her lips like an Instagram girl, which made them both laugh.

Cat opened the envelope and took a few moments to flick through an art magazine.

"What is it?" Angie looked at the empty envelope and then at Cat.

"Oh my god!" Cat shrieked, "I'm in a magazine! Look!"

Angie read the article aloud as they squealed at the end of each sentence.

"Look at those photos too! Go you Cat!"

Cat picked up the magazine looking at the image of herself in front of her paintings, and then glanced over her interview. She had given quite a few interviews recently that they had all began to blend into one another. She had resigned herself to believe that nothing would come from them.

"You come across very well!" Angie clinked cups with Cat and winked at her "This might get you more paintings sold!"

"Oh jeez!" Cat panicked at the thought of all those unfinished pieces she had to get through. "I better get cracking!"

Angie left Cat calling up Jess to give her the good news. Her friend congratulated her, and said she had her fingers crossed that the article would give them more customers at the gallery.

Cat took herself off to her shed, where she threw herself into her work. Spurred on by the article she felt very much like a professional artist. A full-time professional artist, and that felt pretty good.

In a blur, Jess barged into the shed just as Cat was mid-way throwing black paint onto a canvas, as loud classical music blared in the background.

"Oh Jesus!" cried Cat startled, and she turned around so quickly the paint flew across onto Jess's face, hair and yellow corduroy dress.

"Oh no!" Jess held up her hands and looked down at her dress. "Look what you did!"

Cat was wearing her scruffy denim dungarees, which were covered in all the colours of the rainbow from previous splatters of paint. She looked at her friend openmouthed and then couldn't help herself, she started laughing.

"Hey!" Jess's face turned red with fury and stomped her feet like a little girl.

"Well what do you expect!" Cat gasped, looking at her bespattered friend. "I didn't know you were coming!"

Jess stood on the spot looking down. "This is my favourite winter dress!"

Cat sent her friend upstairs to get showered, and gave her a black shirt and jeans to wear. Once Jess came back out, a lot cleaner, Cat tried to save the yellow dress by washing it in the sink.

"What brings you here at this time of the day anyway?" Cat handed Jess a cup of tea and left the dress to soak in the soapy water.

Jess patted her wet hair with a towel and sat down on the sofa. "Yeah, I locked up for the day. I wanted to chat."

Cat felt a knot of concern twist inside her "What? What's wrong?"

"Nothing," Jess reassured her, "calm down, I just wanted to present an idea to you."

Cat settled down on the sofa and listened as Jess ceremoniously asked her to be a business partner.

"But I don't have any experience!" Cat stuttered. "The gallery is yours, I don't want to take that away from you!"

"But you won't." Jess put down her cup and looked Cat in the eye. "I think we can both get something good out of this. Look, if I was able to divide the gallery, that would mean we both could paint part-time, and organise the gallery part-time. It's the best of both worlds! Also I'm acting kind of selfishly too - a gallery in London called this morning; they saw that article in the magazine, and are inviting you to exhibit with them next year! So I'm not asking to work with just anyone. I want to work with a successful artist, and be able to split everything 50/50. What do you say?"

"Oh my god, a gallery in London!" Cat clapped her

hands and whooped. She didn't need to have any time to think, she knew her answer. "Of course, owning and running a gallery was always something I wanted to do. Yes, I'd love to go into business!" The two girls hugged excitedly and chattered excitedly about all the avenues of possibility their new venture together might provide.

29

The days leading up to Halloween saw a flurry of customers come into the gallery. Jess had a huge box of Halloween decorations, with which, along with help from Cat and Andrew, she made the gallery look very festive.

"I love Halloween!" Jess placed the last pumpkin on the windowsill. "Voilà!" She clapped, and they looked around at the unseemly decorations of witches' hats, broomsticks and even skeletons, which were perched on two chairs beside the door.

"Are you sure this looks OK?" Cat mused, looking dubiously at a skull grinning at them from the front desk.

"Aye, some of the locals will just come in to see the decorations." Jess nodded with the side of her mouth curving up slyly. "Last year I sold a painting to James Riley, he came in with his son to see the place all ghoulified! Little did he know that *I* knew he was interested in different breeds of sheep, and hey ho - what do you know? I had some little oil paintings of sheep grazing on seaweed on the isle of North Ronaldsay!"

"You are a clever girl aren't you?" Andrew walked up to her, grabbed her around the waist and kissed her.

"Oh get a room you two!" Cat looked on smiling, with a pinch of jealousy within her, that she immediately extinguished. "What are you planning to do for Halloween?" She asked, adjusting the fake spider's web over the window.

Jess kissed Andrew goodbye as he went off to work, and sighed with a calm smile on her lips. "We were going to watch some scary films. Maybe some old gory ones, popcorn, wine all that. Fancy coming?"

Cat liked the idea of a movie night, but thought it best to leave the two love birds alone while they enjoyed these early days getting to know one another. The idea of being the third wheel didn't sound very tempting.

"I thought I'd decorate the house, and maybe see if I get any guisers!"

"You mean trick or treaters?" Jess said in an American accent.

"No I mean guisers - if I get any kids who come to my house and don't give a decent party piece - a joke, story, song or poem then they are not getting any treats!" Cat wagged her finger.

"Jeez you're so bossy sometimes! Just give them a treat! It's the same thing anyway!"

"No I won't do it, it's tradition here. I won't encourage lazy guisers!" Cat could feel herself getting annoyed as Jess started to laugh.

"Oh, you are funny with your little rules," Jess chuckled.

"But we both had to do a party piece when we went guising!" Cat protested.

"Oh enough of the bloody good-ol' guisers!" Jess bellowed, and the two girls stopped bickering as a client came through the door.

That evening Cat had invited Billy and Jess over for dinner, and had prepared a lamb stew, and baked a cake. The aromas of the sweet buttery sponge, and the rich meaty gravy wafted through the house, making Cat hungry. Billy showed up in his yellow raincoat and wellies, as per usual on a stormy October night.

"No Jess?" She looked outside to see a car drive off in the darkness. Billy sheepishly announced as if instructed: "Jess sends her apologies, she was invited to a last minute dinner at Andrew's parents."

"The cheek of it! And I made loads of food!" Cat showed the old man in.

"She said she'll not be too long, and will pop over later." Billy looked around and smiled. "Nice place, lass".

Cat took his jacket and made the old man welcome. They spent the evening eating, and drinking endless cups of tea.

"It's really good to see you Billy." Cat sat back full and sleepy at the kitchen table after finishing off the last morsels of cake.

"And you, lass." Billy patted his belly. "I've no eaten sae much in a long time. Very kind of you to cook."

"Of course, you did the same for me! You saved my life." Cat poured more tea into their cups.

"Hardly!" Billy laughed, "I just gave you a place to rest for the night."

"And you came to be with me in Glasgow, which meant a lot."

He coughed gruffly and looked a little self-conscious, but Cat continued. "That day you rescued us off the hill, if you hadn't been there I'm sure we would've been hiking those hills through the night! Either that or my weight would've killed Johnny in the end." She laughed, and patted her own stomach.

"How is Johnny?" Billy asked.

"He's good. He called me up a week ago and has asked if he and Mark can come up for Hogmanay." Cat had spent most of her New Year celebrations at home sleeping through to the morning, but this time she wanted to embrace it.

"There's a ceilidh on at the village hall."

Cat cringed at the mention of a ceilidh, the image of being rejected by Patrick still haunted her on occasion. She ignored the nagging, unsettling feeling. "Maybe you could stay here and we could all go together?"

"For you, I'll manage it." Billy patted her hand with a grin.

The night had become colder, so they spent some time in front of the fire drinking Billy's favourite Bourbon. Billy spoke about his years on the fishing boats, from ventures such as swimming with sharks, to lying under the endless flickering of northern lights. "When you're out there, in the ocean." He closed his eyes, sitting still. "You're at the mercy of nature. I've never felt so free, and so alone." He reflected a moment, then started to rummage in his pockets. "I never did show you a picture of Effie." The old man produced a small bundle of photos secured with ribbon, which he carefully untied, and the contents spread on the coffee table in front of Cat.

A black-and-white photo showed a bright-eyed girl with dark, bobbed hair, wearing a wedding dress.

"Oh my goodness, she's beautiful!" Cat picked up the photo and looked at the smiling eyes, a bride on her wedding day.

"Aye...she was bonnie." Billy looked at the photo. "Always happy, always seeing the good things in life." His eyes started to redden, and he rubbed them and coughed.

"How old was she here?" Cat picked up a later, coloured photo of Effie holding a toddler.

"She was about forty I'd say. That's our niece." He pointed to the little girl. "Her sister had a few bairns, and she doted on them. They were like our own, for a while; we'd have them to stay for days on end. Having tea parties, making play-dens, playing catch on the beach. It was a special time."

"You don't see them now?" Cat tucked back a curl behind her ear.

"Nae, life gets in the way doesn't it?" He sniffed. "Everyone leaves home, those bairns are all now spread over the country with their own families."

Cat went through the photos, seeing in each an insight into Billy's life. Picking up another image, she saw him and Effie nestled together on a wooden bench beside the sea. Billy wore a leather jacket with his hair combed back, while Effie was in a peach dress. "Billy - you were very handsome!" Cat giggled. "I bet Effie had to keep her eye on you! I'm sure you were popular with the ladies."

"Not a bit of it, I only had eyes for her." He sipped his dram, looking more happy, and less melancholy than he had when he first produced the bundle. Cat glanced over the other photos until one got her attention. It was much older, and had writing on the back. *Maggie, Sarah and Effie, 1946.* Effie looked about five or six, with two older girls on either side behind her. Effie stood staring at the camera with a serious face, as the two teenage girls smiled with mischief and the beginnings of teenage poise. They stood in front of a gate, and some rose bushes. The scene was somehow familiar. Then it hit Cat, and she froze. The older girl on the right had curly hair that was pinned back, and wore a simple day-dress, her hand resting on Effie's shoulder. Cat's heart skipped a beat, and unsure of quite what was happening, she asked Billy if he knew the children.

"Oh yes. That's Maggie on the left, or Marge as we knew her, and her friend Sarah on the right. They were close. Looked after Effie from time to time." He looked at Cat's pale face. "Are you OK?"

"Billy, do you know this is Marge's cottage?" Her mouth was dry, her head buzzing.

The old man gave a half-smile. "I knew this was her place, but I'd never been inside before to be honest." His face was full of concern as he watched Cat stand slowly. She went upstairs, collected her own photo albums, and walked back down to Billy, who was now standing by the fire.

Cat took out a photo of her mother and her grand-mother. They both had the same nose and eyes, which Cat had inherited in her turn. Cat's mother would say her red hair came from her granny's side of the family too.

"This was my grannie, along with my mum. I kept all my mum's photos after she died." Then she found the picture that had been so similar to Billy's. She took out the black-and-white photo of her grandmother, and of the woman that stood beside her. They both smiled together by a gate and a cluster of rose bushes. This woman was Marge; it was Marge's garden. How had Cat not seen it before? She had gone through Marge's photos with Johnny, but nothing had caught her eye until tonight. She pointed to Billy's photo of the girl standing behind Effie. "I don't know how, but... that's my grandmother".

The evening blurred into a series of questions. Cat examined all her photographs, and Billy's again too. *My*

grandmother Sarah had been at this very house before, but how?
Billy told her what little he knew of the girl named Sarah, as
Cat drank in all the details.

"She had beautiful red hair... all the lads would whistle
at her as she passed by. She'd make her own clothing out of
anything going spare, it was hard to find much during the
rationing." Billy remembered her friendship with Marge;
the two girls would sing together at weddings, funerals and
all the village fairs. "Voices of angels, they had. We used to
joke they'd be the next Andrews Sisters. I think she got
married. Effie didn't speak much of her after a while. She
was a lot younger, see, so she started making friends her
own age, and once the war was over things changed so
much". Billy's eyes started to close, and within a few minutes
he was emitting gentle snoring noises. No doubt she had
poured him one too many drams in the hope of more
stories. Cat fetched a blanket to cover the old man on the
sofa, and then put another couple of logs on the fire. She
texted Jess to say Billy was asleep, and not to worry about
coming over. She hoped her friend was getting on well with
Andrew's parents, regardless. Cat switched her phone off
and went upstairs to lie on her bed, thinking of the white-
haired lady she knew as a little girl, and feeling much closer
to her than she ever had before.

fter Cat had dropped off a somewhat hung-over Billy down at the ferry the next morning, she went back to her cottage and took a look around the rose garden. The iron gate was the same as it had been in the photos, albeit a little worn with time. She peeked in amongst the bushes, not knowing exactly what she was looking for, but continued to cast her eye over anything that might give her more insight into the minds of the women in the picture. She heard the post-van in the distance, but let her thoughts return to Sarah. *Were Marge and Sarah very close?* To think that Sarah had stood in this very same spot as her granddaughter was now.

"What you looking for?" Angie's perplexed face peered over the bushes.

"Come in," Cat opened the gate, "it's a long story, I'll tell you over coffee."

Cat opened up to Angie, telling her all the news from the previous night, not missing out a single detail. She knew the postwoman was a bit of a gossip, but right now she needed advice.

"Wow, I can't believe it. You're grandmother was Orcadian!" Angie gulped down her coffee and slammed it down onto the table with relish. "OK, what you need to do is go to the library in the village. They might have information on the community that used to live here around that time – a census or something!"

"Yes, that's a great idea!" Cat clicked a pen open and noted down a list of places and people to research on a scrap of paper.

"I know the first thing to put at the top of your list."

"What?"

Angie grinned and held out her cup. "Another cup of coffee wouldn't go amiss!"

The library was the size of a small bedroom, even smaller than Cat's own living room. She stood gazing in awe upon entering; she had never seen so many books crammed into every tiny available space. Books lined the windowsills; books lay in piles on the floor, up against walls and covering the tables. The librarian – a stern looking lady with thick glasses, was perched on a chair, fountain pen poised, looking very busy and important, only glancing at Cat briefly as she came in. Cat shuffled and manoeuvred around the miniature towers of chaos that filled the space ahead of her, weaving around the tiny floor to find what she was looking for. A young man with long greasy hair, reading a book with dragons on the cover, sat at a small table in the middle of the room, quietly turning each page mechanically, far away in his own magical world. Standing near him, a mother with frizzy hair and her hands full of books tried to shush her two little boys. The threats of no dinner and no more toys fell on their deaf ears as they both pinched and nudged each other mercilessly.

Cat went up to ask the librarian where she might find local news, and was silently directed to a metal cabinet in the corner, wedged between two bookshelves, piled high, of course, with books. The filing cabinet was packed with newspapers dating back to the 1850s, right through to the recent paper, which had Jess and Cat on the front cover. She glanced at articles from the 1950s, and slightly further back. Looking at the black and white images, and the major events startlingly captured: *"Hitler declares war"* and *"Strikes from the miners"*, Cat examined the papers for what seemed like hours, scrutinising every photograph and name she came across. She knew she was looking for a Sarah. But a Sarah who? Billy didn't know her surname, and she couldn't imagine anyone who would remember just 'a Sarah' who left the island so many years ago.

The librarian came over to Cat and handed her a mug of tea. "May I help?" The lady gave a small smile, and had evidently decided to take pity on her.

"I'm trying to find my grandmother. Her name was Sarah; she left Orkney a long time ago, although I don't know when or why. She used to sing at local events with her friend Marge, who owned Bramble cottage."

"I remember Marge." The lady tapped her finger on her lip for a moment. "I'm afraid I don't know a Sarah." She started to rummage though the newspapers in the filing cabinet herself. "I believe I saw Marge in one of the papers once, but when was it...?" Her fingers lightly touched the tops of the newspapers, flicking them through like an old film reel. "No, nope, not that one..." Then she stopped abruptly, and pulled out a set of leaves. She squinted at the writing, then spread the pages on the small table at the end of the bookshelf. "Yes, this looks to be it. This was Marge when she was very young." There was a small blurry black and white photo of a dark-haired girl wearing a beret and a ruffled shirt, standing next to an older man wearing a kilt suit and holding bagpipes.

"Competition winner Marge Reid is to sing at the opening of the annual gala day in St Margaret's Hope. The event will welcome soldiers to the island, and show local support for the war effort. Sure to be the event of the year." Cat scanned the article.

"No mention of Sarah," she sighed, and sat down. The excitement of finding out about her grandmother had evaporated, along with the promise of new leads. She sipped at her tea, which was now cold, but the sweetness perked her up somewhat. "I'm not sure where to go from here, to be honest!" She gulped the remaining tea down realising she hadn't actually drank anything that day.

The librarian took off her glasses and placed them on top of her pulled-back wiry grey hair. "There's no need to give up just yet," she smiled, and crossed her arms. The library was now empty of people, and the streetlights outside flickered on, casting an amber glow through the window onto the walls.

"It's so strange how someone can be so close to you, but you find out later that you never really knew them." Cat rested her head on her hand. "I mean, how could I not know anything about my own grandmother?" Her eyes cast down to the photograph of Marge looking back at her.

The librarian rested a hand on her shoulder to comfort her. "I'm sorry dear, it's time for me to lock up."

Cat walked back to her car along the quiet cobbled main street. The stillness of the dusk was a little unsettling; no wind, no cars, and no people, just the sound of a dog barking in the far distance. She was about to get into her car when she saw Patrick walking with a girl across the street and down a small alley. Cat could see them reach the end of the lane and turn off. Without anymore thought she quickly and quietly followed them. They appeared deep in conversation, as Cat watched them, feeling awful, but with an unavoidable need to know once and for all, whether this girl was Patrick's girl, or just a friend – *maybe she was just a friend...?* The pair stopped and spoke for a few moments, and then continued strolling up to Patrick's door. The girl touched his arm as they started up the steps, then suddenly kissed him on the lips. Cat felt as if someone had punched her in the stomach. She leaned against a stone wall, hiding in the shadows, breathing deeply, and trying to stop the tears starting down her face. She turned around, and ran back to her car, speeding off into the night, with an overwhelming aching in her heart. She couldn't get the image of the girl kissing Patrick, the same girl that answered the door to her, the same girl that giggled with him at the ceilidh, out of her head. *Just a friend, Cat? You're an idiot!* She thumped the steering wheel with her fists. *How could she be so stupid? Never again would she let her heart open up to another person. She was clearly meant to be alone.*

Cat reached her cottage and went to get her wetsuit. She tried to put on the cumbersome elastic material, but gave up in the end, and marched outside with her towel wrapped around her naked body to meet the gloomy light. She walked down to the shoreline, removed the towel and ran into the waves. The wind had picked up, and the tiny lights of the town in the distance twinkled back at her. She swam until her breath grew hard and heavy, and her fingers and toes began to lose feeling. A streak of lightning flashed, and the rain fell. She began to cry, her sobs consumed by the loud storm arising. Flashes of Patrick came into her head; his kiss, and his touch. Cat felt sure there was something special between them, a primal attraction, and an understanding that she couldn't quite explain. But that didn't necessarily mean they were meant to be uncompromisingly together. Exhausted, she started to swim back to shore. It was then that her hands glided into a large tangle of seaweed. The seaweed grew thicker the more she swam and wrapped its slippery tentacles around her, encircling her limbs. Cat could scarcely see anything in front of her, just the blurred lights of the cottage somewhere away in front of her. In a blind panic, she gasped, and gulped salty water. Coughing and struggling for air, she was pushed underwater by a wave. The sea swelled and the rain lashed down while Cat reached desperately for the surface. In those split seconds, she thought of her mother. She felt her, at that moment, and the warmth of her love surrounded her then, amongst the dark waters, reassuring her. Cat calmed herself down in the midst of the thick strands, focusing on the memory of her gentle touch. Time seemed to pass slowly, but soon the seaweed started to drift away with the movement of the waves, allowing her legs to break free. She swam steadily to the water's edge and dragged herself out of the waves. She collapsed outside her door, coughing up salty water and shaking uncontrollably, but alive. She gave a weak laugh, and went gingerly back inside.

31

Halloween night arrived, and Cat felt, for once, very organised. She had stocked up on sweets and treats, which were now piled high in a big bowl beside the front door, awaiting her spooky guests. She had mentioned to a few people that she would be home tonight, as news would carry fast on the island, and she prepared for the anticipated little guisers coming to her door. Cat loved the old traditions, especially that of carving out turnips and placing a candle inside, which she had prepared earlier, and the jaggy lit-faces looked out of the window awaiting the arrival of whoever was to call on her that night. Her last few days made her realise that she must enjoy these moments in life, and she shuddered at how stupid she had been: *swimming at night and in a storm! Never again!* She was determined to make the most of what she had; she always loved Halloween, so this would be first of many good ones to come.

It wasn't long until she heard cars approaching and a tapping on her door. She welcomed them in, hearing their party pieces and giving them treats in return. Witches, ghosts, devils and monsters showed up one after the other, and Cat loved connecting with the children. She thought of Halloween with her mother, and how they had gone to various parties and dunked for apples. Cat smiled to herself, things were going to be alright; she had her friends around her, and she had herself. Only she could make herself happy in the way that she really needed to be.

The evening grew late, and she was about to blow out the pumpkin and turnip lanterns on the windowsills, when she heard another knock at the door. She opened it to three witches, two tiny girls, holding hands and wearing witches' hats and black dresses, along with their adult-sized companion.

"You don't recognise me!" came the hoarse voice from underneath a thick layer of green makeup and a black wig. "Any chance of a coffee?"

"Angie!"

"I thought you looked unsure - and a bit scared!" Angie laughed, and tapped the two girls on their shoulders. "This is Abbey, and this is Rachel - say hello to Catherine!"

The girls said hello in small voices, and Cat gave them an extra treat while she poured a strong espresso for Angie.

"We've been around the whole village, and there's hardly anyone opening their doors this year." Angie took off her wig and sat on the sofa while the girls knelt in front of the fire, eating their sweets and comparing their hauls with one another.

"I think I'll take them around the next town to a few people I know," Angie drank her coffee, "but I needed this before round two!"

Another knock came at the door and a crowd of wizards, ghosts and ghouls seeped into her living room, as Angie left with her girls.

"Wow what do we have here?" Cat laughed, and was met with a chorus of different children telling her what they were.

She glanced up to their adult, who removed his Frankenstein mask. It was Patrick. "Hi Cat!"

"Oh... Hi, Patrick." Cat reddened.

"I lost a bet," he sighed. "All the parents are down the pub for a few hours while I'm out chaperoning their wee monsters!"

Cat was able to compose herself easier than she had initially imagined, and gave out treats to the kids, applauding the jokes they told her, and pretending to be scared at every roar. Cat laughed at the task Patrick had undertook, as each child started to getting louder and louder, fuelled by the sugary items piled high in their bags.

"Right let's get you all out of this lovely lady's house before she kicks us out!" Patrick shooed the boys to the car and ran back to the front door. He ran his fingers through his wavy hair and looked at Cat, somewhat unsure. Cat casually rested against the cold grey stonewall and waved to the rowdy bunch of kids squeezing into the car.

"I hope you didn't mind me taking them down here, I heard you were welcoming guisers tonight?"

Cat smiled. "Of course Patrick, it was good to see you"

"I wanted to say..." he looked back at the car of shouting boys. "I mean, I wanted to see how you were?"

"I'm fine, you know just working most of the time." Cat folded her arms to keep warm, and nestled in the doorway.

"I want you to know that you've really inspired me Cat. You wanted to paint, and here you are making it happen." He shoved his hands into his pockets. "I wanted to say that I'm writing an album. The gig that you promoted on the radio, well it was fantastic."

"Oh Patrick, that's brilliant news!"

"I've been talking to a record label, a small independent one. But it allows me more control than the big brands would, so we're planning an album. I wanted you to be the first to know."

Cat couldn't help herself, she hugged him. "I'm so happy for you!"

"I think I'm beginning to see the path I want in life. I want to be involved in music, and seeing how you've taken control of your life, well - it's made me look at mine."

Cat stood stunned. *Was she in control of her life*? She certainly wasn't in control of her next words as they fell out of her mouth. "I'm sorry about what happened at the ceilidh. I had too much to drink."

Patrick tilted his head, then his eyes widened. "No, no don't be. I just didn't want to... regret anything." He looked over to the car again, where the boys were now on the car horn and yelling loudly.

Cat clung tightly to herself, against the cold breeze. She was still mortified how she had thrown herself on someone who she had known already to have a girlfriend. She tried to find the words, but before she could open her mouth Patrick cut in.

"I've been meaning to tell you something else, that day at the cafe when we spoke about ourselves... well - there's something I didn't say, and I really should have. I just didn't know how to start explaining at all, and we were having such a good time -" Patrick rubbed his chin in his familiar awkward manner, and looked at the ground. "OK OK! Christ, I'm coming!" he bellowed suddenly at the rocking car-full of cries and shrieks; the boys had the radio on and were howling with eagerness to go on to the next house for more treats.

"I need to go." He started to step away then hesitated. "Sorry." He gave a grim smile and quickly got into the car. Cat stood still, her arms still crossed looking at the car as it rumbled down the road, its lights fading into the distance. She wanted to shut off the longing in her heart. *Maybe he's only looking for a friend to talk to? Either that or he's a good player. Leading girls on and then sleeping with them at his leisure. Well no more,* Cat thought. She was not going to be played for a fool and wait in line as Patrick slowly worked his way through a hoard of girls as and when he felt like it.

32

Cat had spent the day discussing possible new ventures with Jess. She was finally sure that if she focused on her career, she could be happy. Maybe she didn't need some big love in her life anyway, and perhaps the costume dramas she had often watched back in Glasgow had given her an unrealistic view on what life had to offer. She had the gallery, and she had Jess, both of which made her happier than she had been in years. At the moment, she knew she could enjoy what she had, and make the most of it; anything else would happen if it was meant to. As the two girls drank coffee and made more detailed lists of business ideas, the door bell tinkled gently, and Andrew stepped in. Jess ran up to him like a carefree child, happy to show her emotions to the world, Cat had accepted her friend's happiness gladly, and really she knew in her heart that Andrew was the one for Jess. Their new love radiated through them both, it was something special, and Cat knew that Jess deserved every second of it. Andrew laid down a bag of fresh cinnamon scrolls on the table and winked at Cat.

"I hope I'm not too late for coffee? I know these are your favourite Cat, they just came out of the oven at the bakery!"

"Oh, you do know the way to a girl's heart Andy!" Cat poured him a coffee, enjoying their shared sense of humour, present this morning as much as any other.

"Hey what about me?" Jess pouted.

"You like the scrolls too!" Andrew chuckled at Jess's expression and took the cup offered by Cat.

"Sometimes I think you're here to see Cat more than me!" Jess playfully rolled her eyes and peeked inside the paper bag.

"Don't you want your best mate and boyfriend to like each other?"

"We could try to hate each other if you want us to!" Cat laughed, and gratefully took a pastry from the bag.

"Urgh, that's not what I meant, I just..." Jess bit her lip and went pink. "I don't know!"

The day had been quiet, with only one customer picking up their purchase. Cat had said she'd lock up, so Jess and Andrew had decided to go for an early showing of the latest superhero movie, and Cat was happy to decline their offer of being third wheel again. She briefly muttered to Jess that if she never saw another super hero movie, she would die content.

"You sound like an old woman Cat, a movie never did any harm!" Jess chuckled.

"Maybe. But I'm happy to say: I'm only doing things that I want to do from now on, that's the beauty of being single."

"Hmmm," Jess hesitated for a second lowering herself

into Andrew's car, clearly mulling over what Cat had said, and seeing some truth in it, she smiled.

Cat waved to them and spent the late afternoon designing online marketing deals on the computer, as she enjoyed the background music overhead. Then Ella Fitzgerald's heart-rending vocals rolled out from the speakers. Cat lay back at the front desk, enjoying the sweet, lulling notes as she finished up scheduling their first promotion. She thought again of Patrick; she couldn't help it. The music transported her back to that day at the cafe, content with the gentle calm between them as they watched the lashing rain against the window and the people rushing past. Cat got up and went to the back studio where the music system sat, and changed the song to an upbeat 1940s track. She looked around the glow of lights illuminating each artwork on the walls, she had to pinch herself thinking about where she worked sometimes - and a business partner too! She glowed inside - her mum would be proud. Cat smiled to herself, no longer feeling the pain that came from thinking of her mother. She finally felt at peace with herself, and with the memories. Cat peered out the window: only the odd person passed by, saluting her if their eyes met, but otherwise it was quiet, as the cloudy sky grew darker with each passing minute. Cat stared out at the bleakness and thought that perhaps during winter time they should close the gallery and make more time for inspiration, and painting. Jess had thrown out some ideas for business plans for the colder seasons, but it was difficult when most of the island shut down in hibernation for the spring. Cat made a note on a nearby notepad to suggest to Jess tomorrow, and went upstairs to grab a snack from the fridge. She was midway through making a sandwich, lost in her duties for the rest of the day, when she heard a loud bang downstairs, followed by another in the seconds it took her to put down the beginnings of her sandwich. Cat jumped at the noise, a little frightened, but reassured herself something would have just fallen, most likely; a painting, or an easel in the studio area. She slowly made her way down the stairs, in case there was broken glass to take care of, but before she was halfway down she heard another bang, and the unsettling noise of something being dragged across the floor. Cat's heart beat so fast and hard, she could hear it pounding, fearing what she would discover once she opened the door to the gallery. Her brain processed the scene seconds before her emotions and adrenaline kicked in. Several canvases lay on the floor, torn down from the walls, leaving great big scratches on the paint, along with a large pair of open scissors, as if thrown down in fury. The scene was confusing and angry; she tried to let her head catch up to the panic that engulfed her, too scared to look around her for whoever had caused the damage. But as she took a step forward towards the mess, she caught a figure standing somewhere near the doorway out of the corner of her eye. She cried out in alarm, not knowing whether she should stay put and call the police, or run after the culprit herself. Following her instinct, Cat took a leap over her large tree canvas, seeing without really processing the thought, that it had been ripped down the middle, as though cut with the scissors. She ran to the door and outside in the gloomy light could just make out two figures in the distance on the road, wrestling and shouting. She walked into the cold in a daze, unsure of what to do, then froze on the spot, as she recognised that the newcomer was Patrick. He punched the unknown figure, who as Cat moved closer she saw was a younger man, his nose now bloodied as he lunged at Patrick again, making them both fall to the ground.

"Stop it!" Cat screamed.

"Christ, what have you done, Alan?" Patrick bellowed as the young man grabbed him around the neck and smashed his head against the stone road. Patrick yelled in pain and the boy got up quickly, but Cat ran up in front before he could get past her.

"If you don't come back into the gallery now, I'm calling the police. I know your name, Patrick knows you, we'll get to you before you can even leave on the ferry tomorrow!" she panted, looking into a white face staring back at her with rage. The young man let slip an expression of brief uncertainty, then pushed Cat roughly out of the way, making her fall hard.

Patrick held the back of his head and called out after the figure: "Alan, the police will get you - the only way off this island is the ferry, and by god we'll have people looking for you tomorrow!"

The boy hesitated on the spot, and as Cat got up from the ground, composing herself, she knew there was something more to the situation that she had to get to the bottom of; the strange tension between Patrick and the young man was more than just incidental.

"Come into the gallery now, or I'll call the police immediately." Cat brushed off some of the dirt from her elbow and clothes.

"Or I could make sure you *don't* call the police..." The figure turned to Cat with palpable malice, making her chest tighten and her skin turn cold.

"Stop that Alan, you wouldn't do that." Patrick also rose from the ground and pulled himself up to his full height. "Get in there, now!" He pointed to the gallery and Cat swiftly walked back to the welcome glow of the lit doorway, without checking to see if either man were following.

Once inside Cat felt her whole body begin to tremble. She saw the canvases on the ground, and the scissors, and gulped at the work ruined before her.

Patrick came in, hand clasped around the back of Alan's dark hoodie, and pushed him into the middle of the gallery's open space. He took a moment to duck outside to see if there were any onlookers, but again the village was quiet.

"People are going to see us in here, especially after your scream Cat... Can you close the shutters?" Cat's shaking hands locked the door, and pulled down the shutters, shielding them from any prying eyes. Patrick put a hand on her back, and tilted her face towards his. "Are you OK?"

She nodded, unsure of what to say at a time like this. All she wanted were answers, but seeing her work, and the positive progress of the last six months of her life destroyed before her made her want to cry, and lash out at this cruel stranger.

Patrick turned on the young man. "How dare you come here, haven't you put me through enough?"

Alan gave a sarcastic laugh. "How dare YOU come here! Leaving me, taking mum with you! You're a sick bastard, Pat!"

Cat abruptly looked up at Patrick, he turned to her, his face taught with anger and nerves. "I'm sorry you've got embroiled in this Cat, I'm sorry about... this is my brother. Alan."

"Oh I see, not telling anyone about me, is it? Leaving me behind in Ireland with all your other secrets!" Alan spat.

"I don't have any secrets. All our shame is mixed up in you, and what you've done! We had to leave, you were making life too hard for us, and causing mum more grief than she needed in her illness. I'll never forgive you for that. Never," Patrick said quietly through clenched teeth.

"You took her away from me, she was my mother too!" Alan stood tall, inches from Patrick face.

"We gave you enough chances, you never listened - just determined to destroy your life and ours. Jesus Alan, what did you want? Did we not give to you enough? Weren't we there for you when you got expelled from school, and arrested, time and time again?" Patrick flexed his fists, as if ready to fight once more. "You were selfish; all you cared about was yourself, and you believed everything those thugs told you. We couldn't give you anymore. You made mum miserable."

"She made *me* miserable! Not telling me about my Dad for all those years! You two are both as bad as each other – if you don't like it, you just pretend it never happened! You're pathetic!"

"Alan, we've been over and over this. She was trying to care for you, trying to do the right thing to say we both had the same father, to love us both just the same - you just couldn't help yourself snooping through her personal things!"

"I'm glad I did - didn't I find the letters? How could she do that... she was a slut."

Cat froze on the spot as Patrick walked right up to his brother, white with anger.

"What did you say?" Patrick clenched his fists once more and Cat intervened immediately.

"Stop!" she demanded. "You're both in *my* building and I will *not* have a fight in here! I want you to go upstairs and get us some tea, Patrick – there's a bit of whisky left in the top left cupboard if you think any of us can handle it."

Alan sniggered. "Oh, she's got you in your place, hasn't she!"

Cat turned on Alan. "And you can quit that, you absolute...-!" Cat stopped and took a breath. "You and I are going to have a chat - you still haven't explained why you decided to destroy my artwork, and my job. I could still call the police – so I'd stop grinning so much if I were you!" She pulled a seat around from the front desk, fuming. "Sit down here, now." Alan made as though he were about to speak, then considered his options, and grudgingly sat down opposite Cat.

Patrick stood looking on in silence, before Cat realised he was still there.

"Patrick, it's fine let's have tea – please - Alan looks cold, and I am too."

Patrick hesitated, eyes still fixed on his brother.

"It's OK, please Patrick."

The older brother slowly moved back, turning briefly to check on them before he left the room.

"So, where are you staying?" Cat asked softly.

Alan scoffed but stayed quiet.

"Well, my guess is the hostel in Kirkwall." She looked at him intently, and he eventually nodded.

"Alan, I can see you're angry but you're going the wrong way about it. Why would you come into the gallery and destroy my work? I don't know you, why me?" He stayed quiet for some moments but Cat pressed him. "If you need help, I'm sure we can -"

"I don't need help!" he retorted instantly, "it's my bastard brother who needs the help!"

"Alright, well, maybe we all need a bit of help from time to time," agreed Cat with a sigh. "I know I do." She gestured to the destroyed paintings on the ground. "But why would you do something like this?"

"I wanted him to suffer."

"But -"

"You're involved, he cares about you, I could tell! I wanted to teach him a lesson, make him see he can't take everything away from me and be happy himself, like nothing ever happened! And I knew the best way would be through you."

Cat was stunned, but more so for getting out an explanation from this angry boy than by his distorted logic.

Patrick appeared, with a tray of cups and a packet of biscuits. He stood watching his brother, with a mixture of fury and grief flushing his face, and an awkward silence fell upon the three of them. Cat looked from brother to brother; she had to admit that even if they did have different fathers, there was still a striking resemblance. Patrick leaned over to Alan offering a biscuit, and he took one reluctantly, all the while refusing to make eye-contact.

"You never could refuse a Hobnob," Patrick muttered, almost to himself, and Alan gave the smallest smile.

33

Cat picked up the destroyed canvases, and reflected on the time she had put into each one. It was heartbreaking to see them now, savagely attacked and lying in angry strips. Cat anxiously leaned all the vandalised work together in the back studio. She knew she had to let go of the sorrow she felt, as it was useless to hold onto it when the damage had already been done. She doubted whether she could capture those feelings again in her paintings; she had changed since she had painted them; moved on from that girl in the midst of rediscovering herself, at a time that now seemed so long ago. Anger bubbled inside her at Alan's selfish attack; he cared little about the consequences, driven only by the need to create mayhem in the lives of those around him, to replicate what he had experienced in his. But then, had she always dealt with her own problems deftly, without cost to others? She sighed, and began to tidy up any debris left on the floor, leaving the empty wall spaces to await the arrival of Jess. After things had cooled down between the brothers, Cat had sent them away to Patrick's house, where he would

certainly have had to explain to his girlfriend who the
newcomer was! A part of Cat felt sorry for Alan: he had lost
his mother, had felt abandoned by his family, and had so
many questions and doubts about where he came from. On
the other hand, she could see why Patrick had wanted to
protect his mother against the hurt his brother had caused,
jumping in and out of prison with petty thefts and assault. It
seemed messy and complicated, and Cat knew they would
need time if either of them stood a chance at healing their
respective wounds. She swept the floor one last time and sat
back at the front desk, until she heard a car pull up, and
Jess's familiar laugh sound from outside. The car continued
on and Jess came in the front door with a cautious look on
her face.

"Cat, why are you still here? It's really late!" She squinted
at her friend, adjusting her eyes to the bright gallery lights.

Cat locked the door behind her, and led her upstairs to a
comfortable seat for the news she was about to divulge.

"What? Why would someone even -!" She stood
abruptly and marched downstairs again, with Cat hot on
her tails. Jess saw the gaps on the walls suddenly, and
shrieked, then continued through to the studio. "No no *NO!*"
She knelt by the destroyed canvases that were up against the
wall, pulling each one out and examining it, trembling.
"What kind of a horrible bastard *does* this?!"

"He's a troubled boy, Jess. I'm so sorry, I went upstairs for
a few minutes and heard the noise, but when I came back
down it was too late. I'm sorry – I never thought anything
like this could happen here..." Cat leaned against the wall,
exhausted from the day's events, finally creeping up on her.

Jess placed the art down, turning round to her friend. "I
don't blame you, of course I don't - it's not your fault that
some pathetic kid saw fit to destroy something beautiful of

ours." Jess glanced back at the pieces. "Well, it is mostly your work, Cat, I'm sorry."

"But one of yours too Jess!" Cat said gently. "I'll make sure it's paid back to you, or if you still want to go to the police... then I understand. It's your business, whatever you see is the right way, I will support you, fully, I promise. I just didn't want to see him arrested, especially with his record. I suppose I felt sorry for him. Only someone really unhappy would have done this kind of ..." Cat trailed off.

"Cat, he is not our problem!"

"I know, I know. But I know a cry for help when I see it."

"But the insurance... I'm uncomfortable about letting someone off scot-free, just look how malicious this was!"

Cat looked at her friend, unsure what else to say. "Well I can always paint more – and I'll put the profits back into the gallery for the new pieces! I'm convinced it was a one-off thing, otherwise I'd be right with you – he even told me as much - it was to get Patrick's attention. It's that or see someone's life set back another couple of years. I don't know how much more time inside he can take before there's nothing left for any of us to protect."

Jess sighed, rubbed her forehead and put her arm around Cat. "Let's just deal with this in the morning, it's late. Stay the night; we'll know what to do in the morning."

∾

The following day, Cat and Jess decided not to open the gallery. Cat woke feeling an uneasiness at letting Alan go so quickly, perhaps he had absconded on the ferry that morning after all, before the police could be notified? She also hadn't heard anything from Patrick, and began to think the worst. Patrick, understandably, would want to protect his little brother – wouldn't he? At the demand of Jess, both girls went off to Patrick's in search of some answers. Outside the door with the familiar horseshoe, Cat's heart started to thump - *would she see that girl again this time?* She shrugged the feeling off, it didn't matter: either way she and Jess needed to know where the brothers were. They knocked on the door, but no answer came. After several minutes, Cat peered in through the tiny window next to the front door, but things looked quiet and still; all she saw was the same women's red coat on the couch.

She shrugged to Jess, whose face was red with fury.

"I knew it! He's buggered off, and Patrick's chickened out about coming to tell us!" Jess roared.

"You don't know that," Cat tried to soothe her friend.

"Why wouldn't they have come earlier and apologised then? Bloody hell, I should've called the police last night, what was I *thinking*?" Jess raged, and stormed off.

Cat didn't know what to think herself, and her mind swam with unhelpful thoughts. She couldn't imagine Patrick would allow his brother to disappear on them, but perhaps after some time together last night he wanted to save his brother any further time in prison, just as she had. What did it matter if a few pieces of art were destroyed in the process?

Jess slammed the gallery door behind them and went to the phone, she stopped for a moment, and looked at Cat. Cat knew what she meant to do, and nodded.

Just as she lifted the receiver, a tap came from the door, and Cat opened it to reveal both brothers waiting nervously outside.

"Where were you? We came to your house, but no-one was there!" Cat demanded as she let them both in.

"I'm sorry, sorry Jess," Patrick said, his head low, and Cat noticed he was wearing the same clothes as the night before. "We went for a walk, we needed time – to try and talk about things - properly." He looked at his brother for confirmation. "Right?"

"Right," came the Irish accent Cat hadn't noticed the previous night, but was certainly stronger than Patrick's. Alan turned to Jess, who sat staring at him with phone in hand.

"I was just about to call the police," she sniffed defiantly.

"You must be Jess." Alan looked her in the eye briefly, and then cast his eyes everywhere but her face. "I don't know how to apologise properly... You have every right to call the police, I just get so angry sometimes and I don't know how -" His face went pink and he looked up at Patrick for help, but his brother stood still, quietly watching. "No – I suppose I never made myself face up to how I deal with it. I'm very sorry, I'll pay you back, for everything."

"Oh yeah, like you've got a few grand to spare?" Jess scoffed.

He stood still, considering his words. "I do have some money – a couple of hundred – just to start. And I could help you out somehow, do any jobs you might need, anything... until I can make up the rest. Pat says he'll let me stay until I've made up the cost."

Cat watched him closely, the boy was shaking with nerves. Perhaps he had more problems than Patrick had led her to believe. Jess sighed, and finally replaced the receiver. "Well... help us out, you say?"

34

J ess had in fact wrestled with the idea of contacting the police for a little while longer, but had eventually reluctantly agreed with Cat that the issue should be resolved without the authorities. The following day Jess got the gallery spring cleaned by Alan, who had shown up to everyone's surprise, able and willing to work. Jess had curtly shown him the cleaning cupboard and left him to it, while the girls discussed ideas to generate other revenue in the business. Much to both Jess and Cat's surprise, Alan gradually scrubbed down the whole place, taking breaks only when the odd customer came in. Jess decided to make the most of their free labour, and asked Alan to organise the painfully messy back studio the next day.

"Now - don't even think about more vandalising, Al! Or I will hunt you down personally," she said in a low voice, and left him to do his worst in the studio.

"You know, I think you're actually enjoying this Jess," Cat whispered, when the girls were alone together.

"I am a little," Jess giggled, "but don't tell him that!"

⁓

A week had passed, and like clockwork Alan would come in each morning to complete his duties. Cat no longer felt any uneasiness at him being there, so much so that he would be left to run errands or jobs for them, freeing up more time for the girls to paint. One evening when Cat locked up the gallery, she went into the studio to check on Alan. He was leaning on the giant table, scribbling on a sheet of paper.

"What are you doing?" Cat asked suspiciously, as he stood up quickly and hid the paper behind his back.

"I packed up all the older paintings, and organised them by name-of-artist. So... they can be posted next week." Cat had given him the dull task of arranging and packing any unsold work from previous exhibitions, and she was heartily glad she had been able to delegate the job.

"Thanks Alan. But - what are you doing *there*?"

He shook his head and waved his hand dismissively. "Just doodling that's all." His face turned its usual tinge of pink when he spoke.

"Can I see?" It was a request that Cat knew he would need to submit to.

He closed his lips tightly for a moment, and placed the page back down on the table. His bright eyes shot her a scared look that Cat knew all too well. He was laying himself open to judgement. Cat took in the frantic pencil etching, unable to see what the drawing was exactly. It expressed pain and fury, whatever was going on in Alan's head was reflected clearly back at her through the movement and sweep of the drawing.

"I like it," Cat said simply to the stunned boy.

"Why?"

"I'm seeing into you, through your work. There's a lot of emotion in this. Do you usually express yourself like this?"

Alan snorted, and Cat realised she would have to choose her words wisely with this audience.

"I mean, do you draw often?"

He shrugged. "Sometimes, if there's free paper around."

"Do you enjoy it?"

"Sometimes." He shrugged again.

Cat led him out, mulling over things as she locked the gallery up for another night, the drawing still lying face upwards in the centre of the table.

Cat took the time to set up paints, a canvas and an easel in the main gallery. It was the day that they were closed to customers, and Cat had been taken suddenly with an idea, and wanted to test it out. Alan knocked at the door and she took him through to the display area.

"What's going on?" He was instantly suspicious, but Cat reassured him quickly.

"We're closed today, so you'll have no interruptions. I thought maybe you'd like some time to do more drawing. You don't need to show anyone, this can be just for you to play around with. I've laid out some paints if you want to add colour. So go for it, whatever you want to do." She quickly corrected herself: "On the canvas or the paper I've given you, I don't want to see paint anywhere else, OK?"

Alan nodded in a daze, dropped his shoulder bag to the floor, picked up a paint brunch, and examined it as though it were a live animal.

"I'll be back in a couple of hours, alright?" she called over her shoulder as she made her way to the door.

"You're going to leave me here, by myself?" he stuttered.

"Yeah, why not, you've proved yourself reliable recently, so I want you to play around today, no jobs to do. OK?"

He nodded slowly, and Cat hoped that her trust wouldn't be betrayed. Without any more ceremony, she quietly left the building, hoping that she had made the right decision, and that the gallery would still be in one piece when she returned.

A few hours later Cat reappeared at the studio door, both anxious and curious at what she might find. She unlocked the door to a bare-chested Alan sweeping his hand over the canvas, spreading scarlet red paint over a darkly abstract piece. Cat was delighted with what she was witnessing, he seemed fully absorbed in his work, and intent on expressing something in particular. As the bell above the door tinkled, he turned around with a jump, startled to see company.

"How's things Alan?" Cat asked nonchalantly, as she placed her handbag on the front desk, and pretended to shuffle through some papers. The last thing she wanted was to draw too much attention to Alan's work straight off the bat.

"Yeah, er... fine." He stood still, looking from the painting to a distracted Cat. "Erm, thanks for letting me play around with the... stuff."

Cat scanned through the paperwork on the desk, "Hmmm? Oh yes, of course, sure. How did it go?" She sauntered over and glanced at the painting. It was certainly an angry piece, but there was a kind of beauty there too, lurking beneath. "That's fantastic, Alan." She smiled at the awkward half naked young man, covered in paint.

He smiled at her for the first time, a broad, genuine smile, and Cat lit up inside. "I'll maybe clean up, and be on my way." He picked up the brushes and went to the back studio.

Cat stood, arms folded, in front of the brave painting, lost in the light and the shade. She had had another of her ideas, and that smile was proof that she might be on the right track after all.

35

The next morning she was woken by her phone buzzing loudly, Cat patted her bed, squinting in the early morning light, trying to find the unwelcome source. She was greeted by a curt voice on the other end of the line.

"Miss MacGregor, it's Mrs Grey, at the library. I may have what you've been looking for. Please come in today, I'll be here till 5pm." Mrs Grey hung up before Cat could get a word in edgeways.

Cat summoned herself out of bed, and put on the thickest jumper she could find, along with jeans, a wooly hat, scarf and pair of gloves. Her house was freezing, but rather than light the fire, she decided just to leave immediately, with all her layers on. The library would be warm anyway.

Cat parked the car outside, feeling nervous and intrigued at the same time. She entered the little room again and found a group of young children and their parents crowded around a lady reading a story. The scene was very heart-warming but did present an obstacle with regards use

of the peripheral space. A few older pensioners read newspapers at the only other table, discussing the headlines of
the day with one another. Cat looked over to the librarian,
who was behind her desk, and waved to get her attention.
Mrs Grey wore an aptly-coloured tweed suit, and manoeuvred round children and chairs to hand Cat a sheet of paper.

Cat looked down at the photocopied page, covered
neatly with old-fashioned handwriting.

The librarian wore thin spectacles today, and through
them looked at Cat with excitement. "It's a birth certificate."

"Oh I see." Cat didn't see at all, it was still too early in the
morning for her without her first cup of coffee.

"Look at the name," Mrs Grey pointed to the written
scroll at the top of the paper, "Sarah Campbell."

Cat gasped. "It can't be!" And scanned the words:

Sarah Campbell, born in Kirkwall infirmary 1928.
Mother Mary Campbell
Father Angus Campbell

"I have a friend who is very good at this sort of thing."
The librarian pursed her lips with satisfaction. "Also, I
couldn't help myself. So it looks like this may be who you're
looking for?"

"My grandmother," Cat breathed out, and touched the
name.

Cat met Jess at the gallery to discuss business. The road was
now coated in a fine sheet of ice, making the whole island
look like a giant frosted fruitcake. Cat's nose was permanently red, and her hands could never get warm, no matter

how thick her gloves were. She drank the hot tea Jess issued to her and savoured the heat as it enveloped her throat. The day was quiet on the street, with only the odd person passing by; each walking as slowly as the next, trying not to slip on the frozen cobbles. Cat also updated Jess with the new details of her grandmother.

"Apparently she left the island when she fell in love with a soldier in the war. They moved to Glasgow, but sadly he passed away shortly after. Then Sarah met and married my grandfather, and had my mum!" Cat thawed her fingers over the small heater that gently rotated side to side in the gallery, making her move with it to get every last bit of heat. "Jesus it's freezing!"

Jess wore a dark green jumper-dress and fleece-lined boots, and was glowing like a girl in love. "Really?" she sipped her tea and smiled in a daze. "I hadn't noticed!"

"That's because you're high on love drugs!" Cat mocked.

"Maybe you're right" Jess sighed, "I'm just so happy, I met Andrew's parents again last night and they are lovely. I feel light and free." Jess then tucked her blonde hair behind her ears and focused her attention back onto Cat. "I'm sorry Cat. I've been a crap friend!"

"No you've not, don't say that. You're just a little distracted, and happy, I can't begrudge you that!"

Jess nodded. "Anyway, that's so crazy that your gran was from here, does that mean you have family here? You know, like, distant relatives?"

"I never thought of that!" Cat couldn't believe the connection she found with the island. Hidden away for so long, she had had the nagging feeling that something was trying to come to the surface. Like a creature underwater, waiting, something beautiful and filled with opportunity. This was why she had come to the island; not to run away from a failed relationship - her grannie Sarah had been calling her all this time.

Cat's thoughts, full of newfound family members, suddenly presented her with the fact that she hadn't seen Alan or Patrick over the last couple of days. "How are things with Alan?" Cat mouthed quietly, unsure if he was cleaning some corner or other quietly in the background, wanting to be unobtrusive herself.

Jess swiped some image or other on her phone absent-mindedly. "Oh I gave him the day off, he's been in constantly until now, and to be honest he's done everything I could get him to."

Cat glanced around at the polished wooden floors and sparkling windows. "He has done a good job."

"Yeah, definitely," Jess mused. "He even offered again to pay me money for the damage he caused."

"I'm glad to hear it."

"But I think he's made amends now. I even taught him a new skill - showing him how to make up framing."

Cat clenched her teeth; Jess had often tried to teach her the techniques involved in frame-working, but cutting each piece to precision was not Cat's forte. "And how did he do?"

"He's a natural. I think he could do woodwork; it could make him a good living, especially when he goes back to Ireland."

Cat felt a dull pain at the thought of losing another friend on the island. "Is he leaving so soon?" She tried to hide the disappointment in her voice.

"I reckon so, he can't stay here forever." Jess shrugged and popped her phone in the desk drawer. "Jeez, these winter months are quiet! I'm so bored!"

"Well... actually, if you're bored... I had some ideas I

wanted to float past you." Cat brought out her trusty note-book and felt a flicker of new excitement.

After Cat finished her tea, she was ordered home by Jess, who was sure there was to be a snow storm coming.

"But they didn't say anything about a storm on the news this morning."

"Maybe not, but I feel it in my bones."

"What does that mean?" Cat snorted, chuckling at Jess's serious expression, "are you a witch who can see the future?" She collected the empty cups and walked to the back studio.

"Actually, I *am* from a long line of healers," Jess nodded with superiority. "And we all know that healers were "witch-es", once upon a time. She air-quoted and rolled her eyes. "Well, greedy powerful men decided they were!"

"OK, in that case I better go!" Cat kissed her friend on the cheek. "Don't want you to put a curse on me!", and she ran off before Jess could pinch her.

Cat called into the library on her way back to her car and spoke with Mrs Grey about possible relations. The old lady clapped her hands at once and went to get the pen and notepad that were a permanent fixture on her desk.

"So, I can check with my very informed friend, and I might do some searching myself. Otherwise, why don't you come over to mine tomorrow and we could look together? I can show you how to research, I have my family tree on my dad's side completed right up until the 1500s!" The librarian nodded, looking very proud of herself. Cat couldn't help but admire her; she seemed so organised, but couldn't under-stand how she worked so efficiently in the clutter of all those books.

They arranged to meet the next day, and Cat, feeling elated from the day's events, decided that she would bake a cake for Mrs Grey as a thank-you gift. She got back into her car gratefully on the clear icy afternoon, and started off homeward bound at a snail's pace.

36

C at lit the fire, trying her best to warm up the cold cottage. The chill refused to leave, however, so she dressed in all manner of different layers, pulling on anything remotely clean that she could find, and started baking. The smells of cinnamon and spices floated through the house. She had classical music on very loudly and hummed to the orchestra. Her favourite piece came on over the speakers as she turned up the volume even more; two female voices sang out the *Flower duet, Lakmé de Delibes* and she pirouetted in the living room, humming along to their lulling angelic harmony. In that moment she felt like a ballerina in a fairy story, and danced her heart out, letting her body move in any way it desired. Then a knock came at the front door. Startled, she almost crashed into an armchair, and peered hastily out the window to see a tall figure by the door. She couldn't make out who it was as they huddled into the shadow of the porch. The sky above was covered in thick dark clouds, and the sea ahead roared and sprayed across the rocks at her usual swimming spot.

Patrick smiled as she opened the door. His chin was

stubbly again, and his curly head of hair was covered in a black beanie, making his green eyes stand out.

"Hi, I was just passing and I thought I might drop by?" He bit his lip slightly, and smiled. Cat had to stop herself from swooning. *Not this time.*

She invited him in and caught sight of herself in the living room mirror; her hair was scrapped back in a messy bun, and she was wearing about four jumpers, and a bright yellow scarf tightly wrapped around her neck. *Oh well, doesn't really matter,* she thought. *I don't want him anymore anyway.* She put on the kettle and gestured for him to sit at the kitchen table.

"What's that smell? It's like... burnt curry?"

Cat looked at him confused, then gasped and frantically opened the oven door to a very blackened smoky cake.

"Oh no!" She threw the cake tin down on the table as the smoke alarm blasted above. Cat opened her small kitchen window while Patrick wafted tea towels under the smoke alarm, trying to get the sirens to stop.

"You made a curry cake?" Patrick shouted over the noise and his constant fanning.

"It was a spiced cake!" Cat roared, annoyed at the disruption he had caused. All this was his fault really; regardless of whether her ballerina action had had anything to do with burning the cake, she was sticking to that theory for everything from now on. She ran through to open the front door to find it was already getting dark outside and snowflakes were falling gently. The smoke alarm stopped, and the house was silent. Patrick followed Cat and leaned against the doorway to find her open armed and catching snowflakes on her tongue twirling on the spot outside.

"You are such a big kid, you know that?" he chuckled. "It's only a bit of snow!"

Cat had not actually seen snow in years, but it reminded her of Christmas time. Sledging with kids in her neighbourhood, then her mum calling them in for hot chocolate and mince pies. Her feet would be freezing cold in her wellies but she hadn't cared, all she had wanted was to sledge and build snowmen all day long. She spun around in the gloomy light, surprised at how short the days were this far north.

"Come in you crazy girl, it's cold!" He rubbed his arms and hands. He was wearing a light-coloured Aran jumper and dark jeans. He removed his boots and placed them at the door, revealing bright orange and green striped socks.

"Wow, you really are Irish, right down to your feet!" Cat giggled, and walked in, closing the door on the snowy afternoon.

"The cold is making you silly in the head. Now, make yourself useful, go put another log on the fire and I'll make the coffee."

"Yes sir," she teased, and fuelled the fire. A moment later he came out with two cups and sat on the sofa next to Cat.

He looked around the room and sipped his drink. "It's looking good Cat, you did well."

"You did do a lot of the work, remember - thanks again for helping me." Cat went quiet and awkward. Looking back to those days, there seemed to be some serious fireworks between them both, only for her to discover that they had never really started after all. Well, maybe on her side. She sipped her coffee. "Hey!" She smelled the dark liquid. "You spiked my drink!"

"I didn't spike your drink, I just made it taste better. I thought a little Irish coffee was a good idea!" He had a twinkle in his eyes which Cat casually ignored.

"How is Alan? He didn't want to come over with you today?" Cat changed the subject with ease.

"Oh Cat, I'm sorry, I thought you knew - he left today."

"What? But... I thought he would stay longer? He never said goodbye."

Patrick gave a grim smile. "He decided it was best. He called to the gallery to tell you, but I think you had left." Patrick rummaged in his pocket and produced an envelope. "He wanted me to give you this."

Cat opened the envelope, to find a wodge of money stuffed inside, along with a single-sided letter. "I can't take this, he needs the money, I'm sure!" Cat protested.

Patrick's eyes remained fixed on hers. "He knew you and Jess wouldn't take it otherwise, so he wanted me to give you it in person."

Cat opened the letter reading the hastily scrawled words:

"Thanks Cat, for not calling the police, and for giving me time. I'm sorry for what I did."

"He's off to sort out a new job in Ireland, but I think he'll be back. There's still a lot to patch up between us, but something's changed. I don't know if it's just being somewhere new, getting away from our town, and the memories, and the people, or that we have just one another now..." He trailed off, and sipped his coffee thoughtfully.

"He might also, in time, want to find his biological father," Cat suggested softly, unsure of what reaction she might receive by addressing the fact out loud that they both came from different paternal beginnings.

"Yeah, you could be right." He nodded briefly and let out a breath. "Things are better, and I know you are a big part of that."

Cat blushed, shaking her head a little, refusing to take

the compliment, and started talking about her recent new undertaking.

"Swimming everyday?" Patrick shouted? "But it's freezing in that water!"

"Honestly, it's not so bad once you go in, I've started just going in wearing my swimsuit. Come on, I thought you were a strong Irishman, not a wee wimp!"

"Oh jeez I'm not sure I could do it!" He shuddered. "Maybe once in a while, but not everyday!"

"I'll need to get you in the water, I'm sure you'll change your mind!" *Was she flirting with him?*

"You really are a mermaid aren't you?" Patrick shook his head slowly his expression changing into awe. Cat turned to him with a puzzled look. "I had a dream about you after the first time we met, you were swimming in the sea, leading me to dry land. It was the strangest dream..." He said, his words drifting to a stop.

Cat turned to face the fire. She stared into the flames and was momentarily lulled by the cracking of the logs. She felt at peace with herself, happy in her own life. *I can't do this anymore.* She sighed and prepared herself to be honest. *No more.* "You said... you said you were passing by? I'm at the end of a single-track road for a mile. You can't be just passing by, Patrick?" Cat looked at him quizzically, but all he did was smile, and continue sipping his drink. "Look Patrick, it's nice to see you. You were really good to help me with decorating this place, I owe you, but -"

"Yes, you do." His eyes twinkled, but this time Cat was *absolutely* going to ignore them.

"But, sorry - enough is enough. What's... going on?" She looked directly at him. "I'm sick of the games."

Patrick sat very still, his smile fading with each passing instant. "*You're* sick of the games?" He took off his hat and ruffled his hair, agitated. "Each time I meet you, you treat me differently. I don't know where I am with you."

"Oh come on Patrick!" Cat protested, but then couldn't help thinking of their previous meetings; her swooning over him, then shouting at him, then throwing herself at him, then being angry with him, then aloof... She didn't know what to say. So she just sat there, unable to look at him.

He sighed. "But I can't stop thinking about you. Every day, hoping I would see you, just catch a glimpse of you."

"What?" The word caught in her throat. Cat couldn't move.

"I came here tonight, against my better judgement admittedly, as, well - I know we can't be together, given you have a boyfriend. I just needed to tell you, it's been eating away at me." He gulped the rest of his drink and placed the cup on the table. The moment seemed to last an eternity and all Cat could do was stare at him, speechless. "I shouldn't have come." He got up to leave. "I don't know what I was thinking, I just -" he stuttered, "I just wanted you to know I think you're beautiful". He shook his head in gentle disbelief, turned to leave, stomped his wellies on and walked out the door. Cat was still in utter shock and by the time she got up to try to catch him, he had driven off. The snow continued to fall heavily, and was already lying thickly on the ground.

"Damn it!" Cat didn't know what to do. It was too dangerous to drive; she didn't trust her little car. *Jess was right, it's turning into a storm after all.* She closed the door that Patrick had left open, shut off her lights and sat down, contemplating what to do in the darkness, with only the glow of the fire. *What just happened?* Cat's heart thumped so hard in her chest, she almost got up to run after Patrick in the snow, but realised she would be walking at least a mile in this snowstorm, before anyone found her on the road. She paced her living room, asking herself questions but not getting any answers. She needed help, so she called Jess immediately and explained what had happened with Patrick.

"Uh... yeah I know?" Jess said in bored tone. "Of course he liked you, but you told me you weren't that interested in him, and you wanted to concentrate on your work?"

"I didn't say that! I mean, I didn't tell you!" Cat looked for the words. "But I thought he was a player, you know a different girl every weekend. I saw him with a girl a few times recently and -"

"Well I don't know about that, but I did understand he liked you – it was pretty obvious, Cat! - and you weren't that interested after the night you snogged him... oh yeah, then Johnny came up and you didn't speak about Patrick after that at all, really."

Then it hit Cat: Patrick had thought Johnny was her boyfriend. *Surely it was obvious he was just her friend?* But then, maybe to someone on the outside, it may have looked differently; Johnny was attractive, and had been entirely affectionate to her in public. *Had she been treating Patrick all this time just like she had treated Dave? Was she always going to be afraid of letting anyone in?* The fear of not telling anyone about how she felt was beginning to haunt her. She hadn't even confided in Johnny about Patrick.

"Oh no... " Cat jumped at the knock on her door. She rang off the phone and opened the door to find Patrick, breathing heavily.

"It's too dangerous out there, my car skidded into a ditch."

Cat took him in and placed him in front of the fire. She poured him a shot of whisky to steady his nerves.

"You're shaking really badly." She touched his cold fingers. "Are you OK?"

"I'm fine, I just wasn't expecting the snow to be that thick. I've never seen it that bad on this road." He drank the whisky deeply.

"Patrick, are you with someone?"

"With someone? No? It was just me in the car!" He seemed confused, then looked away from her back his now empty glass.

"No, I mean, I saw you with the girl at your house."

He looked at her blankly. "I haven't been seeing anyone."

"I saw you... kiss the other night, at your house... and she was at your house when I called around before, too."

"I didn't know you came to the house?" Realisation dawned on him, and he sighed, exasperated. "Clare, you must mean Clare."

Cat searched his eyes for more information, hoping in her heart, for some reason, that the answer to her next question would be a no. "Is she your ex, back from Australia?"

Patrick shook his head. "She's my housemate's girlfriend. She was coming over all the time, and then she started to come over when he wasn't there... and say she'd wait for him... I didn't mind her, but she was my mate's girl. I didn't want to tell him – I didn't want to tell anyone! - but yes, she kissed me the other night outside the house." He turned to Cat. "But believe me, I was never interested in her, in anyone else but you. Though, when I saw you with your boyfriend at the ferry..."

"He's not my boyfriend!" Cat blurted out. "He's a friend, one of my best friends. He's married too; he was going through marriage problems, so, I was here for him - only as a friend!" The noise of the crackling fire continued as a silence fell between them.

The snowstorm outside whistled and whirled around her cottage, but Cat didn't care. What mattered was right here, this second, with Patrick.

"So you were always single? When we kissed... until now?"

"And you too?" Her heart pounded.

They both nodded their replies and laughed.

Cat rubbed his arms and hands without thinking. "You're still shaking."

Patrick touched her cheek with his cold hand.

"Am I?" He took her hands in his and kissed them. "I want you, Cat." Then pushing back her hair, he took her head in his strong hands and kissed her softly. Cat could feel the musician's calluses on his fingertips as he pulled her forwards. She knelt into the gentle movement of his lips, then passionate hunger consumed them both. Clothes came off so naturally and so quickly in between breathless kisses, neither wanting any moments wasted between them. They locked together on the sofa; Cat wrapped her legs around him as his firm body held onto her tightly. He kissed her neck, as she untied her hair, letting her curls fall loosely over her shoulders. He ran his fingers through them, his touch continuing down her bare back before stopping to look at her. "You are so beautiful." Cat couldn't wait any longer; she wanted him with everything she had, and pulled his mouth onto hers again. The light from the flames danced up and down the walls, as he broke away, and knelt down on the floor by the fire. He held out his hand to Cat, and she went to him.

37

The next morning Cat woke to make them some tea, leaving Patrick snoozing under blankets of all colours and sizes, draped over the bed to keep the cold out. She wrapped herself in her dressing gown, ventured downstairs, and opened the front door to a freezing cold morning; the sea rumbled before her, and white snow covered everything. It was a beautiful sight, as gentle snowflakes fell from the sky, promising more cold weather to come. She wasted no time getting back upstairs to Patrick, and handed him a cup of tea. He propped himself sleepily up against the headboard, and let Cat nuzzle into his chest.

"There's a blizzard starting out there. I just heard on the radio that all ferries are off, and people are advised to stay at home."

"Oh - so I have to stay here until it clears?" He grinned down at Cat.

"Looks like it!" Cat ran her fingers down his chest and stomach. He was strong and lean, and happily for Cat his interest in the tea didn't last long. His arms tightened around her and they disappeared under the covers once again. Hours passed, and the snow continued to fall gently outside, undisturbed.

≈

Night descended, and Cat lit the fire. Nat King Cole played softly in the background whilst the gentle flames crackled. She poured a glass of wine for them both while she rustled up a simple beef stroganoff. Patrick picked up the wooden spoon and sipped the sauce.

"Hey!" Cat pulled the spoon away. "It's not finished yet, you do not disturb an artist at work do you?" She adopted a theatrical French accent. "Go make yourself useful and set zetable!"

"You're very bossy do you know that?" Patrick chuckled and pulled Cat to him; kissing her neck and making her want him all over again.

Cat had laid a blanket on the floor beside the fire and scattered some cushions to sit on for dinner. The coffee table was moved sideways, and set with plates and cutlery, as Patrick came through with two large glasses of wine. Cat looked around at their makeshift luxury. She loved Bramble cottage. It had given her so much already; nurturing her talent and helping discover her family. And now being here in the space with Patrick felt right, giving life back into the building, making it a home again.

Patrick served up the food and sat down on a cushion beside Cat.

"This is all very bohemian," she laughed.

≈

Relaxed and very full of food they both lay on the floor next to the fire.

"I'm so thankful for this snow," Patrick said, stroking her neck. "If it wasn't snowing, I wouldn't have banged my car up and had to come back here last night. It forced me to make a decision. I'm pretty stubborn at times, and all I wanted to do was get away last night, thinking you didn't want me."

Cat touched his lips. "We both know now." They kissed, and Cat laid her head on his shoulder. "Hey!" she exclaimed suddenly, "I never told you I found out that my grannie lived near here, did I?" She told Patrick about her recent findings, with the help of Mrs Grey, and the photos that Johnny and Billy had unearthed.

"That's a bit spooky!" Patrick stroked Cat's hair as she lay her head back on his chest. "I mean, of all the places you could have decided to go, you came to the very spot your grannie was born!"

"I guess!" Cat lay still, enjoying his touch. "I do think it was there, somewhere in the back of my head, like a distant memory lurking in the wings, until finally there was too much evidence to ignore! When I saw the island that day in that magazine, it seemed familiar. And thinking about it now, I saw it at a time I really needed to."

He reached over to the table for the bottle of wine, trying not to move Cat's head and refilled their glasses awkwardly. Cat felt the gentle rise and fall of his breathing as she stayed close to his chest, gently lifting his shirt up and stroking his stomach underneath. Patrick pulled Cat's face to his, kissing her slowly as they slipped into endless moments lost in one another's arms.

∽

The phone rang early the next morning, and a sleepy Patrick held it out to her, his eyes half-closed.

"Ms MacGregor? It's Mrs Grey the librarian."

"Oh my goodness, Mrs Grey I'm... I'm so sorry I didn't call, I, er... completely forgot I was meant to come over yesterday!"

"Oh my dear that's fine, I assumed there was no way you'd be over – we did have a blizzard after all!"

"Thank you, Mrs Grey! So... what can I do for you?" Cat was relieved; choosing between Patrick's warm, glorious body and the prim but kind librarian was no choice at all, really, especially in the winter.

"Can you spare some time to come over later today? It looks like it'll be safe to travel now. I have some exciting news for you."

EPILOGUE

That year the snow cleared midway through December, but a persistent frost arrived instead, covering the island in a glittering white glaze. Cat and Patrick hopped in Cat's car with a bag full of wrapped presents, which Patrick stuffed into the backseat.

"Cat, you really need a bigger car," he half-groaned, half-laughed, trying to make room for the bag.

"Hey don't mock the Beetle, it's fabulous - and it makes me look cool!" Cat glanced in her mirror and put some red lipstick on.

"That's no reason to have a car -"

Cat turned her head and gave him a look that made him stop short, and they both laughed.

"Come on get in, or we'll be late!" It took Cat a few tries to start the car and a look from Patrick.

"You're right, I don't know what I was thinking - this is a great car" Patrick suppressed a smirk and looked away from Cat's now reddening face. Several minutes later they finally left the cottage in a cloud of smoke.

"Are we picking up Jess and Andy on the way?"

"No, they've decided to go to Andrew's parents first. But should see us later for drinks" Cat thought of her two friends happily; Andrew was the best partner she could have imagined for Jess. He encouraged her as a painter, and was always bursting full of ideas for the gallery. After what had happened with Alan, Cat and Jess had agreed to look into helping other young people like him, with the end-game being an exhibition of their work in the gallery, and a talk about the relationship between art and mental health. Cat was very excited by the prospect, and had already started looking at application forms, and booking research trips to similar retreats the following year. Patrick and Andrew were also becoming fast friends, with Patrick taking a new interest in diving. He was even due to go on a dive on New Year's Day, which Cat thought somewhat over-ambitious; she would most definitely be recovering from the night before safely in bed! Cat looked over to Patrick and grinned. She had already fallen head over heels for him and even just looking at him still made her melt. Cat caught herself daydreaming, and focused on the road ahead; the Beetle needed all the help it could get in the frost.

In a short time they approached the large house on the outskirts of Stromness. The driveway led up to a charming stone house with a huge green wreath on the front red door. Fairy-lights covered the windows, and were draped around the small trees that surrounded the house.

"Oh, it looks gorgeous! They put so much effort in!" Cat parked the car and took in the whole view, enchanted at the chocolate-box Christmas scene before her.

Patrick lumped the big bag over his shoulder to the door, which opened wide to a beaming Monique, wearing a red sequin dress.

"Welcome darlings!"

Two small girls ran up to the door wearing Santa hats and red tutus. "Is this our new auntie, Cat? Auntie Cat! Auntie Cat!" They chanted jumping up and down on the spot.

"Now calm down girls, this is your..." Monique stopped and looked to Cat to clarify.

"Cat is my second cousin, so she is family, and of course she can be your auntie." Monique's husband Iain came up behind the excited girls. "Let her in Monique, it's freezing outside!" He tutted and rolled his eyes as Monique and the two girls fussed over Cat and Patrick's coats.

They entered the lounge room and saw a couple of familiar faces, and wished everyone a Merry Christmas. Billy came up to them, and hugged Cat.

"You look bonny, lass!" Billy smiled, then shook Patrick's hand. "I say you must be the most handsome couple in Orkney!"

Iain handed them both a glass of wine. "It's lovely to have you both here."

Looking down, Cat noticed the red holly jumper Iain was wearing, and his red corduroy trousers. "You all look very festive!"

Iain looked down at himself and chuckled. "Yes, it's a little tradition here. The girls love it. And when I say the girls, I mean, Monique particularly!"

Cat laughed and looked down at her plain blue dress. "I think I should've made more effort to look festive!"

"Oh I'm sure the girls will give you a Santa hat or something. But there's plenty of time to prepare for next year!" Iain winked at her, and Cat felt tingles down her arms. *A family. I have a family.*

He introduced Cat to other people sitting in small clusters around the room, all of whom shook hands with her, welcoming her to the family. Then the familiar face of Mrs White appeared. Iain gestured to the old lady, "And of course, you know our teacher, Mrs White?"

The old lady walked up to Cat and grabbed both of her hands in hers. "But what you didn't know is that I'm Iain's mother!" She smiled over to her son "You're grannie was my mother's sister." Mrs White touched Cat's face. "And I must say, now that I know who you are, you look just like Auntie Sarah. Same hair, same nose, same eyes!" She smiled and chuckled. "Oh my dear we've got so much to catch up on! I have plenty more stories to tell you!" Mrs White squeezed Cat's hands.

"Oh mum don't tell her about the selkie girl!" Iain moaned in tones akin to those of a mortified teen.

"You think I'm going to leave out any facts whatsoever about her family history?" Mrs White raised her eyebrow to her son.

"That's just folklore – not facts!"

"Maybe. Maybe not!" Mrs White beamed at a bewildered Cat.

Iain and Monique went through to prepare the dinner, while Patrick pulled out the bag of presents, and the two fair-haired girls squealed delightedly and clapped. They had opened their gifts in an instant, tearing the wrapping paper off in a frenzy, then ran through to show their mother and father. Excited with their new fairy outfits, including crowns, wands and wings, the girls wasted no time in redressing, and pretending to cast spells on people.

Patrick spoke with one of Cat's newly-introduced second cousins, but was otherwise in his element, knowing everyone else already; a local lad, after all. He sat on a chair with wine glass in hand, looking relaxed and chatting about his new business venture. "A local music venue, kind of a cross between a coffee shop and a bar." He talked about his plans and various ambitions; after the success of recording his own album he had certainly been inspired to do more.

Everyone passed around gifts, sipping wine and laughing.

Patrick came over and put his arm around Cat. "Well my love, how do you feel?"

"So happy - what a crazy year it's been!" Cat touched the new engagement band on her finger. "Do you think we've rushed things a bit?" She chuckled.

"I don't know, maybe." He smiled. "All I know is from that first day on the ferry you captivated me – seasick or not! I love you Catherine MacGregor." He kissed her on the lips. "Our first Christmas together".

Cat smiled and held his hand. "Our first of many."

ALSO BY CLAIRE GILLIES

Coming soon...

From Scotland With Love

AFTERWORD

This book took a long time to write. I mean...a really long time! After spending years working in offices, I was becoming increasingly less and less fulfilled with the 9-5 daily grind. This book started initially from my own daydreams of escaping to somewhere new and living a creative life. It was during this time that my husband and I decided to go and live in the Orkney Isles. Moving from the hustle and bustle of Melbourne city life to go to the other side of the world, was a big change - I didn't really know what to expect! As soon as I landed on the island I was confronted with a horror of "what have I done?!" And my writings of "On The Edge" was put on hold for many years while I opened up and let myself experience the ups and downs of living on an island.

I have loosely based Cat on my experiences, and even now after leaving Orkney many years ago, it still was and will remain a big part of shaping my life and who I've become.

I look back on that time with fondness and wanted to

capture the feelings of freedom and excitement. I hope you enjoy coming along on the journey.

ACKNOWLEDGMENTS

There's so many people who I'd love to thank.

Mum and Dad - who I believe I got my words from. To my dad, his endless stacks of hand written songs, poems and little thoughts and humourings, I think (or really hope) have passed down to me. Mum, who secretly is a beautiful writer, but would only keep to writing Christmas letters to distant family every year. I will always be thankful to you both for the endless encouragement.

Grace - Giving me confidence in my work, your editing has made this book possible!

My good friends who I'm so lucky to have in my life still...

Hayley, who has always been around to give me a "kick up the arse", you inspire me continually.

Sue, the first person I showed my work to, and who I was gobsmacked to find out actually liked the book. You gave me belief in myself and I treasure you.

And to Eamonn, always bringing light into my life with a smile on your face. I'm so very lucky.

ABOUT THE AUTHOR

Born and raised in the Highlands of Scotland, Claire's homeland continues to be a stream of inspiration for her.

Claire currently splits her time between Scotland and Australia with her lovely Irish husband. She is a cat lover (without the cat) and can be found either drinking coffee, eating a slice of cake, watching a costume drama...or consuming another glass of wine!

www.clairegillies.com

Printed in Great Britain
by Amazon

84263092R00162